MICHAEL R. JOHNSTON

THE BLOOD-DIMMED TIDE

FLAME TREE PRESS
London & New York

For John and Karla,
who taught me to dream big

CHAPTER ONE

Tajen Hunt

I stood in front of a huge window overlooking Earth and fingered my collar. Kiri slapped my hand. "You're going to mess it up after all my hard work."

"It itches."

"It's cut almost exactly like the uniform you wore for more than a decade."

"I hated how that felt, too."

She tried not to laugh, but her smile gave her amusement away. "It'll be over in a bit. Liam's on his way." She gave Katherine Lawson, my second-in-command of Earth's space forces, a long-suffering look. Katherine said nothing out loud, but her expression made it clear she got my niece's point, and agreed.

My partner, Liam Kincaid, entered a few moments later, skidding to a halt just outside the room. He composed himself before entering the observation lounge. A small group of friends stood in loose ranks, which parted to let Liam through. His suit was as elegant and uncomfortable-looking as mine; Ben Denali stopped him halfway through the crowd, reaching to adjust the suit. After a few seconds of shifting and tugging at the jacket, Ben flicked Liam's hair back into place, gave him a once over, then nodded decisively and pushed Liam toward the front of the room.

"Sorry," Liam said. "Had a little training accident to deal with."

"Everyone all right?"

"Yeah, everyone's fine," he replied. "But I had to give my team The Talk. It took a while."

"The Talk" was what everyone called Liam's patented "This is why you listen to me, morons!" lecture. He'd given it enough times in the year since we took Earth back from the Zhen and began training our defense force volunteers that it was nearly a rote speech. It was also entertaining enough that an audience inevitably formed as he was giving it. I looked him in the eye and raised an eyebrow at him. "You sure you didn't embellish it a bit for the audience and lose track of time?"

"Of course not!" he said in an aggrieved tone. Then, after a beat: "Maybe a little."

"Well, you're here now," I said, offering him my arm. "Shall we?"

He linked his arm with mine, and we turned to Katherine. She smiled and looked around the room. "We who stand here today have been witness to several 'firsts.' We are the first humans to see Earth in over a thousand years. We are the first humans to break free of the Zhen Empire and declare ourselves free of their treachery. And now, we in this room are witnesses to the first marriage ceremony since we founded our colony."

She took a breath, looking down at the book in her hand, and said, "When Tajen and Liam first met, it was an instant connection. They got along so well, and so immediately, that it took the rest of us by surprise. And their attraction was obvious to us all, too. So much so that the rest of us had a betting pool going for how long it would take."

"I won," Ben drawled, drawing a laugh from the audience.

"Indeed he did," Katherine said, her sour tone cueing even more laughter. She waited for it to die down, then said, "Liam and Tajen have written their own vows, which they will give now."

We turned to face each other. We'd agreed Liam would go first. "Tajen, I was no saint before we met. But the moment you first spoke to me, I knew that I was going to spend my life mooning after you. Do you remember your first words to me?"

"No," I lied.

"'Who the hell are you and what are you doing to my ship?'" he quoted, getting another laugh. "I was smitten. You cannot imagine how relieved I was to see my affections weren't one-sided." He paused and smiled. "I pledge myself to you, and to our family, blood and chosen both. From you I will hold nothing back, and give wholly of myself. I am yours, for now and always."

"Liam, I first saw you half buried in my ship's electronics bay, with only your legs sticking out. And even then I knew you'd be trouble. I tried not to fall for you, but… it was impossible. We live a dangerous life, but I want to spend as much time with you as I can, for as long as we've got in this universe. I am yours, for now and always."

We placed our hands over each other's hearts. Katherine said, "Liam Kincaid, do you take this man as your husband, to love in all ways, for as long as you can?"

"I do."

"Tajen Hunt, do you take this man as your husband, to love in all ways, for as long as you can?"

"I do," I said, unsure whether I was going to cry or grin like an idiot.

"Then by the power placed in me by the Provisional Government of Earth, I now pronounce you married."

Before the words were finished, Liam and I were leaning in to kiss. We were just about to complete the act when the sudden blare of the Earth Orbital Station's alert klaxon pummeled my ears. My comms implant sounded, a panicked voice filling my head. "Captain Hunt, this is command. We're reading seven ships coming out of slipspace."

I was running for the tower before he was finished speaking, Katherine and Liam on my heels. I took the stairs two at a time, stumbling into command. The officer on watch, Kaz Simmons, welcomed me with a salute. I'd tried to put a stop to that, but nobody would listen to me. I ignored the salute until I realized he wasn't going to stop until I returned it. I sketched a quick salute and snapped, "Report!"

Simmons answered in the precise speech that I'd grown accustomed to from him. "Seven ships, all of Zhen manufacture. They came out of slipspace, then used chain drive to get to the inner system. They're waiting just outside lunar orbit, as I instructed them to."

"Who are they?"

"They claim to be refugees. Lead ship is called the *Stellar Wind*, registered to the Faded Sky Shipping Cartel. The captain is Liz Orozco." He cleared his throat. "She is refusing inspection, and she is asking to speak to you directly, sir."

I motioned him to put it on the screen and stepped into the comms' visual pickup. "Earth command to vessel *Stellar Wind*. As you've been informed, all ships coming to Earth are required to submit to inspection. I'm told you don't want to. Explain yourself."

The woman who appeared before me was in late middle age. She looked almost embarrassed when she recognized me. "Captain Hunt, it's not that we refuse inspection. As I've tried to explain to the young man, we're carrying some…well, something that could get us in trouble. We wanted to explain to someone in charge what we've got aboard before you scanned us. Tempers flare, and that could be a disaster, you see."

I raised an eyebrow. "And what is it you're carrying?"

"Weapons, Captain."

"What kind?"

"Mostly ground – about a hundred Zhen pulse rifles, some smaller sidearms. But we've also got fifteen starfighter-class pulse guns, ready for mounting, and a few crates of explosives. It's all yours."

"And you're asking…?"

She grinned. "Nothing, sir. But I suspect you'll need 'em. I had 'em sitting in my – well, my *employer's* – warehouse. Thought you could put 'em to better use here than he could."

"We could indeed, Captain Orozco."

She looked embarrassed. "Please, call me Liz. I'm not a captain. I stole this ship and will be turning it, too, over to your colony."

"It's not *my* colony. Liz, I'm grateful for what you've brought us, but I'm going to have to ask you to stand down and submit to inspection. Nobody gets—" I was cut off by a new alarm blaring across the command deck. "What the hell?"

In the battle tank, one of the ships in the *Stellar Wind*'s formation was accelerating toward the station. "What the hell is this?" I snapped at the screen.

Orozco blanched. "I don't know!" She pointed to someone outside the field of view. "Get him on comms!" she shouted. "Deveraux, what the hell are you doing?"

I couldn't hear the reply, but Orozco's eyes widened, and she drew a finger across her throat, then turned back to the pickup. "Captain Hunt, he's lost his mind, says he's here to—"

I cut the feed and turned to the defense officer. "Fire on that ship!" He relayed the order, and the station gunners, as well as the system patrol ships that had responded, focused fire on the vessel. I could see, though, that as powerful as our guns were, they weren't going to be enough. The freighter was too big, and our ships were too few.

"Sir! Another ship on the move!" the sensor officer called.

I looked up at the holotank and cursed. "Get Orozco back!" I roared.

The comms officer signaled me, and Orozco appeared before me again. "What the hell is going on?"

She waved her hands in a warding gesture. "I don't know!" she said.

I started to give the order to fire on that ship too, but stopped when I realized what was happening. The second ship was on an intercept vector with the first. As the two connected, the smaller ship crumpled. Her drives blew, and the small ship was gone.

I looked at the plot and realized the freighter had been knocked off course; it wouldn't hit the station – but it was headed right for one of the arms of our shipyard. I turned to the comms officer. "Signal the shipyard and tell them to evacuate."

"Will they have time?" Katherine asked.

I didn't look at her as I replied, "Not all of them."

We watched in sick horror as the freighter slammed into the shipyard. Moments after impact, the freighter's drives blew, and the resulting star vaporized half the dock and numerous ships. "Brace for impact," the comms officer called, and we all grabbed for supports.

When the shaking was over, I looked to the watch officer. He scanned his boards and said, "No casualties on the station, sir. But the shipyard...." He gestured at the screen.

Now was not the time to berate a civilian-trained crew member on military protocol. I walked over to look at the screen.

We'd lost over half the shipyard, and what was left was in pretty bad shape. Barely any of our docked ships had managed to detach and get away in time. The loss in lives was devastating. I cleared my throat and spoke softly to him. "Get a list of the dead. The council meets in an hour. I want a detailed status report by then."

"Yes, sir."

I turned to comms. "Get Orozco back on screen."

"Yes, sir."

I looked back to the screen, which was showing Orozco once more. Her face was pale, her breathing shallow.

"What the hell happened?" I said.

"Captain Hunt, I'm sorry," she said. "Deveraux...he had told us he was one of us. But when he tried to ram your station, he broadcast a denunciation. He said that we – and you – are criminals, making things worse for people back on Zhen and Terra."

I blinked, not knowing what to say. I'd known there were human elements that didn't approve of what we'd done, taking the Earth from the Empire and declaring it our own. Despite finding out the Zhen had wiped out Earth civilization and then lied to us about it for eight hundred years, despite the Zhen treating us like second-class citizens, despite everything they had done, many humans still thought of the Zhen as the good guys. After all, they had found our drifting, nearly dead colony ship. They had saved our people, given us a home. It didn't seem to matter that that had happened centuries after they'd already destroyed our homeworld while we'd been drifting through space. The Zhen Imperial news sources had taken advantage of this divide; there were commentaries all over the slipnet about us, making us out to be villains and cutthroats who had turned against the 'benevolent' Empire. Far more humans and Zhen than I had ever thought possible just fell for that nonsense without a second thought.

"The second ship?" I asked.

"The *Avo Grande*, captained by Mel Kramer. She sent a message just before impact. All it said was, 'At least I saw it. This way, my death means something.'" She paused, clearly emotional. "She was a Dreamer, Captain. The day your message was broadcast, she called me. It was she who convinced me to come." She paused to get a grip on herself. "She was dying, you see. She wanted to die on Earth."

I nodded. "How many were on her ship?"

She attempted to smile but faltered. "That's the one piece of good news. She didn't have any. Her ship was a scout-ship she'd bought secondhand. She didn't have space for a crew. She'd planned to volunteer it for your defense fleet."

"What about Deveraux's ship?"

Orozco looked down, troubled. "Well...there we weren't so lucky. The *Harbinger* had a crew of five, and six passengers. But he had all the weapons in his cargo."

"I don't care about the weapons," I said. "Tell me there were no kids on board."

"No, none."

I let out the breath I hadn't intended to hold. "Well, that's something." I looked to Katherine. We'd been working together long enough now that we didn't really need to speak. She nodded, and I turned back to

Orozco. "Given what's happened, I'm almost sorry to say it, but we still need to complete the inspection."

She nodded. "I understand, sir."

"When that's done, though, assuming – as I do – that nothing untoward is found, you and your fleet are home. Welcome to Earth."

"Thank you."

As her visual faded from my view, I turned to my chief of security. "Be thorough – don't cut any corners – but try to be respectful to them. They've just lost people." I glanced back at the wreckage of the shipyard. "As have we," I added.

"I think we can handle the job, sir." She saluted and left the control room.

I led Liam into the hall, then sighed as my NeuroNet displayed a priority message. I turned to Liam. "So much for the celebration," I said. "Diana's called an emergency meeting. I'll catch up with you at home?"

"Of course," he said. "I might as well go out on that exploration survey I was putting off." He leaned in and kissed me, his lips tender.

I breathed in his scent as we separated. "Bad timing," I muttered.

"Seems like that's a way of life around here," he said.

★   ★   ★

The new Earth Council gathered in the colony administration center's conference room an hour later, mugs of steaming tea in our hands. Since we'd defeated the Zhen force that had tried to pry us off the reclaimed Earth a year ago, we'd been rebuilding the civilization they'd destroyed over a thousand years before. Many humans had left Zhen and Terra, the human colony world in the Zhen Empire, and taken up residence on our ancestral homeworld.

It was still a rough world, with a lot to be rediscovered, but it was coming along nicely. We'd built a small city, with the astoundingly unoriginal name 'Landing', and were moving outward slowly. There were some isolated settlements on other parts of the planet, some with reclaimed Old Earth names, and some with names inspired in the years of what was now becoming known as 'the Big Lie', the period of time in which we'd thought of the Zhen as our saviors, and not the architects of our misfortunes.

I had never intended to become the leader of a colony, so when the original group of colonists who arrived with me had tried to make me the colony's head, I immediately, without reservation, refused. We held elections a few weeks later, and chose Diana Adakai, a woman from Terra who had come with the first wave of humans, to join us. She headed a large group of people she called 'Diné', who she told me had worked very hard to remain 'whole' during the eight hundred years of the Big Lie. Ben had joined them, and was learning the language. It turned out his mother had been one of them, but he'd been raised by his father and hadn't learned as a child.

Diana sat in her place at the head of the table and looked around the table. "While we have urgent matters to discuss, let us begin with the standard reports, please," she said, setting her cup down on the table.

Kiri, to her immediate left, spoke first. "Network security has been upgraded with a new cypher," she said, brushing her red hair back from her face. "I removed the Zhen back doors from all the software – and, by the way, you're not paying me enough. It was damned difficult to do without crashing the whole system. We're continuing to scour the system for more software traps, but I think we've got them all. We're also replacing some of the most vulnerable Zhen equipment with Kelvaki equivalents, giving us another layer of security."

"What about comms?" I asked, from beside her.

"All the ships in the fleet are now using the same comms equipment, and they're protected by a Kelvaki encryption code. So far as we or the Kelvaki are aware, the Zhen haven't broken this encryption. We'll continue to update the keys and frequencies often."

Diana nodded. "All the ships in the fleet," she repeated softly. Her eyes met mine, and she sighed. "How many is that now, Tajen?"

I took a deep breath as I composed my answer. "Not enough," I said. "We've only got two squads left – twenty-four ships in total. The Zhen attacks of the last month have been whittling us down even before today's disaster."

"What are they doing?" she asked.

I frowned; we'd discussed this before. I realized she was asking for the benefit of the others around the table. "It's an attrition tactic," I said. "They could just come in with a huge fleet and overwhelm us, but the Zhen like to toy with their enemies when they can. This is designed to brutalize us psychologically. They want us at the edge so they can just push us over. They don't just want to take Earth back. They want to break us completely as a people."

"How many personnel did we lose today?"

"One hundred and fifteen," I said.

"How long can we survive with our current numbers?"

"If they continue this campaign?" I bit my lip. "Maybe six months, at the current rate. But I'd say probably less – a lot less. My pilots were already beginning to fray. Today may have accelerated the process."

She frowned. "So. We need more ships."

"Yes."

She met my eyes briefly, then turned to another member of the council. "Let's hear from exploration."

Neil McShane, a tall man with a patrician nose and an elegant accent, said, "We've finished the flyovers of this continent," he said. "We're definitely in what was once called North America, somewhere in the old American Southwest."

"Have you found signs of any other Zhen bases?"

"No. We have found signs of survivors after the Zhen invasion, but nothing recent. My team is still divided over whether that means they all died out eventually, or if they're still out there somewhere, in hiding." Neil shook his head. "We're looking, I promise you. But there isn't much out there besides plants and animals. Even the ancient cities are pretty much gone. It's been a thousand years, after all, and the Zhen bombardment reduced most of the cities to ruins. In some places you can't even tell that millions of people lived there, once."

Diana said, "Keep looking, but priority is finding any Zhen outposts, for now." She turned to the next person around the table. "Jim?"

Jim was a barrel-chested man with a magnificent beard and moustache. He'd been a doctor on Terra and had been elected by the first group of civilians to administrate the day-to-day operations of the colony while Diana focused on the big picture. "We've got the land for the next batch of housing set up – we're going to start the replicators working today. One of my guys created the plans – they're going to be nice places, not cookie-cutter like the originals."

"Have we got enough raw materials to do that?"

He gave us all a huge smile. "Yes. The last group of civvies that arrived brought a construction rig, remember. They knew exactly what we'd need. Mind you, we could always use more."

"Fine. How's the militia coming?"

Our militia commander, a former infantryman called Driscoll – I never did figure out if that was his surname or his first name – grimaced. "I'm doing my best, but we need better weapons."

"What about your personnel?"

"The people I'm training are okay, but if we get more military types," he said, glancing at me, "I'd appreciate them being sent my way."

"We'll see what we can do," I said.

*　　*　　*

Liam came in the door of our shared quarters just as I was taking our dinner out of the cooker. He looked at the plates and cocked his head. "Roast rations A or B?"

I grinned. "One of each. With some additions from the hydroponics bay."

"Well, that's something. Let me shower first." He headed for the shower and stopped, turning. "Unless you want to join me?" he asked, waggling his eyebrows.

I raised my left eyebrow and snorted. "My husband, you are very pretty, but *way* too filthy. Get cleaned and we'll eat."

As he showered, I plated our food and set the table. When he came out, pulling his shirt on, I noticed a new bruise on his torso. "That looks bad. What happened to you?"

"Ah, it's nothing – I fell down an old shaft in a cave."

"That's *nothing*?"

"Well," he said, "it hurt like hell. But we had a field medic with us. I'll be okay. And it was worth it." He indicated the plates. "Which one's mine?"

"Take your pick. Why was it worth it?"

He considered the plates. Like all human rations, they only vaguely resembled the foods they were purported to be. They were bland, but we'd learned over the years the best ways to modify them to make them palatable. "I've always hated A," he said offhandedly, as he took the B plate.

"Bastard," I said with a grimace. I took the plate he'd left behind. "You're lucky I love you."

He snorted as he sat down at the small table. "You're lucky I *let* you love me."

I tried to give him a hard look, but I couldn't stop grinning at the dumb joke. "So, the cave?"

He took time to eat a few bites before answering. "I fell in the hole, and it was deep. Luckily, we were wearing emergency grav-harnesses, so the fall wasn't as bad as it could have been – the harness kicked in, but not soon enough to give me a soft landing." He took a drink before continuing. "Anyway, there was a hallway at the bottom – there were some remnants of old signs, but nothing still legible. But we think, from the railings and some old stuff down there, that it was a tourist stop once."

"In a cave?"

He spread his hands wide. "They were magnificent – formations like I've never seen anywhere else. And it was huge. The whole thing was about two hundred feet below ground, and cold. It looks like it was used for storage, once – probably got used just after the Zhen destroyed everything. I was thinking we could do the same, just in case."

"When the Zhen come back, you mean."

"Yep. Put some food and weapons in there, and it becomes a bolt-hole if we need it."

"Sounds like a good idea. You run it by Driscoll?"

"Yeah, he liked it. Started things in motion already."

"Good, I—" We were interrupted by the door chime. "Ah, hell," I said, and used my implant to tell the door to open. Diana Adakai stood in the doorway. "Diana, come in. What can I do for you?"

"Oh, I'm sorry. I didn't intend to ruin your dinner," she said.

I gestured her to a seat. "Don't worry about it. The food was crap, anyway."

She smiled as she came in and nodded to Liam. "I've got an assignment for the two of you," she said as she sat.

I took the seat across from her. "Yes?"

"We need more ships," she said. "We need more guns. We need trained pilots to fill in before our trainees are ready. I want the two of you to go to Kelvak and get them for us."

"Kelvak isn't a shopping mall," I said. "And my last communication with Dierka suggested he was at the end of his ability to send help."

"I know, and I thank Dierka for all the help he's given us in the past – I have a small idea of how much it might have cost him, politically. But the fact remains, we need help, and the Kelvaki are the only people in a position to help us – unless you'd like to ask the Tabrans?"

"It…wouldn't be my first choice, no," I said.

"There you are, then. Of all our people, you're the only one who has a chance of convincing the Kelvaki. So, I want you to go there, and find out what we can do to earn more help from them." She gestured to Liam. "And because I know you have a tendency to get in trouble on your own, I want Liam there to keep you out of it." She glanced at him and added drily, "You'll have to keep an eye on him as well, I have no doubt. But as you've just been married, I don't think either of you will mind that aspect of your trip."

I ignored her salacious expression. "Not that we have much, but what am I authorized to offer?"

"Short of giving away our homeworld, Tajen, do whatever it takes." She rose and moved to the door. "My analysis – based on your reports, of course – tells me that we have, at best, twelve weeks at the current rate of attrition before we're out of ships. Please take that as your deadline, but – don't shave it too close, please."

"Of course. I have one thing to do, and we'll leave immediately after."

"Excellent." She left.

I looked at Liam. "I guess we get a honeymoon after all. Can you pack us up? I have to go talk to Katherine." I left before he could say anything.

★   ★   ★

On my way down to Katherine's quarters, I thought about how to say what I needed to. By the time I touched the annunciator beside her door, I thought I had it ready. I hoped so.

When the door opened, Katherine looked at me oddly. "Something wrong?"

"Not really," I said, as she ushered me in. "I'm being sent on a mission to Kelvak."

"To get more ships?" She whistled. "Good luck with *that*. My understanding of the situation there isn't perfect, but it doesn't seem like that'll be easy."

"It probably won't be," I said. "But while I'm gone, I need someone to manage things here. You're my second, so you're up."

She froze for a moment. "Tajen, I'm not sure I'm the best—"

"Katherine," I said, dropping my pitch, "let's cut the shit, okay?" I kept eye contact with her until she agreed. "Good. You were a great captain when you had *Maggie's Pride*, and you've been a perfect partner ever since. Right up until Takeshi died." I held her eye. "And then you folded."

She wilted. "I couldn't save him," she said.

"No. And nobody else could have, either. But your brother didn't die because you screwed up. He died because a Zhen soldier got too close, and we were all too far away." I reached out and put my hand on hers. "The point is, it destroyed your confidence. And I get it – of course I do – so I let you fold. We were in crisis and we needed to keep moving. But it's time to remember."

"Remember what?"

"That you are a damn fine commander."

"Sure, for a merchant—"

"Nope," I said, cutting her off. "A damn fine commander, full stop. Katherine, I need to go away, possibly for quite a while. I need to know someone who has a karking clue will be in charge here while I'm gone. Someone with the same training and ability to think on their feet I have. Someone who can make hard calls. I need *you*."

She pursed her lips, thinking. "All right," she said finally. "But you need to promise to get your ass back here as soon as possible. If the war gets hot again while you're not here, I'm going to kick your karking ass."

"You have my word," I said with a grin.

"You're goddamn right I do," she said, rising to grab a bottle of whiskey and two glasses. "Now, have a drink with me before you go. We need to make sure we're on the same page with the fleet assignments."

"Absolutely," I said.

★　　★　　★

I talked with Katherine for over an hour. When I returned to my quarters, I found Liam sitting on the couch reading. As I entered, he waved his hand and the book's projection faded from view. "Ready to go?" he asked, standing. "I packed for both of us. Gear's already on board."

"Did you get my—"

"Blaster?" he asked. "Yes. And I also got your best cloak, and that weird badge Dierka gave you. All on board."

"You're amazing."

He furrowed his brow at me. "Why are you always telling me things I already know?"

We made our way back to the docks and boarded my ship quietly. When we got to the bridge, Kiri, my eighteen-year-old niece, was sitting at her accustomed place at the flight engineer's console. "Hey, guys!" she said brightly.

I looked at Liam. "Did you call her?"

He shook his head.

Kiri beamed at me. "Diana told me she was sending you. I decided to go with you."

"Kiri, you're needed here," I said.

"What's that ancient expression? Oh, right – *bullshit*. Tajen, all I'm doing here is maintaining the colony's systems and updating the security codes every few weeks. Jonn can handle that. You're not taking Ben, right?"

"He's busy with the medical clinic here."

"Then you know as well as I do that you're going to need me."

"And how do I know that?"

She gave me that look she reserves for special occasions, the one that seems to say I am being particularly stupid. "When have you *not* needed me, since this all began?"

Liam chuckled. "She's got a point."

I gave him the *you're not helping* look, took a deep breath, and let it out slowly. "Fine, you can come," I growled. "Stow your gear."

"Already done," she said with a shit-eating grin. "Ready for departure, Captain."

I pointedly turned away from her and continued to the pilot's chair. Liam took his place beside me, and we quickly brought the engines up and did our preflight checks. Once we had clearance, I disconnected from the station, brought us about, and began heading for the jump point at the edge of the system. "Activating chain drive," I said.

As our drive opened up, Liam grinned. "I love that sound," he said. "The way the drive cycles up, and then drops an octave as we go luminal."

I smiled. "I've always loved it. In training sims I got in trouble once because I dropped in and out of chain drive just to hear it cycle again."

We lapsed into a companionable silence, mostly because it was still late night for us. As we approached the jump point, I brought us out of chain drive and slowed us, bringing us to a relative stop just inside the system's jump limit, the point at which jump drives could operate without interference from the star's gravity.

"Jump solution is locked and loaded up," Liam said.

"Kiri, check his math," I said.

"Hey!" Liam cried, as Kiri brought up the jump plot and ran her eyes over the lines of code.

"Eh, it checks out," Kiri said. "More or less." She winked at Liam. "You know, for a ground-pounder."

Liam had been studying to be a pilot. He knew it was only a matter of time before I put Katherine in command of a ship again. He also realized that while he was an excellent soldier, he needed another job if he was going to be flying with me a lot – which he was, considering our relationship.

"You two do realize, I hope, that not only did I qualify as an astrogator last month, but the ship's computer has already checked my jump plot?"

"Of course," I said, as if it was obvious – which, of course, it was.

"Yeah, I know," Kiri said.

"Then why the song and dance?" Liam asked.

I grinned. "Because it's *fun*." Kiri nodded in agreement.

He turned back to his board. "I hate you both."

"I'll make it up to you," I said, as I brought the jump drive online and pushed the throttle forward. I watched as the stars elongated into lines, and then disappeared in a flash, replaced by the disconcerting, weirdly shifting colors of slipspace.

"Yeah? How?" he asked.

I gave him the full force of my 'Pilot's Grin', that mix of cocky arrogance and total confidence that I'd used to blind many a starry-eyed young man across space before I'd met Liam. "We're gonna be in slipspace for three weeks," I said, "and we're alone on board."

"Uh, hello," Kiri said.

I gestured at her. "Well, okay, she's here. But she's," I said, giving her a mock glare, "a total bookworm who will give us at least twelve undisturbed hours so we can—"

"Sleep?" Liam said.

"Exactly," I said, trying to stifle a yawn.

"You guys are already a boring old couple," Kiri said.

"Shut up, you," Liam and I said together. The two of us unstrapped, and I clapped Kiri on the shoulder. "In all seriousness, it's late and we need sleep. We'll see you when we see you." She nodded, and we headed off to our quarters.

CHAPTER TWO

The first few days in slipspace are always productive. I finally get around to various maintenance tasks I've been meaning to do for ages, get some reading done, maybe play some games. But eventually, if the trip is long enough, once I've done everything I need or want to do, I end up in the cockpit, bored out of my mind.

This trip, it took me four days.

Kiri was working on some project in her quarters, and Liam was working out in the small gym we'd installed for long voyages. Having grown bored with watching him, I'd returned to the cockpit, my home-away-from-home. I was sitting in the pilot's couch, my feet up on my console, watching the weird colors of slipspace go by, when something out there caught my eye.

Slipspace is weird, but the weirdness is always moving, always flowing, like liquids of varying viscosities and colors trying to mix and never quite managing. Nothing out there stays still. Nothing is constant except the ship you're on.

Something out there was pacing us.

I took my feet down and sat up straight, leaning closer to the glasteel viewport. I could barely make it out, as if seeing through thick fog, but there was something there. I thought I could see some light limning the edges of the object.

I set my implants to record the image, but almost as soon as I did, it seemed to move away, and disappeared.

"What. The. Shit?" I said out loud.

"You know, looking out into slipspace is a good way to make yourself crazy," Liam said, entering the cockpit.

"Yeah," I said. "I might be halfway there."

"I won't argue that," he said, "but why now?"

I gestured outside as I sat back. "I could have sworn I saw something out there."

He sighed. "Well, you wouldn't be the first."

"Yeah."

Kiri entered the cockpit and took her usual seat. "The first what?"

"To see something out there," I said, gesturing to the ports.

"I thought nothing lived in slipspace?"

"Nothing does," I said, "so far as anyone knows. But pilots have been claiming to have seen something for centuries. The Zhen even mounted an entire expeditionary force to try to find out if there's anything out there."

"What happened?"

"Only one ship came back."

"What did they say?"

I shook my head. "Nothing useful. Most of the ships got lost in a gravitic anomaly deep in slipspace. A few got lost on the way back. Just... faded off the scanners of the one remaining ship."

"So there might be something out there."

"Maybe. Could all be spacer nonsense and coincidence too," I said.

Liam took a small flask from his pocket, held it up briefly, and said, "To weird spacer lore. May it never get us killed." He took a drink and replaced the flask. "I'm headed back to the galley. It's lunchtime. Anyone hungry for anything specific?"

"Food," I said absently.

"Helpful," he said. As he left, I could hear him down the corridor, talking to himself. "Always with the helpful requests, he is." Something banged, as if he'd tripped over something. "Fuck is this?" he cried.

"Oops," Kiri said. "I think I left my tools in the hall." She scurried off, and I could hear her and Liam arguing good-naturedly about who was more annoying.

I turned my attention back to the view into slipspace. "Where are you?" I said to nobody in particular. "What are you?"

I must have sat for half an hour, just gazing into the void. Once or twice, I thought I saw something, but it invariably turned out to be a trick of the light, or a shadow of slipspace energies reflecting off my ship.

Liam returned and handed me a small bowl of something hot and steamy. I sniffed at it and smiled. "I didn't realize we had any chili," I said.

"I froze some the last time you made it. Thought I should bring it when we packed up for the mission."

I took a bite of the very spicy mixture of *tlal* meat and spices, chewing with pleasure. Legend had it that the dish was adapted by one of the earliest human colonists, recreating a beloved dish he'd learned at his grandmother's knee. Even though the spices we used now were very different from the spices used on Old Earth, it had the flavors described in the books. I was hoping to find the original plants in the wild and recreate the original recipe, but so far I hadn't found anything that matched the pictures we had. And cows had gone virtually extinct with no humans to care for them; as near as we could tell, they'd been so changed by centuries of breeding they couldn't live in the wild. A few tiny herds had been found that were close enough to their ancestors' size and physiognomy that they could survive, but the Zhen had preyed on them fairly extensively. We'd decided it was best to leave them in peace.

Liam broke the silence. "You think we'll ever be able to use cow meat instead of tlal?"

"Maybe," I said. "Remember that group on Terra that figured out how to grow meat in a lab?"

"Yeah," he said. "But the Zhen outlawed it."

"Right. They think it's unclean to eat something created in a lab. Goes against their predator instincts." I waved my spoon in the air. "And I think it was part of their whole project to direct our development – since they didn't like it, they made it illegal for us too. But now? We can do it on Earth, and we don't even have to kill one of the few remaining cows."

"But we'd have to get a sample," he said. "Wouldn't that mean having to kill one?"

"Why?" I asked. "If all it takes is a gene sample, we can probably get that without killing. And if we can't, well, maybe it's better not to. And if that fails, well, it may not be Zhen-approved, but we can do okay with plant-based proteins."

"Sure we could. But why? You've never had a problem eating animal flesh before."

"It's what I grew up with. I'm not sure I'll ever have a *problem* with it, per se. But I'm starting to wonder if doing things the Zhen way might be a problem beyond the obvious. Why do it their way if we don't have to?" I shrugged. "I don't know the answer, I'm just asking the question."

"Fair enough," he said.

Kiri came in. "I heard you guys talking about meat. You do realize most of the tlal meat the Zhen eat is synthetic, right?"

"What?" I asked. "But fake meat is illegal."

"Officially. And officially, it's all real. But only the Zhen:ko get real meat."

"How do you know that?" Liam asked.

"I found it in an old file," she said. "The Zhen government made vat-grown food illegal when we started doing it, but they've been growing it in labs for centuries now. They just don't tell anyone."

"That doesn't make sense," I said.

"It might, actually," Liam said. "They tell the people what they feel the people need to know. Believing it's all taken from animals preserves the narrative of Zhen:saak:arl." He held up his hands in a gesture of benediction. "The Struggle is All. The Struggle is Holy. We Must Fight For What We Have," he said, quoting the Three Tenets of Struggle. He dropped his hands. "On the other hand, when was the last time a Zhen actually *had* to fight for their food?"

He had a point. "The Zhen:ko are a collection of bastards," I said.

"No argument there," Kiri said. She gestured to the viewport. "Any more sightings?"

"No," I said. "I guess I'm just going crazy."

"No argument there," she said, an innocent smile plastered to her face.

★　　★　　★

Later that evening, shiptime, the three of us sat together in the mess hall for a dinner Liam had come up with. He claimed it was an old stew recipe his family had handed down since the Rescue. "So, what are we likely to find on Kelvak?" Liam asked.

"How much do you know about their political system?"

"Not much. I learned a little when I was taking lessons in the language, but it was surface-level stuff about the Great Houses of the Assembly."

Kiri added, "From what I remember, each House oversees one aspect of their infrastructure – the original Houses were formed by the first Ascendant of the Kowali clan when they took power."

"That's right," I said. "I wasn't aware Kelvaki history had been added to the curriculum on Zhen."

"It wasn't," Kiri said. "But I read a lot."

Liam grinned. "So, what, they add a new House every time technology advances?" He set a bowl in front of me.

"No, that would be insanity." I poured him a glass of wine and passed it over. "Most of the time, new tech is folded into a House that already covers that area – each Great House contains several smaller Houses." I took a sip. "Anyway, most of the Houses are *rev*, a family House-name – like a clan. But the *rev'na,* the Great Houses, have functions besides clan structure. They each oversee several *rev*, and have nominal control over some industry or piece of infrastructure. Sometimes a *rev* is elevated to a *rev'na*, but it's usually a reward for a *tor'rev* who's done something for the Assembly." I sipped my wine and said, "It hasn't happened for a long time."

"Tor'rev?" Kiri asked.

"The head of a House," Liam said. I touched my nose and pointed at him.

"What's the head of a Great House called?"

"Same word," I said.

"How many Houses are there, now?" Liam asked.

"Dozens, maybe hundreds of regular Houses. But only twelve Great Houses."

"And every Great House has a seat in the High Council?"

"Yes."

"What does the Ascendant's House oversee?"

"The Assembly itself," I said with an airy gesture. "They guide the Assembly's policy and oversee contact with outsiders."

Liam took a bite and chewed it, a thoughtful look on his face. "So, what's our plan?"

"I've sent ahead to Dierka. He'll meet us when we arrive in-system. We'll discuss the current situation with him and get his advice before we do anything else."

"See?" he said, smiling at Kiri. "I keep telling people, he's not just a pretty face."

She gave him a disgusted look. "Please leave me out of your flirting. You two are gross."

"We are not 'gross', Kiri Hunt, and I'll thank you to remember it," Liam said before leaning over the table and pursing his lips. "Give us a smooch, smoogly-woogly."

I stared at him, and said, deadpan, "For that, I am not kissing you ever again."

He sat back down and grinned. "Liar," he said, taking another bite.

I didn't let my amusement show, but took a sip of my wine, met his eyes, and said, "We'll see."

★   ★   ★

We came out of slipspace in the designated arrival zone. Immediately, my system notified me of seventeen weapons locked on to my ship.

"Kelvaki control, this is Tajen Hunt on the Earth vessel *Something Cool*. I am here to speak to the Assembly High Council on behalf of Earth."

"Stand by, *Something Cool*." None of the weapons targeting us released their lock; in fact, ten more guns locked on while we waited.

"Is this normal?" Kiri asked.

"No," I said. "It's never happened before."

"I think I might know why," Liam said, flicking his display at me. The graphic leaped into the air between us, my NeuroNet implants showing it as a hologram. Liam gestured, and a section lit up red. "There's a Zhen Imperial courier out there, and it's got six *Karnakkar*-class fighters escorting it."

"Shit," I said.

"Think they knew we were coming?"

I shook my head. "Probably not. But the Empire's been looking at the Kelvaki for a while. They don't like that Kelvak helped us take Earth, even if it was unofficial."

"It's going to make our job harder," Kiri said.

"You are not wrong. Any activity from the Zhen since we got here?"

Liam didn't take his eyes off the board. "No, but— Wait. We're being scanned."

"By the Zhen?"

"Yeah. No weapons lock – and the Kelvaki seem to have weapons locked on them too."

"Interesting. I wonder what—" I was interrupted by the comms system.

"Zhen courier *Her Will* to Kelvaki command. The Zhen government protests the presence of the human ship. We demand you refuse them entry to Kelvak and order them to leave Kelvaki space immediately. They have no diplomatic standing and may not speak for any part of the Zhen Empire."

"Oh, that's great," Liam said. "We're already—"

"Shhh," I said. "Wait for the reply."

A few moments later, the Kelvaki channel lit up, but it wasn't the original voice. I smiled as I recognized Dierka's voice and acid-laced tones. "Kelvaki control to *Her Will*. I do not care for your tone, Zhen. You do not command here. The Kelvaki government will welcome both your parties. You may both make your respective cases to the council.

"If *either* of you fires on the other, the offending ship will be destroyed, and the Kelvaki will immediately fully ally with the other.

"If both ships fire, then *both* ships will be destroyed. In addition, your missions to Kelvak will be forcibly expelled from our space, and the Kelvaki Assembly will consider itself at war with both the Zhen Empire and the planet Earth. Do not try our patience."

The channel went dead.

"Wow, that was...." Liam began.

"He's bluffing," I said. "Oh, not entirely – if they fire on us, the Kelvaki will blow them straight to hell. And if I was dumb enough to fire, he'd shoot us down too – he'd have to. But ally with the Zhen? Dierka would be five days dead before he even considered that."

A few moments later, the channel came to life again. "Attention Earth vessel *Something Cool*. A Kelvaki tender will rendezvous with you shortly; at that time, you will surrender your ship to the control of a Kelvaki Assembly pilot for docking. Until then maintain your present position. Any deviation from these instructions will result in your immediate destruction."

The comms signal ended, but almost immediately, my implants informed me of a communication incoming on my personal NeuroNet channel, with a Kelvaki origin code. Only one person in Kelvaki space had the code for that, so I allowed the connection. The same voice from before said, "I am bid to tell you that you are welcome, Tajen Hunt, but that the situation is difficult. You are asked to do your best not to make it more so." The comms signal faded again.

"Well, that's great," I said with a sigh. "Here we are, on a time-sensitive mission, and the karking Zhen have to show up and complicate things."

Liam waved a hand in their general direction. "It's what they do," he said.

"Now what?" Kiri asked.

I looked at her. "We," I said, drawing out the vowel, "do exactly what we're told to do, so they don't blow us up."

"I meant after that, obviously." Her tone made it clear she didn't think much of my answer.

"Wish I knew," I said. "I'm pretty much making this up as I go along."

★   ★   ★

An hour later, the tender vessel arrived. The ship got permission from me to link up via airlock, and attached to the side of my ship. Once the inner door of the airlock opened, two Kelvaki arrived. One of them was eight feet tall and about half that from shoulder to shoulder. His face was dominated by a mouth fully a foot across and bristling with teeth. In short, he was a mountain of reptilian muscle I knew quite well. "Dierka!" I said. "I didn't expect you to come yourself."

"Well met, *draka*," the heir to the Kelvaki throne said, baring his teeth and unsheathing his claws in greeting before retracting them. I returned the predatory grin, baring my teeth, stunted and dull as they were compared to a Kelvaki's, and steeled myself as he came closer. I braced as he swatted my shoulder as gently as he could – which still knocked me on my ass.

When I was younger, I'd served in an exchange program with the Kelvaki military for a short while, and Dierka and I had ended up the last survivors of a battle during the Third Marauder War. Out of that experience had grown a fierce friendship. He regarded me as his *draka*, his brother-by-choice, and every damned time we met up, he thumped me off my feet. I climbed back to my feet gingerly. "Dierka, I keep asking you to stop doing that," I said, rubbing my shoulder.

Kelvaki didn't smile like humans. They showed amusement by twitching their long, pointed ears. Dierka's were fairly well dancing. "And I keep telling you 'no'," he said, chuckling the awful and disconcerting Kelvaki equivalent of a laugh. True to Kelvaki custom, he then got right to business. "You have chosen your time to approach us poorly, Tajen," he said.

"As you saw, the Zhen are already here, and they are…" he shrugged, "…not happy, shall we say."

"What are they mad at you about now?"

His ears twitched. "They're Zhen. What are they *not* mad about? But mostly they are angry because we helped you take your world back. They are here to tell us that they will overlook it – and to demand that we 'not interfere in the interior workings of the Empire again,' or we will be at war." He hesitated before saying, "I do not like to say this, but their threats are working. My uncle is doing his best, but the majority of the Council does not wish war with the Zhen." Dierka's uncle was the current Ascendant, and due to an 'accident' we all believed, but couldn't prove, had been organized by the Zhen, Dierka was now the heir to that office.

"They know the Zhen will come for them eventually, right?"

"Some do, some will not admit that probability even to themselves."

Liam spoke up. "Whom do we have to convince?"

Dierka seemed to ruminate for a moment. "The Ascendant is already on your side," he said, "and so is Skaaran of House Makann, and Jinnka of House Lakor. But Skaaran has relatively little influence, and while Jinnka controls our ground forces, that is only one third of our military." He sighed. "So, essentially, you need to convince them all."

"All of them?" Kiri asked. "Not just a majority?"

"No," Dierka said. "In matters of war, the entire High Council must agree."

"You have any leverage on any of them?" I asked.

"No," he said. "While I'm sure that such exists, I am not aware of any of it."

"That's where I come in," Kiri said. "All I need is access to your systems."

"You really think you can hack an alien computer system?" I asked.

"Who said anything about hacking?" she said, a disdainful look crossing her features. "Just hook me in and watch me find you some leverage."

"Worth a shot," I said, looking at Dierka.

"I'll get you an access code," he said to Kiri. "One not traceable to you," he added with the Kelvaki equivalent of a wink, "in case you decide to look in places you maybe should not."

She gave him her brightest smile. "You know me so well."

Dierka stood, and finally gestured to the smaller functionary beside him. Like all Kelvaki women, she was smaller than the males, closer to human proportions, but with the same overall appearance, and the same fearsome teeth and retractable claws. I'd heard some say that history had forced the women to become even more dangerous than the men. Having served with several in my time among the Kelvaki, I believed it. "This is Injala," he said, "a servant of my House. She will advise you throughout your stay on Kelvak." He gave me a penetrating look. "I trust her with my life."

I cocked my head. "How many times has that come up?" I asked.

"Six," he said.

Injala immediately said, "Eight."

Dierka looked at her. "Eight?"

"Yes, my lord."

"Huh," he said. "Wait. Are you counting that idiot yesterday?"

"Of course."

"That was *nothing*!"

"He had a bomb strapped to his torso, my lord."

"Oh," he said. He stood there, silent, then shrugged it off and turned to me. "Injala will begin by piloting your ship in." He waved at me once more and headed for the airlock.

As it closed, Injala turned to me. "If you are ready, Captain Hunt?"

"Of course," I said, gesturing toward the cockpit. "This way."

CHAPTER THREE

"Why," Councilor Aljek said with a snarl, "do you think you can come here and demand our aid?"

I blinked. "I *demand* nothing, General. I am *requesting* the Assembly's aid."

"The question remains," he rumbled, coming very close to me and leaning down to look me in the eyes, "*why?*"

I did my best to appear unintimidated and glanced at the Ascendant, who sat calmly watching the proceedings. He hadn't said a word since he welcomed me, but his eyes were active, flitting back and forth between the various councilors and myself. He gave no indication of even noticing I was looking at him.

"Forgive me, *Kaar* Aljek," I said. "Kelvaki isn't my first language. I'm afraid I don't fully understand you."

He growled, his lip curling back from his fangs, turned away from me, and began pacing the council chamber floor, his arms rising in a gesture that said *do you believe this shit?* "Do not play the fool with me, Tajen Hunt. I am well aware that you are fluent in *two* of our languages, including the one we are speaking now."

I inclined my head, conceding the point. "Forgive me," I said, "but I am unclear whether your intent is to ask why I am here requesting your help, or if you are actually asking why I felt it was possible to do so?"

I could hear his teeth grinding from ten feet away. "The former," he said, his voice edged with the effort to control his temper.

My arms rose slightly from my sides, then fell again. "We are dying," I said. "If the Zhen continue their campaign, there will be nobody left to protect our world."

"It is not your world, Tajen Hunt," came an unmistakably Zhen voice. I turned and saw a Zhen:ko standing in the doorway. Like all Zhen, he was taller than humans. And though he looked less dangerous than the Kelvaki warrior, the lean muscles of his body were more than enough to do damage to my relatively weak flesh. That wasn't what scared me, though.

Most of the Zhen in the Empire are Zhen:la. Their skin ranges from pale to deep green, and they're slightly taller than humans. This guy was a Zhen:ko, a member of the ruling caste, and as such, his scales were a deep red. He was on the high end of Zhen height at nearly nine feet tall, placing him on equal footing with Aljek, whom he regarded over my head. "It is ours." The crest atop his head, which tended to signal Zhen emotion, lay close to his skull at the moment.

I frowned at him, and turned to make sure the council members could see my expression. "You're kidding, right?" I asked. "By what grounds could the Zhen claim Earth?"

One of the councilors said, "Despite the lack of protocol displayed, this council recognizes Ambassador Gelka of the Zhen Empire."

"Thank you, Kaar Siiren."

Siiren's voice turned cold as she said, "But I would like an answer to Captain Hunt's question."

Gelka's crest extended fully, betraying his surprise at her directness. "By right of conquest!" he snapped. "We took the Earth! That makes it ours!"

Councilor Skaaran shifted position in a manner which, to Kelvaki, signaled irritation. "If I stride over there and take your weapons and jewelry from you by force, does that make them mine and end your claim to them?"

Gelka faced Skaaran directly, settling into a ready pose. "Try it and see," he snarled.

"Honored sirs," Jinnka said, "this posturing is unworthy of this chamber and gets us nowhere." She turned to me. "Captain Hunt, would you like to respond to Ambassador Gelka's point?"

I sketched a Kelvaki salute to her. "I would indeed, Councilor." I turned to Gelka. "You say the Earth is yours because you took it by conquest."

"Yes," he growled.

I spread my hands. "But we took it from you – by conquest. Why should the Empire not recognize *our* claim by conquest?"

He snarled. "Things have changed, as you well know."

I smiled. "I know that they've changed, yes. But how much? While the conventions of Zhen:saak:arl are well known in the Empire, they have never been recognized by interstellar law. They are not even universal within the Empire – despite whatever force of conquest is used, theft is illegal in the Empire, is it not?"

Gelka gestured *grudging acceptance*. "Imperial Law has changed in this manner, yes," he said, "but the Earth was taken in a time when Zhen:saak:arl was the governing principle of the Empire."

"So, your argument is that it was legal for you to take Earth and destroy our people, but it's not legal for us to retake Earth from you, because you changed the rules between the two events?"

He gestured *irritation*. "What have 'rules' to do with conquest?"

I paused to take a deep breath and calm myself. I was in no mood for his game, and I was sick of playing it. Balancing my weight very carefully, I said in a soft voice, "Even war has rules, Ambassador. Or have you forgotten about Imiri?"

His rage response kicked in before his brain could stop it, and he swung a clawed fist at my head. I danced back out of range but did nothing more. The guards around the chamber, though, immediately drew their weapons, drawing a bead on the ambassador and his guards.

Gelka froze, aware of how I'd baited him. He collected himself. "I apologize for the breach of conduct, Ascendant," he said. "I…humbly… ask for a recess." He refused to even look in my direction.

The Ascendant waited several long moments before answering. "While I understand your desire, the business of the Kelvaki does not start and stop at the pleasure of the Zhen. We will continue the meeting that was in progress before you arrived, Ambassador. You may go."

Gelka's crest expanded with his fury, but one look at the guards stopped him from saying anything. He swept out of the room, his own attendants following in his wake like leaves caught in a gust of wind.

Councilor Siiren rose from her seat in the circle around the outer edge of the room. Like all female Kelvaki, she was slighter than the men, making her just slightly taller than me. She stepped softly to my side, and her hand rose to rest briefly on my shoulder. "You said earlier, Captain, that without our help, there will be no one left to defend Earth. We do understand this." She looked at Aljek, and her expression hardened into one of disgust. "What my *esteemed* colleague is asking, is why that should concern *us*?" She looked at Aljek. "Yes?"

He glanced at me, then at her. "Yes," he said grudgingly. "Though I would not have phrased it quite so ineloquently." Siiren's ears quivered with amusement; she knew damned well he would have.

I glanced past Aljek to the Ascendant, who was leaning forward in his throne, his eyes fixed on Aljek. I suddenly realized that I was standing in the middle of a power play that ultimately had nothing whatsoever to do with me or with Earth. I was being used as a convenient lever to move a difficult piece in the Assembly's game of rule. I took a moment to consider my words carefully, then moved to the center of the chamber, turning to face Aljek and the Ascendant both.

"Right now, my lords, we humans are holding the attention of the Zhen on us. We took the world they had claimed back from them, and then we destroyed one of their flagships. They are angry – at us, for now." I spread my hands out, as if questioning. "When they finish with us, my lords, then they will turn their eyes – and their ships, and their anger – toward you."

Aljek sneered at me. "So you say. But you have not supported this claim."

"Allow me to rectify that," I said briskly, and turned toward the display holo in the middle of the chamber. I flicked my right hand toward the display, and my implants, reading my intent, sent the prepared data packet to the holo, which obligingly animated a light leaving my hand, expanding into an image in the center of the room. "Shipyard production at the Empire's primary military shipyard. Note the date, sir." I flicked my left hand, and another data packet leaped from my hand to the display, the two adjusting sizes to display side-by-side. "Patrol route changes logged within the last six months. Note the increase of patrol squadrons along the Assembly's border zone." I paused. "I've always felt border lines in space were a bit of a joke, but you'll notice how close to your border systems the ships are coming. Well within scanning range of *Klintaan*-class reconnaissance vessels." I flicked my right hand again, and another graphic sprang up. "Troop movements." Another flick. "Recruitment numbers over the past four years." I waited a moment, and then said, "Any questions?"

Jinnka and Aljek, commanders of the Assembly's ground and space forces, pored over the data as Siiren rose to join them. She looked over the data for a time, then turned to me. "How did you get this information, Captain Hunt?"

"I regret that I cannot answer that, my lady," I said with a Kelvaki-style bow, "but I cannot endanger my sources." She gestured an acceptance of that and turned back to the data.

I faced Aljek. "We are both men of war, sir, so let me speak plainly. The Kelvaki forces are formidable, but we both know the Assembly is no match for the Empire if full-scale war breaks out. Not yet, anyway. Simply put, the longer you help us survive, the longer you have to prepare for the inevitable war with the Empire, and the more likely you'll have an ally when they eventually come for you."

Another council member rose from her seat. "You would have us use your people, your world, your *children* as a buffer to slow down the Empire," she said. "What kind of person are you?"

I met her eyes. "The kind that must play the hand he is dealt."

The Ascendant rose from his throne. "Thank you, Captain," he said. "My council and I will take this matter into consideration. Until we call you back, please enjoy our hospitality. You are also welcome to travel freely in the city, of course." He signaled the door guards, and the door opened. Liam rose and joined me, and with a bow to the Ascendant, we left the chamber.

★　★　★

As we neared the residence we were using, Injala seemed to materialize beside me. "That was well done, Tajen Hunt," she said. "Successfully baiting the Zhen into such a breach of protocol will bring some toward your position. However, you made one error."

"Oh? What's that?"

"You embarrassed Aljek. That will likely cost you."

"Yeah, well, he's an ass," I said.

"Ass?" she said, her face noting confusion.

"*Lanka*," I said, and her features shifted to amusement.

"You're not incorrect in your assessment, Captain, but he is nevertheless a powerful being. It is perhaps unwise to make an enemy of him when you need his approval."

I stopped suddenly, and she turned back to me quizzically. "Are you fucking kidding me?" I asked her.

She took a moment to parse the question, then said, "I am not kidding with you, no."

"I'm not an idiot, Injala. Your people used me against Aljek. Don't maneuver me and then chastise me for doing what you clearly wanted me to do. My people had a saying, back on Earth: 'Don't pee on my leg and tell me it's raining.'"

"I believe I get the point, Captain."

"I hope you do," I said. We arrived at the door to our residence, flanked by two Kelvaki guards in the livery of the Royal House. Liam greeted them and entered. I turned to gesture Injala in before me, but she was gone. I quickly activated my sensory implants, switched to infrared, and saw her walking away under a cloaking shield. "I hate when she does that," I muttered.

"What was that about Imiri?" Liam asked as we went inside.

I grinned. "Oh, that was me baiting the ambassador. And he rose to the bait brilliantly."

Liam fixed his gaze on me for a moment. "Yeah, that part was pretty obvious. Reckless, but obvious. But my question was asking for the details."

"Oh. Well, Gelka used to be military. Imiri was a colony that tried to break away from the Zhen. His methods of stopping the rebellion outraged the public and caused a ruckus in the Talnera that forced the Twenty to come down on him. That's why he's a diplomat now, and not commanding a ship."

"Too important to shitcan him forever, but too problematic to keep in the command chain?"

"In a nutshell."

"Nice guy," Liam said. "Glad he's here and not planning the response to Earth."

That raised the hairs on the back of my neck. "Yeah," I said.

"Well, I'm a bit gross," Liam said as he walked toward our bedroom. "I need a shower. And then maybe——"

The door chimed, and I groaned. "Close the door, we've got company!" I called to Liam, then went to the door and opened it, expecting Injala to have returned.

My breath caught when I saw the Zhen at the door. Before I could move, he held up a hand in a warding gesture. "I am not here for blood, Captain Hunt."

Behind him, a pair of Zhen guards stood nervously, their gazes flicking between me and the Kelvaki guards, whose ears were twitching.

I examined him for several seconds. This guy was wearing the symbols of the Zhen diplomatic service, which like all things in the Empire, was part of the Zhen military. I was still officially an enemy of the Empire, and I'd just embarrassed the ambassador, so I wasn't expecting a nice social visit. On the other hand, attacking me here would probably get him killed and the Empire at open war with the Kelvaki, if Dierka had anything to do with it.

He cocked his head at me. "You appear to be trying to decide if you can safely let me in," he said. "If it will help you feel better, I shall leave my guards outside, and your Kelvaki guards may enter and witness this meeting."

I smiled. "I don't need the guards to feel safe from you. By all means, enter." As I stepped aside and let him pass, I reflected that I'd probably been played. But the die had been cast, so I let it go. That said, I made sure to stay several feet outside his reach. With a thought, I sent a message to Liam apprising him of the situation and told my NeuroNet to start recording everything I heard and saw. "Now, what do you want?" I asked.

"I am Kor—"

"I don't care who you are," I said, interrupting him with a wave. "What do you want?"

"I am not here to make a request. I am here to make you an offer."

I simply stared at him and waited.

He realized I wasn't going to ask. "Your destruction of the *Chon:ak:al* was quite a blow to the Space Force—"

"Thanks," I interrupted. "I'm quite proud of that."

"Yes," he said, bristling slightly. "I'm sure you are. It set our plans back several months, and gave you room to fortify your illegal colony. It was quite well done, honestly. But," he said, holding up a hand as if to stop me from interrupting again, "you must know that all you did was buy some time. We will regain our footing, and we will be back."

"We'll be ready."

"Perhaps," he said. "Perhaps you will defeat us again, and our response to *that* will be rebuffed, and again, and again, until we decide to leave you alone." He made a gesture, as if weighing possibilities. "Or, we will come back in force, destroy your colony, kill your people, and retake Earth for ourselves. Or perhaps we will simply decide to bypass all that and leave you alone, now. The choice is yours."

"What. Do. You. Want?"

"We want you."

"You have *got* to be kidding," I said.

"Not at all. I have been sent to inform you that if you turn yourself in to our government, we will leave Earth alone forever. We will also guarantee the freedom of your crew, with full immunity from prosecution for the crimes they have committed alongside you."

"And what becomes of me?"

"You, I am sorry to say, will be tried in the Imperial courts. You will of course be found guilty, publicly and officially stripped of your status as a Hero of the Empire – which of course you realize has already happened unofficially – and executed. But your friends will be free."

"Bullshit," came a new voice. I turned and saw that Liam had entered, his blaster out and leveled at the Zhen. "You will not take my husband," he said, his voice ragged.

"Liam, stand down," I said calmly.

"Tajen, you can't possibly—"

"Liam," I said quietly. He looked at me a moment, then lowered his gun.

"He's not wrong, though," I said as I turned back to the Zhen. "It's bullshit. We didn't just embarrass the government, we showed the galaxy the Zhen can be beaten. There is no conceivable way the Zhen government will ever let that stand unpunished. You just want to use my execution as a way to demoralize my people, and maybe buy a little time to prepare your forces to steamroll over them right after the trial." I affected an expression of deep thought for a moment. "Probably the plan is to attack even as the sentence is carried out." I looked at Liam. "Sound right?"

"It's what I'd do," he said. "You know, if I was an untrustworthy *shken* like the One."

The Zhen functionary drew himself up in outrage. "How dare you insult—"

"Oh, *stop*," I said, irritated. "The One is as untrustworthy as a wild *shken*, and you know it. She'd kill you herself if she thought it would get her something. Hell, comparing her to the *shken* is actually unfair to the *shken*. At least they're just acting on instinct. The One could choose better, if she wasn't such a—"

The Zhen drew himself to his full height. His crest stood straight up, and his claws unsheathed – an incredibly rude action to his people, in a meeting like this. "Be careful, Tajen Hunt," he spat. "Insult our leader one more time, and I may forget about the guards outside."

"Try it," Liam snarled, and I heard the click and whine of his sidearm priming to fire.

I waved Liam back without looking at him, and grinned at the Zhen. "She's not my leader. Now. Take this message back to your superiors, and be sure to phrase it exactly as I tell you. Ready?"

He nodded, murder in his eyes. I sent a signal to the door, which opened. I held a hand out toward the door and said, clearly and distinctly, "When you come for us, we'll be ready. Until then…. Fuck off."

He left, and I shut the door after him.

"Was that wise?" Liam asked.

"No," I said. "But it was a hell of a lot of fun."

CHAPTER FOUR

A week later, I left the offices of a minor ally of Lord Aljek, shaking with frustration. Liam rose from his seat in the waiting room and crossed to me. "How'd it go?" he asked.

I said nothing until we had left the building and were on the street. "Lady Akkal is *terribly* worried about the *poor* humans and their fate if the Zhen return, but she just *can't* go against Lord Aljek without losing her position in the House, and she hopes we *understand* that she will do whatever she can behind the scenes, but cannot help us openly."

"Your impression of her is uncannily accurate," he said with a shudder. "At least she'll help behind the scenes."

I glanced at him. "You believe that?"

He sighed. "No, not really." He glanced at me, and then said quietly, "You know these people better than me. What's going on here?"

"The problem, my love," I said with a grin, "is that while I know some things about the Kelvaki, they are incredibly opaque in many things. I know the basic structure of their government – each House controls various functions of government, the heads of each House sit on the High Council, the Ascendant guides overall policy, blah blah blah. But how that actually works in practice? It's confusing as hell, and it's constantly shifting. In order to get anywhere, we'd need a better snapshot of the council politics, and even Injala can't help me there. She spent two nights trying to get me to a basic understanding, but I just can't grasp it long enough to know what to do. It almost doesn't matter how good a case I make for helping us. They're playing an internal game, and without the right leverage in that struggle, I can't move anyone."

He shook his head. "I guess that—" He stopped suddenly, at the same moment that an URGENT CALL bulletin came up in my visual field. "Are you getting this too?" he asked.

"Yes," I said. I accepted the call, and Kiri's face appeared in a corner of the field. "What's up, Kiri?"

"Nothing good," she said, "but it isn't something I want to say over the air. Even our encryption may not be enough. When can you get back?"

"We're on our way now," Liam said.

"Make it fast," she said, and cut off.

Liam sighed. "Guess we don't get that dinner date."

"I'll make it up to you," I said.

"See that you do," he said with a wink.

We took a flyer back to our residence. As we neared the guard station, one of them nodded to me and signaled the door to open. As we passed through, I thanked them. Kiri was waiting for us inside, pacing.

"What's the problem, kid?" I asked. Normally she'd give me a raised fist, or at least a glare, over being called that, but today she didn't react to it.

She said, "I think the Zhen are going to assassinate Dierka."

"What?"

She crossed the room to her computer and swiped at the display area, then 'threw' me the data, my NeuroNet linking to both hers and the computer to display the data in the air between us. "This is a series of communiqués between the Zhen government and their ambassador. See this?" A word repeated several times flashed red.

"Why are we concerned with offers of some *uktatha* to the Kelvaki?" I asked.

"*Uktatha* are good eating," Liam said. "Probably a good market for them here."

"Wait," I said. "That doesn't make sense. Kelvaki body chemistry is markedly different from the Zhen's. A lot of their foods are toxic to the other." I pulled up some data and frowned. "She's right – *uktatha* are poisonous to the Kelvaki. There's no way they'd buy them even if the Zhen offered them."

Liam said, "Maybe the offer's one of their 'calculated insults'."

"Maybe, but take a look at this," Kiri said. She added new information beside the first. "These are messages we got when we raided that Imperial Intelligence node last year. Right after you left Zhen:da, messages went out to several ship captains, putting them under the command of Solaar Den'sho. And *these*," she said, bringing up another set, "were to Den'sho himself. They order him to follow you, give him your NeuroNet tracking information, and then tell him to be sure he kills 'the *uktatha* at Akhia'."

Liam said, "You think '*uktatha*' is code for Dierka."

Kiri nodded.

"Eh," I said. "It could be code for me."

"No," she said. "The code for you is 'shitworm'."

I stared at her while Liam began laughing. "You're not serious."

She just blinked at me a few times.

"Okay," Liam said. "Let's say you're right. Let's turn the information over to Kelvaki Intelligence."

"No," I said.

"No?" Liam asked.

Kiri frowned. "Why not?"

"We're going to handle this ourselves," I said.

Liam pursed his lips a moment. "I get where you're going," he said. "If we handle it for them, we not only bypass their politics, but we show we're capable of helping them out."

"Right," I said. "And—"

"I'm not done," Liam interrupted. "I see where you're going, but it's a bad idea."

"How so?"

"We have no idea what Kelvak's intelligence people are aware of, or what they're doing. We could walk into the middle of something and screw it up."

I thought about it, and he was right. "Okay," I said, "how about this – we follow the leads we have, try to see if Kiri is right and gather evidence. Once we have proof something's up, we take it to the Kelvaki."

Liam didn't look entirely convinced, but he agreed.

"Okay," I said, turning to Kiri. "Let's find this asshole."

★　　★　　★

After a week of searching, we still couldn't find the asshole. If I'm being honest, we couldn't even prove there *was* an asshole. We'd traced the finances of the ambassador's delegation, but found nothing. If there was an assassin here, they weren't being supported by the embassy, at least not in any way we could track. But right now, I had more immediate problems.

I was standing in the council chambers again, arguing – again – with

Councilor Aljek. "Ridiculous!" he spat. "You would have us send our best unit to your defense?"

"Nonsense, Aljek," Councilor Jinnka said. "You are exaggerating the effectiveness of the Dekka'ka."

Aljek sneered at Jinnka. "I do not need a ground-grubber's analysis of my forces."

Jinnka merely smiled up at her comrade in arms. "Perhaps His Excellency has forgotten that before I was ordered to take command of the Assembly's ground forces, I *led* the Dekka'ka?" she asked in a solicitous tone.

"I have forgotten nothing," Aljek replied. "But I have made improvements to the unit since those days."

"Oh, is *that* what you call your decisions?" she asked.

Aljek folded his hands behind his back and drew breath, but before he could speak, a new voice cut through the room. "Enough of this!"

Both Jinnka and Aljek turned toward the dais, where the Ascendant stood. He stepped down and looked both Aljek and Jinnka in the eyes, then brushed past them and spoke directly to me. "These games must be tiring for you, Captain Hunt."

I searched for a politic answer – or at least a clue what he wanted to hear from me. I was clueless. So I merely said mildly, "They would certainly be more amusing if I knew what their goals are." I paused, then said, "Other than His Excellency's apparent desire to refuse to help my people."

"Perhaps I can be of assistance. Jinnka," he said, gesturing toward the other Kelvaki, "is interested in helping your people. In addition to her admiration of your cause, she finds you, personally, amusing and worthy of our aid." I heard gasps from around the chamber. The Ascendant glanced at Aljek, and said, "My space commander, on the other hand, doesn't actually care whether or not we help you, just so long as Jinnka is inconvenienced and, if possible, humiliated."

The other councilors, many of whom had been speaking softly with each other on the edges of the room, turned to face the Ascendant in shock. A couple of them even stood, the muscles of their arms and legs quivering with outrage. Siiren's face fell as she placed her head in her palm, a very human gesture that might have been theatrical.

What's going on? Liam sent via our NeuroNets.

He just put his foot in it, I sent. *Dierka once told me that the biggest sin in Kelvaki politics is to make the secret game public.*

What's he playing at?

No idea, I replied. I turned to look for Injala. She was standing beside the throne, where she always stood during council sessions. I wasn't as familiar with female Kelvaki as I was the males, but she didn't look happy, and I wondered what had happened here besides the obvious.

For his part, the Ascendant seemed to realize he'd made a mistake. His breathing slits closed so tightly they made a slight sound when he exhaled. He said calmly, "This session is adjourned. Return tomorrow," before simply turning and leaving. Injala flashed me a hand sign I'd come to know meant I'd be seeing her later that evening.

★ ★ ★

"Anything?" I asked Kiri as we gathered for the evening meal.

"No," she said. "I've been watching the Zhen delegation's dispatches for days. There's nothing. No hint of an assassin anywhere. Maybe we were wrong."

"'We'?" Liam asked slyly as he sat at the table.

I brought the serving bowl of stew to the table. Liam cocked his eyebrow and looked at it. "Did you make this?" he asked, careful to keep his voice neutral.

We'd had to bring our own food with us on the mission; Kelvaki food was disgusting to human palates. But we didn't bring anyone to prepare it, figuring we'd be good enough. Liam was a passable cook, but the first time he'd tasted something I made, he'd sighed and said sadly, "I miss Takeshi." Takeshi had been an accomplished chef, and his death at the hands of Zhen last year had robbed us of more than his company.

"No," I said defensively. "Kiri made it."

"Oh, all right then," he said, reaching for the ladle. I growled at him, but only playfully – he was totally right to avoid anything I cooked except chili. Everything else I made was overdone, often to the point of inedibility. For fifteen years I'd lived on other people's cooking and pre-prepped ration packs. Even NeuroNet 'skill packages', meant to teach one to cook, had never helped my kitchen skills; after a while I'd stopped even trying.

Thinking of the NeuroNets made me pause. Every adult citizen of the Empire has a NeuroNet installed in their brains. They're used to do nearly everything, from making calls to conversing silently to operating equipment to creating visual information links.

My own NeuroNet had been upgraded considerably last year when I busted through the blocks placed on the military-grade system I had in my head. I could do things with my NeuroNet that most people couldn't do, especially humans. We'd tried to enable some of my new skills in the civilian models most humans had, but they didn't work without the military-specced hardware, and we hadn't found any humans who'd managed to keep their military 'Nets like I had, so far.

And then it hit me.

I reached out with my own 'Net to test my theory, using the sensors embedded in my brain to locate nearby systems. I could see Kiri and Liam at the table. I turned to look at the door, and through the wall, I saw the two Kelvaki guards on-station. Their systems looked different – I could, if I wanted, make contact with them, but it wouldn't be as easy as making contact with an Empire-made system.

"I think I know how to find the assassin," I said.

"What?" Kiri sat back from her bowl of stew and stared at me. Liam looked at me, but it didn't stop him from continuing to shovel stew into his face.

"We've been trying to do this like detectives," I said, "and getting nowhere. The Zhen are just too good at this, we're *not* detectives, and we were never trained as spies."

"Okay," Kiri said, "so what's the breakthrough?"

I tapped my forehead. Kiri frowned and shook her head, then her eyes widened. Liam grinned, then went back to eating.

"How?" Kiri asked.

"The Kelvaki use a different kind of system," I said, pointing toward the wall, "and the Zhen override suite can see them all. I can see the guards even from here. Their systems look different in the visual overlay. If I link up with something that can see the whole city, I bet I can sift through and find all the Zhen-made systems. Then it's just a process of elimination."

"What if it's not?" Liam asked.

"Don't borrow trouble," Kiri and I said simultaneously. We grinned at each other; those words were Hunt family wisdom handed down for generations.

Liam stared at us both a moment, his face completely neutral. "I hate you both," he said.

"Liar," I said.

He opened his mouth to answer, but Kiri interrupted. "So, as much as I love watching you two do this," she said, before opening her mouth wide and gesturing into it with her fingers as if trying to vomit, "maybe Tajen should get on that?"

"You're no fun at all," Liam said.

"*So* no fun." I rose and went to the couch, calling up my 'Net's access HUD.

Kiri brought over a Kelvaki computer. "This has the access code Dierka gave me. It'll let you log in to any civilian system."

I closed my eyes and accessed the local slipnet connection nodes. It wasn't necessary, really, but I liked to cut myself off from the real world when doing anything that required concentration. I envied Kiri, who could do this kind of work with her eyes open while playing a game, but her system wouldn't be able to see the differences in systems like I could.

While the Kelvaki slipnet systems weren't identical to Zhen models, they were similar enough that I was able to maneuver the system pretty easily. It didn't actually take me long to identify all the Zhen-made systems in the city. But there was a problem.

I'd been operating on the assumption that Zhen systems wouldn't be common. But there were hundreds of the damned things in the city. The open market had flooded Zhen-made systems into Kelvaki space. There were doubtless differences based in the differing physiologies of each species' brain, but those differences weren't obvious enough for me to find them. I gave up and withdrew from the system.

When I shut down, I opened my mouth to speak, but was interrupted by the door signal. I simultaneously received an 'all clear' signal from the guard outside, so I opened the door breezily.

"Injala," I said to the Kelvaki woman at the door. "Come in."

She stepped inside and took both my hands in hers. "Good evening, Captain," she said. "I come with some information, and an invitation."

"You are quite welcome here," I said. "We have a small supply of Kelvaki refreshments. Would you like anything?" I waggled my eyebrows. "I even stocked some *jiran*."

"You stocked *jiran*?" Injala looked shocked, which made sense – *jiran* was one of the Kelvaki foods that would kill a human who tried eating it.

"It's one of Dierka's favorites," I said. "I could prepare some for you?"

She looked hesitant, and finally said, "I am uncomfortable with the idea of you endangering yourself – contamination would be bad for both of us. How about *I* prepare it while we talk?"

"Of course," I said, and led her to the kitchen.

I put the sealed package of *jiran* on the counter and tried not to shudder at the feel of it in my hand. I sat back and watched as Injala opened the package and dumped the contents onto a cutting surface. She unsheathed one of her finger claws and began to cut the gelatinous mass into strips. "You are doubtless wondering what was happening today," she said, carefully not looking at me.

"The question had crossed my mind, yes," I said.

"I do not need to imagine why. To see the Ascendant show his *chralak* like that—"

"*Chralak*?" Kiri asked, settling onto a stool beside me.

"His inner voice," I said. "He outright said what Aljek wants."

"And?"

"To the Kelvaki," I said, "that's the height of bad manners."

"It goes beyond manners," Injala corrected gently. "The *chralak* is the secret face of all Kelvaki. To show it is to betray yourself – it is something one normally shows only one's mate."

Kiri frowned. "But doesn't everyone know what he really wants, already?"

Injala's ears flicked. "Well, yes, in this case. But among Kelvaki, there is what is known, and What is Known. By stating it in an open meeting, the Ascendant not only embarrassed Aljek, but he made it clear, without intending to, where *he* stands on the issue – and incidentally made the entire council aware that they cannot trust him."

"Why not?" I asked. "I gather something is wrong with him, but what?"

Injala stopped slicing the *jiran*, then took a moment to throw out the discarded bits. She placed the strips she'd cut on her plate and pushed a button, signaling the countertop to clean itself. She gestured to the dining table, and we joined Liam there as the kitchen wall opened several ports, allowing a swarm of tiny robots to flood the countertop and scrub it clean before disappearing once more.

Injala led the way to the sitting area, where she perched on a chair, not waiting for it to conform to her body's dimensions. She settled into it as it finished adjusting, then popped a tiny piece of *jiran* into her mouth, chewed it, and finally swallowed, before saying, suddenly, "The Ascendant's mind is unraveling." She waited a moment, and then said, "It will not be long before Dierka is called to lead the Assembly."

I stared at her. "What do you mean, it's unraveling?"

Her earflaps closed tightly, and she seemed to draw in on herself as nearly every muscle in her body tensed. She very deliberately relaxed before turning fully to me. "I mean exactly what I say. We call it *shiralak*. He is losing the ability to control what he says, and to whom. In time, it will get worse. Eventually, his brain will forget to run his body. Then he will die."

Kiri shuddered. "We have something similar among humans, but we found a cure for it. Can nothing be done?"

"No," Injala said. "We looked into this, but the cure your people use depends on the NeuroNets and nanite-based medicine. But *shiralak* is caused by those very things. It is a reaction, uncommon among our people, but not unknown, to the lifelong presence of neural computers."

"Is there no way to cure it?"

She tilted her head to the right momentarily., "We could, of course, program his neural computer to take over his autonomous functions, but his mind would still be unable to direct his actions properly. He would become a *ssirakk*, a Kelvaki in form only. In the end we would have to put him down. Far better, it is felt, to let him pass naturally."

I sat forward, my elbows braced on my knees. "So today – how much damage was done, really?"

"To your cause, or to the Ascendant?" she asked archly.

I winced. "Both."

Her mouth twisted in a sardonic grin. "To your cause, none." At my surprised expression, she said, "You realize, of course, you were never going to get what you came here for. Which," she added as I took breath, "does not mean you will leave empty-handed. But there is no force in the Assembly that could make Aljek give you what you want…and his agreement is mandatory, where disposition of the space forces is concerned."

"And the Ascendant?"

"His position is almost as precarious as yours," she said, her voice trailing off. She stared into space for a moment. "It is not long now before he will have to step down."

Liam sat forward. "And then Dierka becomes the Ascendant?"

"Yes," she said.

"When that happens, can he help Earth?" Kiri asked.

"No," Injala replied, "not in the way you are thinking. While we try to project an image of the Assembly as a harmonious collection of peoples, the truth is that we are somewhat more fractious than we appear. Dierka will have his hands full consolidating his power and holding the Assembly together, possibly for quite some time. Earth, I am afraid, must stand alone." She looked like she was sorry to say it.

"But all is not lost for your people." She rose and walked toward the door. As I rose to join her, she plucked a small folded piece of flimsiplast from her belt pouch. "Tomorrow, the three of you are invited to this address," she said, passing it to me. "Be there at the Hour of Singing. I think you will like what you see." She didn't wait for an answer, but slipped out the door.

We took our dishes to the kitchen and placed them into the cleaner. Once Injala had been gone for a few minutes, Liam got out a small scanner and began to sweep the apartment, paying special attention to anywhere Injala had been. She was on our side, but she was also a Kelvaki Assembly intelligence officer; we weren't taking any chances. After he'd scanned the room, he shut down the device. "We're clear," he said. "What did you find?"

"A dead end," I said. "I should have realized the Zhen-made models are just as numerous here. There's no way we could track them all."

"I was afraid that might be the case," Kiri said.

I glared at her. "Why didn't you say something?"

"I thought maybe you knew something I didn't." She sighed. "Where do we go from here?"

"I guess we go to this meeting of Injala's tomorrow, first. Then we'll figure out our next move before the next Council meeting."

*   *   *

We arose before dawn and got dressed in the soft twilight of a Kelvaki morning. Apparently, our guards had been told what was going on, because the car was already there for us when we stepped outside.

As we flew across the city, Kiri kept her face practically glued to the window. Liam and I traded grins at the sight. Most of the time, I forgot how young she was; she appeared – and acted – like someone several years older. But today she looked not a day over her age. I also tended to forget that she'd never left Zhen:da before the day we'd fled the Zhen last year. Kelvak was a place I'd visited many times, but for her it was the first non-Zhen world she'd seen aside from Earth itself.

"I know you're laughing at me," she said without turning. "And I don't care."

"We're not laughing," Liam protested. "Just being amused."

"Yeah," I said. "It's not often you look your age. We're just enjoying the sight."

"Enjoy this," she said, flipping me off.

I thought about retorting, but the car suddenly banked and began to descend. "What's at the address Injala gave us?" I asked her.

"Not sure," she said. "I looked up the address but couldn't find anything in the databases It was marked with a governmental secrets code. But that doesn't look like a government building."

Liam leaned over and checked the window on her side. "I recognize that emblem," he said. "That's Kaatlak Weapons Systems. They're one of the big Kelvaki weapon designers."

"Interesting," I said.

The car landed, and when the door rose, Injala stood waiting for us. "Welcome, Captain Hunt," she said as we exited. "Liam, Kiri." She ushered us toward the building's entrance. "Please, follow me." She led us inside, where we were checked in and scanned for weapons.

Once cleared, Injala led us farther into the building and underground, where we entered a transport station. We were ushered into an enclosed tram where we did our best to get comfortable on the Kelvaki-sized seats before the tram began traveling through a dark tunnel, gathering speed quickly.

"What's this about?" I asked Injala.

Her ears quivered. "There is something Dierka wishes you to see."

"Which is?"

"You'll need to wait, I'm afraid."

In a surprisingly short time, the tram climbed back up to the surface. We'd clearly left the city behind. I looked around briefly and realized we were in the Maka Wastes, an area of Kelvak that had been damaged centuries ago by war.

"Couldn't we have just flown here?" I asked Injala.

"No," she said. "Civilian flights are prohibited over the Wastes, and we needed to avoid military means today."

The tram came to a stop in a small, luxuriously appointed station. A Kelvaki woman stood waiting. As we left the tram, Injala nodded to the woman, who bowed in return. I filed that away; I hadn't realized Injala's status was so high.

"Allow me to introduce you, Captain Hunt," Injala said. "This is Administrator Shalara. Kaatlak Weapons Systems is her domain." She turned to Shalara, and said, "Captain Tajen Hunt is the emissary from Earth we spoke of."

"Pleased to meet you," I said. "This is Kiri. She's my computer expert, and this is Liam, my second-in-command – and partner."

"Indeed," she said. "Welcome to my domain. If you will come with me, I think we have something you will find quite interesting."

She led us all through a nearby door, where the three of us stopped in surprise.

"Whoa," Kiri said.

I couldn't disagree. We were standing in a small observation post overlooking a vast battleground, the ceiling hundreds of feet above us, the hard-packed ground a maze of obstacles and gun emplacements.

But immediately before us, standing in ranks just below the observation post, were dozens of what appeared to be humanoid robots. Each stood about six feet tall, with white armor plating over their chassis. Instead of humanoid faces, each had what looked like a Y-shaped window. A red light pulsed on the necks of each of the robots.

"Behold the newest weapon in the Kaatlak arsenal," Shalara said.

"Battle drones?" Liam said, a little dismissively. "I once participated in a 'friendly' battle between Zhen infantry and some Kelvaki battle drones.

We destroyed them. All we had to do was take out their central processing coordinator, and they all went dead."

"Ah yes, the Jenaa 427 exercise," Shalara said. "I was the lead scientist for that project. We have made substantial improvements since then. Unlike the model you faced, these have no centralized battle processor. While the units do communicate to plan strategy and give orders in their hierarchical structure, each unit is fundamentally autonomous. If a command unit is removed from the network, a drone is chosen by the network to become the new command unit."

"How did you manage that?" Kiri asked. "Even with modern Kelvaki systems, that's a lot to ask of mobile weapons platforms."

Shalara said, "It was difficult. I trust you will understand, however, why I do not choose to answer your question." She turned to me. "What is your opinion, Captain?"

"They're impressive enough," I said. "But why make them human-sized, instead of Kelvaki?"

"Oh, we have Kelvaki-sized drones as well. However, these were created with the defense of your world in mind. They should be able to use any and all weaponry or vehicles your people have. Would you like to see what they can do?"

"By all means."

She waved her hand at a console, which lit up with a tactical map. "I will split the drones into two forces," she said. "One will operate autonomously, but you will control the other side's tactics." She must have sent a command through her own NeuroNet, because suddenly the drones' triple-lobed visor slits lit up with an orange glow. Half the drones turned and ran toward a 'building' set up on the battlefield. "All you need do is direct the drones in defending that 'installation'. The other drones will be trying to take it intact, with a secondary objective of destroying it if it cannot be taken. I will give you a few minutes to familiarize yourself with your forces."

"All right," I said. "Liam, you're up."

Liam stepped up to the command console for our 'side' and spent a few minutes examining the various capabilities of the droids and the controls. After a few moments, he moved them into various positions around the installation. When he was finished, he turned to Shalara. "Ready," he said.

Shalara nodded, and the fight began.

The drones started out in a pretty standard attack, splitting into two smaller forces, one attempting to distract the defenders – Liam – with a frontal assault, the other circling behind under cover.

"Yeah, that's not going to work," he said, his fingers flying.

I spent fifteen years learning to fly like I was born in space. The lessons on strategy and tactics were equally applicable, because the service isn't stupid, but I was far more effective with a ship around me. Liam, though, had spent an equal amount of time learning to kick ass on the ground. He played the console like a virtuoso. When the drones bypassed his sentries, he grinned and adjusted his drones' positions.

His grin lasted about thirty seconds.

First his brows furrowed, and his lips turned downward. Then, after a few more moments and a few frantic orders relayed through the console, his eyes grew wide and he looked quickly at me before turning back to the console. Only a minute or two later, he threw up his hands.

"We lose," he said. "They're good. They've totally outclassed my drones."

Shalara waved a hand at the console, and the battle ceased. "Karr' nok tor!" she called out. The drones all stood back up. One of them walked toward us with an easy gait, stopping just under the railing separating us from the battlefield. It threw me a salute and said, in an almost-perfect human accent, "We hope you have enjoyed our demonstration, Captain Hunt." Its voice was as human as the accent. I stepped closer.

"Where was your voice sampled?" I asked it.

"I am afraid I do not know how to answer that," it said.

"We sampled their voices from human film records," Shalara said. "But they are heavily manipulated. While not entirely unique, there is care given so that no drone working in a group sounds like another in the group. Each is slightly different, to enable humans to tell them apart. Of course, in production we can also give them distinctive livery to further differentiate them, should Earth choose to purchase them."

"And if we don't?"

"I am certain we could find buyers for such equipment, if your people are not interested."

"Oh," I said, "I think you know as well as Injala here that we'll be interested. With whom do we negotiate?"

"I can negotiate with you, or we can send a salesman to Earth to speak to your leaders, as you wish."

"Let me contact home and find out what my government wishes to do," I said.

She bowed in agreement. "I will leave you to my assistant, then," she said, and walked out of the room.

Injala and the Kelvaki attendant ushered us back to the tram, which began the journey back to the city as soon as we were seated.

"Well, that was interesting," I said to Injala. "Is that your way of telling us there won't be any official help?"

"You might think that," she said. "I could not possibly confirm or deny any such thing." She inclined her head for a moment. "But a wise man would make plans for the worst possible outcome. As I believe I mentioned last night."

"Yes," I said. "I think—" I was interrupted by a comms signal indicator. I blinked and sent a command to accept the link, and my vision changed to show Dierka's face floating a few inches in front of my face.

"Dierka!" I said. "To what do I owe the honor?"

"I have some time to myself, for once, and I thought it would be nice to have lunch with my honored *draka* and his family," he said. "Are you free?"

I looked to Injala. "Are we free to meet with Dierka?" She nodded, and I said, "It looks like we are."

"Splendid!" he said. "I shall direct your driver when you return to the city."

"Dierka," I said, "tell me you're not keeping tabs on me."

"Why would I lie to you, *draka?*" He signed off, laughing that horrible Kelvaki laugh, and I couldn't help but laugh with him.

It was the last time I'd laugh on Kelvak.

★   ★   ★

The aircar landed in a public plaza, and we got quite a few angry looks from Kelvaki civilians as we climbed out. Those looks disappeared when Dierka came striding out of the plaza's hotel and greeted us. Some of the Kelvaki genuflected and moved on, others stopped and stared at the Kelvaki who would, in a relatively short time, be their leader.

As the car lifted, my eyes followed it – and widened as I saw a telltale glint on a nearby rooftop. "*Down!*" I shouted, diving for Kiri. Liam crouched low and hit Dierka at the knees – and bounced off the Kelvaki's much larger frame. Fortunately, though, Dierka had been trained similarly to Liam and I, and he threw himself at the ground a moment later as a blast of plasma hit the spot where he'd been standing. Fortunately, he managed not to land on my husband's comparatively fragile body.

Liam rolled to his feet quickly and scanned the rooftop. I painted the location of the assassin with my NeuroNet and sent it to him via battle-link. As Dierka's bodyguards flooded the plaza, guns out, Liam and I took off running toward a nearby staircase.

Halfway up, I spotted the assassin as he reached the landing above us. Seeing us coming up, he fired a couple of wild shots our way and ran off down an attached skyway toward the maglev station.

Neither Liam nor I had been hit. "He's human!" Liam said as we pursued the assassin. "What the hell?"

Rather than waste breath speaking out loud, I sent a reply via the NeuroNet. *Humans have worked for the Zhen before*, I reminded him. As we chased the assassin, I noticed there was something odd about his gait.

The assassin made it through the closing doors of a maglev train. Liam and I stumbled to a stop as the train took off, accelerating quickly. Liam threw his hands up. "Damn it!"

"Not over yet," I called, running over to an antigrav flyer kiosk. I quickly waved my hand over the NeuroNet interface to wake it and acquire a key code. Once I had it, I jumped onto a flyer and called over my shoulder to him, "I managed to tag him with a tracker. Come on!"

He grinned and jumped onto the saddle behind me, his arms wrapping around my torso as I gunned the engine and took off after the train. The flyer's display screen notified me I'd been fined 150 *kiln* for the unorthodox and illegal takeoff. Liam put his mouth near my ear. "You're expensive, you know that?"

"I'm worth it," I called over my shoulder. "I see the train ahead!" I quickly opened a window in my visual field and zoomed it in on the train. "Looks like there's an emergency hatch in the middle of every car," I said. "Pretty big one, too. That's our entrance. Be ready." I pushed the flyer hard, and it managed to get us to the last car before the machine's engine started to protest at the speed I was pushing and faltered.

"Go!" I shouted, bringing the flyer in low over the train. Liam dropped over the side, grabbing on to a maintenance handhold. On the train, a window shattered outward, and the assassin leaned out and took a shot at the flyer, burning through the front cowling and hitting the engine.

The flyer bucked and I fought to control it, swinging wide away from the train and then veering back. I gathered my legs beneath me, then jumped as high as I could while using my NeuroNet to activate the flyer's air brakes and drop thrust. The flyer slid out from under me, and as my boots made contact with the train, I fell backward, Liam barely managing to grab my hand and keep me from going over the edge. I laughed, and then winced at the sound of the flyer crashing on the tracks behind us. "We're not making friends of the locals, here," Liam said. "Let's try to minimize damage and keep the civilians out of harm's way." I made my way to the nearest hatch.

I managed to override the hatch, and we dropped through the hole into the train. The assassin was heading through the door to the next car, and without stopping to think, I raised my own pistol and fired. Several Kelvaki screamed and ducked as my shot hit the door, missing the assassin as he ducked behind it and made his way farther up the train.

I followed him, trying not to step on the Kelvaki who were now picking themselves up off the floor they'd dove to when I fired. A small Kelvaki child yipped in alarm and scrambled up into her father's lap as I neared them, her eyes glued to my gun. Her father eyed us with suspicion and wrapped his arms around her. "Don't worry," I said to him. "We're here to catch a criminal. Sorry for the fright." I followed the assassin through the door, hearing Liam behind me talking to the father, but I couldn't make out what he said before he followed me.

When we reached the next junction, I crossed the small platform between cars and triggered the door just before a series of blaster bolts hit it. I threw myself back, stumbling into Liam. We fell, arms and legs tangling. The target stalked toward us, and I pointed the gun between my knees and fired, hitting him in the chest. He staggered back, then turned and fled to the next car while we struggled to our feet.

I glanced out the window and cursed. "We need to hurry," I said. "We're pulling into a station. If he gets off we'll lose him in the crowd." Shoving my way between Kelvaki passengers, I pushed my way up the car, ignoring their grunts of annoyance. Once or twice a larger Kelvaki male turned to me, angry, but backed down when they saw my drawn blaster. I saw Liam frown at me, but I didn't have time for that conversation just now. An assassin in the employ of the Zhen Empire had tried to kill one of the few friends I had left. I wasn't going to let them get away with that.

As the train stopped, Liam and I took up station at the nearest doors and watched passengers disembark farther up the train. "There he is," Liam said, pointing.

I raised my blaster and aimed as I stalked toward the assassin. The crowd began to scatter as they noticed me. The assassin took note and ran along beside the train toward the front of the line. I followed, using my targeting system implants to compensate for motion.

As soon as I had a shot with nobody else in the way, I fired. My target dodged and the shot missed. The assassin spun and fired back, the first shot going wide. As I dodged the second, I activated my NeuroNet's stealth system, which should have removed me from the assassin's perceptions.

It didn't work.

The assassin kept firing, stalking toward me, and my NeuroNet informed me I was being targeted by *three* weapons. I ducked behind a large planter box as bolts from three different guns impacted on the other side, chewing through the plascrete. Liam dropped down beside me. "We're being shot at," he laughed.

"I thought you'd appreciate it," I said.

"Oh, I do," he said with a grin. "You know I love this shit." He popped his head over the planter and ducked back down as another blast hit. "He's coming around your side."

I readied myself, gathering my legs under me. As the assassin turned the corner, I launched; my left hand slapped the gun out of the way as my right slammed into his solar plexus.

My punch rocked the target back, but now that I was up close, I saw immediately it wasn't going to do enough – my opponent wasn't a human male after all, but a Kelvaki woman. "Oh, shit," I said. As she swung her free hand toward me, I ducked back, reaching for my dagger – and cursed when I realized it wasn't there – hadn't been there since I'd left it embedded in Kaaniv's throat on Earth a year ago.

The assassin used my distraction to kick me; I went down hard. I rolled away from the stomp she aimed for my head. As I kicked my legs backward over my own head and rolled up and over onto my feet, I heard

Liam call my name and looked just in time to see a dagger skittering across the ground toward me. I snatched the weapon into my hand and rose, dodging another shot in my direction and closing once more with the assassin. I had to change my strategy to account for the biology; Kelvaki, of course, have much different vulnerabilities than humans.

We traded a few blows back and forth before I finally saw an opening and took it, stepping into her guard and slamming the dagger into her side. Her eyes went wide as I slammed the dagger home, and she collapsed to the ground. I'd placed the knife very deliberately; it wasn't a lethal wound, but it would keep her out of action.

Liam dropped beside me. "I got the other two," he said. "No telling if there's anyone else out there, though." In the distance, the klaxons of approaching emergency vehicles sounded.

"Why are you trying to kill the heir?" I asked the assassin.

She looked at me with a snarl on her lips, but said nothing. Something in her eyes flashed, and I realized what she'd done just in time to shove Liam over sideways, pushing him away from her just as her body exploded. The shockwave of the blast forced us to slide several yards across the plascrete. My face burned like fire, and I could hardly breathe. I could hear civilians screaming in pain and fear all around us.

As the emergency vehicles landed, I tried to rise, but fell back, slipping into unconsciousness.

CHAPTER FIVE

Katherine Lawson

When Tajen made me commander of Earth's fleet in his absence, I was proud to serve, and thankful for the trust he'd put in me. Right now, though, I was ready to punch that son of a bitch right in his stupid face. We'd had several emergency scrambles since Tajen left, and this was the third this week.

"I can't believe this is happening again," I muttered as I strode into the station's command deck. "What've we got, Simmons?" I yelled over the sound of alarms blaring.

"Ships jumping into the system," my sensor officer said. He touched a control, and the alarm sounds muted on the command deck, though I could hear them continuing from outside. I nodded thanks to him, and he continued reporting. "They're hot-jumping into high orbit," he said. That meant that the ships weren't using a standard protocol of jumping to a known point, but jumping toward a system and allowing the gravity well of their target to yank them out of slipspace. It was a dangerous tactic, because if you miscalculated, your ship would either come out *inside* the planet, leading to death, or you'd plow right into the atmosphere, which was probably also leading to death.

Hot-jumping was something you'd only use in two circumstances: either desperation, or an attack. And I had a feeling it wasn't desperation.

"Can you ID the ships?"

"Working on it," he said. "Interceptors are arriving on— Interceptor flight fired upon! They're Zhen!"

"Here we go," I said. "Launch everything we've got!"

"Already done," my XO replied.

"You're in command, Lise," I said, moving toward the exit. I stopped short when Simmons stepped into my path.

"You should not," he said.

"Simmons," I said, "please tell me that you're kidding."

Simmons looked at me, his bald head shiny under the station's lights. "I am not kidding," he said. "Captain Hunt would not appreciate you throwing your life away."

"Thanks for the vote of confidence," I said. "But I'm going." I strong-armed him out of my way and went down the corridor toward the nearest airlock, where my ship was berthed. Simmons followed me.

"Commander Lawson," he said, his measured tones calm as usual. "While I understand your desire, one more ship out there won't matter."

I spun to grab Simmons by his shirt, then spun and shoved him into the wall. "It matters to me," I said. "Now, you have two choices: you can shut the hell up and go back to command, or you can come with me and help me live longer."

He cocked his head at me. "I will help you," he said.

"Good choice," I said, letting him go. We made it to the ship and locked it down before heading to the bridge. Simmons took the copilot's chair while I strapped in and brought the ship to full power. I didn't bother to request clearance from command, but simply undocked. I locked my nav system on to the developing fight and angled for it at full burn. "Set 'em up and I'll take 'em out," I said.

Simmons began assigning targeting priorities to the ship's gunnery system. The moment we entered weapons range, I fired two missiles at a Zhen bomber that was making a run on the station, pursued by smaller fighters. My plasma fire overwhelmed their already weakened shields and the bomber disintegrated under the combined fire of several Earth ships. Unfortunately, he got a missile off just before exploding.

"Gamma group, take out that missile!" I said. "You're on stray duty – make sure nothing hits the station."

"Acknowledged, leader," the Gamma commander said.

I locked on to a ship of a similar size to mine and headed for it. "Deploy ECM," I said to Simmons.

"Deploying ECM."

As the electronic countermeasure system came online, doing its best to block the Zhen ships from locking their weapons on us, I angled for a better firing solution on the ship I was chasing. I fired into their shields with everything I had. My eyes kept flicking to my own displays, where I could see my computer's best guess at how much of their shields remained.

"Come on," I growled, as the shields of the Zhen ship held steady.

Impacts on my own ship caused it to shake violently, and I had to break off my pursuit. "Shrak!" I yelled. My implants identified the ship firing on me, and I started evasive maneuvers to try to get out of their firing cone. "Damn it!"

"What is the problem?" Simmons asked.

"I can't get out of their firing cone!" I snapped. "And you can't use contractions!"

"I can," he said, his hands flying over the controls, "but I choose not to."

"Why?" I asked, pulling the stick all the way to the left.

"It is my way," he said.

"It's damned annoying," I said. I noticed a Zhen ship flying in from the side and dove to avoid its fire. Only then did I see the full squadron of fighters that would shortly pass through the same space I was in. I quickly rolled the ship, barely missing the gun pods of a fighter as it flashed by me.

The fight had quickly become overwhelming. We'd all known the Zhen were whittling us down, getting us ready for this attack. If we'd had more time, maybe Tajen would have returned with Kelvaki aid. But time had run out, and we had to play with what we had available.

"All fighters, target their command ship," I said. It was a desperate move, but I didn't have many others at my disposal. To Simmons I said, "Patch me through to command."

"It's done."

"Command, this is Lawson. I'm ordering all ships to focus on their command ship. With luck, that'll pull everything off you long enough for you to activate Contingency Exo."

"Commander...are you sure that's the best plan?"

"Lise, they've got us," I said. "There's no chance in hell we can beat the force they've sent to take us out. But if we can't win, we can at least give them some setbacks. Do it."

There was silence for a moment, and I wondered if Lise, too, was going to question my orders. "Understood, Commander. Contingency Exo is in effect." I could hear the evacuation alarms sounding in the background.

"Good. See you on the ground, Lise."

"You'd better."

Contingency Exo was a last-ditch effort to deny the Zhen the use of the station. The personnel aboard would eject in the station's lifeboats, which were all programmed to get them back to Earth.

Once that was done, the station's reactor core would be ejected outward, the attached thruster packs guiding it toward the closest enemy capital ships. If we were lucky, it would go critical in the middle of the Zhen ships, taking at least a few of them with it. And immediately after ejection, a series of explosives buried in the station's infrastructure would start blowing up, turning the entire station into a cloud of shrapnel.

Odds were, we wouldn't get anywhere near lucky enough for the core to take out the command ship. Even so, the resulting interference, as well as the giant cloud of spinning metal and ceramic shrapnel, would cause problems for any ships still in orbit.

"All ships, Contingency Exo is in motion," I said. "Once you get the all clear, break for Earth. Make landing and report in to colonial admin."

The ships all acknowledged, but looking at my computer's tactical display, I wasn't sure we'd all make it. "Simmons, you probably should have stayed on the station," I said. "I'm not sure we'll make it back to Earth."

"It seems not," he said. "Still, I did learn what I needed to."

"Yeah, what's that?"

"Perhaps later," he said. "Now is a time for fighting, not conversation."

I laughed even as I steered the ship around a fireball that moments ago had been one of my fighters. I guess I'd gotten used to Tajen's flying; the guy couldn't shut up even in the middle of battle.

I slammed my thrusters to full and resumed a straight-line course for the other side's command ship. "Find me something to break before we get shot down," I said.

"Here," Simmons said moments later, flicking a target lock to my board. "That's their main slipnet transceiver. Without it, they will find it difficult to send word back to Zhen:da. Communications will have to be transmitted via courier, which will take roughly two months, according to my calculations. It should throw their forces into disarray, at least temporarily."

"Unless they get it fixed quickly," I said. "They've got to have spares."

"No," he said. "It's too big. Destroy the assembly and they'll need to get new gear from the supply ship, and that," he said, highlighting a cloud of debris in my vision, "was destroyed a minute ago by Beta group."

"Well, nice work, Beta. All right, let's take out that transceiver. Give Beta group the targeting information and tell them to form on us."

I led Beta group in, slaloming the ship through incoming fire like I was possessed. At one point I slammed the ship into a corkscrew maneuver that got me unscathed through a volley of plasma fire.

As I passed through that, I realized four ships were headed right for me from dead ahead. If nobody moved, I was going to hit at least one of them. I held my finger down on the firing stud, pouring plasma bolts into their shields as they got closer.

One of the approaching ships lost their shield in a brilliant flash. The pilot must have been surprised, because he made a rookie error and tried to pull away. He flew right into a shot that would have missed him, his cockpit shattering and his ship plowing into his closest neighbor. Only two ships were left, but they were still closing fast.

"We are in danger," Simmons said. "If you—"

"Shut up," I snapped. At very nearly the last possible second, I turned the ship on its edge and sailed between the remaining two fighters. "I've got this."

"Clearly," he replied. He 'tossed' the next target to my side of the board. "I will leave the flying to you."

"Good plan." I vectored in toward the new target, a gunnery emplacement on the leading edge of the command ship. I locked on the gun with a torpedo and waited for the computer to give me a firing solution. As soon as the computer worked it out, the weapon fired.

Almost immediately, the command ship's guns began to fire interceptor charges, trying to knock the torpedo out. I made their job harder by locking and firing two more torpedoes, then switched to a different gun and started firing at their interceptors.

The first torpedo was hit and knocked out of action, but the second managed to get through the interceptors and hit the gun emplacement, which instantly became a mess of metal and plastics. The third torpedo impacted a few seconds later, making the hole bigger and causing secondary explosions inside the ship's substructure.

That was the good news.

The bad news was that I was so busy firing my torpedoes that I didn't see the Zhen on my six until he fired on us.

The explosion threw us violently against the straps, and alarms began blaring. "Beta flight, continue on to the transceiver," I said. "I'm going to slap this guy around a bit. Be with you soon as I can." I signed off the comms and shook my head as I pulled the ship into a tight loop, trying to get behind the Zhen. "Simmons, I've got a new job for you."

"Yes?"

"Whenever I start talking like Tajen Hunt, smack me."

He looked at me for a few seconds. "Am I to start this immediately?"

"Yes!"

"Very well." He reached over and smacked the back of my head.

"What the hell was that for?"

"You were sounding almost exactly like Tajen."

"Great," I said. "Everyone's a crit— No," I said, as I saw him reach for me. "You know what? Stop doing that job. That was a bad idea."

He regarded me silently. The Zhen bogey was good; I was struggling to get behind him. "It did seem a stupid plan," he said. "You have spent many hours with Captain Hunt. It seems likely his personality may have rubbed off on you a little."

I pulled back, bringing the pitch of my ship up to align with the Zhen. At the same time, I used the top thrusters to push my ship downward, keeping my forward-firing weapons pointed at the Zhen.

Which is probably why I once again missed someone on my six. This time, their missile hit me solidly, slamming through my shields and exploding right up against my engines.

The blast sent us spinning. I reached for the controls, but the ship was spinning so fast I couldn't quite grab on to the flight stick. I leaned against the straps, reaching as hard as I could, and—

I came to, strapped into a different seat. "What the hell?" I said, shaking my head.

"The ship is inoperable," Simmons said. I looked around and saw him sitting next to me. "So I brought us here." He glanced at the hatch readout next to me. "Launch in ten seconds."

"Then what?" I asked. "We're so far out of orbit, we're not getting back. Hope you're ready to meet some Zhen up close."

"We will see," he said. "Launching now." The pod launched a second later, the G-force slamming us into our seats. The pod's steering nodes tried to get us around the debris, but judging by the sluggishness of the pod's movements, at least one of the nodes had been damaged.

We drifted in the pod for some time before I got impatient. "Come on," I said.

"Patience rewards those who wait," Simmons said.

"What the hell is wrong with you?"

He opened his mouth to answer when the pod was slammed by something, sending us into an uncontrolled tumble. I was slammed against the harness and a terrible screeching filled my ears. But the last thing I remember is Simmons, sitting calmly in his seat, smiling at me.

CHAPTER SIX

Tajen Hunt

I learned later that I spent three days unconscious in an infirmary, healing. When I woke, the Kelvaki Security officers in the room handed me replacements for my burned clothes – but not my weapons – and escorted me to a waiting car, which took us directly to Government Center. I was marched – they did it politely, but it was a definite march – into the council chambers.

I was relieved to see Liam and Kiri there, and quickly gave both of them a hug.

"What's our status?" I asked Liam quietly.

He gave me a smile. "Our usual."

"Shit," I said.

A voice rang out across the chamber, speaking Kelvaki. "The High Council of the Kelvaki Assembly is now in session." I turned to regard the council, and my heart sank. Not a one of them – not even those who had been on my side before – wasn't scowling in my direction. The Ascendant gestured to his seneschal, who stepped forward.

"Tajen Hunt," the seneschal began, "while this body thanks you for your willingness to help us, we must condemn your flagrant disregard for public safety. Your actions resulted in the injury of forty-two Assembly citizens."

I felt the blood drain from my face. I opened my mouth, but the speaker continued. "Only luck prevented any deaths when the assassin's bomb exploded. Such reckless endangerment of our citizens cannot be—"

The service door behind the Ascendant opened and an aide rushed up to him and whispered in his ear. He frowned and got the distant look that meant he was accessing something on his NeuroNet, then turned to Injala and gestured to us. She, too, got that distant look, and then her eyes widened and she rushed to me.

"Tajen, you must go."

"Back to the residence?"

"No." She glanced at Liam and Kiri. "We've just received word from a scout team – stationed in the Sol system. They broadcast a coded message as soon as they exited slipspace."

I suddenly knew exactly what she was going to say. I wanted to stop her, to keep the words and the fear I'd been living with for a year now from becoming reality. But I couldn't.

"A little less than two weeks ago, the Zhen invaded Earth and retook the planet."

Kiri's face hardened and she said, "What about the colonists?"

"Our scouts didn't stay long, but it seems they have set up an occupation force." She turned back to me. "The Ascendant wishes it were not so, but we have also received word that the Zhen ambassador is on his way to demand your arrest and extradition to the Empire. We cannot protect you without getting drawn into war. He asks you to leave our space immediately."

"No help, then," I said. It wasn't a question. "Fine. Let's go," I said to Liam and Kiri. I turned and strode from the chamber, my husband and niece in my wake.

We hurried through the offices to the arrival zone and immediately got into our transport. We asked to return to our residence to gather our gear, but the car went in a completely different direction. "What's going on?" I asked the driver.

"Orders, sir," she replied. "We are to avoid known routes so as to prevent the Zhen from seizing you."

"Have the Zhen threatened any such—" I stopped when she held up a finger to silence me.

"My apologies, Captain," she said. "New orders: apparently there are Zhen Imperial agents at your quarters. The guards are delaying them, but I am instructed to take you directly to the highport."

"Shit," Liam said.

The car rose steadily, breaking through the atmosphere and heading straight for the station. Two Kelvaki escorts dropped into place on either side of us, where they remained until the car passed through the highport station's forcefield. At that point they turned, as if on patrol, and began to circle the station's perimeter.

The car landed in the vast bay, and we were met by Kelvaki guards in full armor and carrying large rifles. They escorted us through security and to our ship's docking port, where Injala stood waiting for us. I frowned. "How did you get here so fast?"

"Kelvaki Intelligence must keep *some* secrets," she said.

I let it go. "Here to say goodbye? I'm sure you have more important things to do."

She made a gesture of negation. "I am here to deliver the word of the Council," she said. "The Kelvaki government regrets that it must refuse further aid to the people of Earth. Earth's status within the Empire is an internal Imperial matter, and we cannot risk open war with the Zhen."

"Given how things have been going, I assumed that would be the case."

"However," she said, sounding amused, "while we cannot risk open war, there are other ways to fight than in the open. I shall accompany you to Earth, where I shall act as an advisor to you."

"Injala, no offense," I said, "but I've fought in wars before. I know how the Zhen fight."

"Yes," she said. "But I have fought in other wars, and I know ways of fighting which you have not been taught. My job is to teach you." She held up a hand. "This is the order of my liege, Dierka. I cannot refuse. Do not place me in the position of explaining to Dierka why his draka refused the aid he offered."

I could have argued, but the Zhen might have been coming any minute. I was sure the Kelvaki with me could hold them off, but I was also sure that doing so would ignite an incident that wouldn't win me any friends with the Kelvaki – and I was already on thin ice with them.

And, hell – Injala was probably right. While I was pretty good at war, I was mostly good at space war, and if the Zhen were occupying the planet, we were going to need more than my skills. And since I'd been trained by the Zhen, as had every other human fighter, we might be locked into methods and ideas the Zhen would expect. Maybe Injala could help.

"All right," I said. "Welcome to the crew."

★   ★   ★

I went straight to the cockpit and started the engines spooling up. "Kelvaki control, this is the *Something Cool* requesting departure clearance."

A female Kelvaki voice responded. "*Something Cool*, be warned there is an Imperial task group in-system. Kelvaki ships are en route to escort you to the jump limit. You'll be cleared as soon as they are in position."

"Understood, control." I turned to Injala, who had followed me into the cockpit. "Well, have a seat. Not that one!" I said as she moved toward the copilot's couch. "That's Liam's seat. Take that one." I waved to the engineering console. As she settled into the couch, I grinned. "You sure you want to be here? It's possible we won't make it out of the system."

"I'm where I need to be, Captain."

I frowned at her. "'Need'?"

"Yes."

"I admit you may have some ideas that could be helpful. But I took Earth without you once. Pretty certain I can do it again."

"Tajen Hunt," she said, "may I tell you a true thing?"

"Sure," I said.

"You are a *klintaka*."

I laughed. "You are not the first to say that. You won't be the last."

"I am not finished," she said primly.

"Oh. Do go ahead."

"You are a brilliant tactician, and from what I have heard, a fantastic pilot. But you are also a liability to your people."

"How so?"

"You are reckless. Tell me, did you ever think it might have been a good idea to come to us about the assassin? To let us handle it?"

I frowned. "He – she was right in front of me. What was I supposed to do, let her go?"

"Yes."

"Are you kidding? What would that accomplish?"

"For one thing, we'd have caught her alive."

I stared at her, my eyebrows rising toward my hairline.

"We had an operation in place. We'd been shadowing her. We had agents ready to snatch her once she got back to her home. Your actions not only resulted in injured civilians, but they scuttled our chance to find out who she was working with. And by extension, you ended the chances we could do more to help you than was already set in motion.

"If you truly want to help your world, then you need to do better than simply leap without thinking. I know you love the action and danger, but not everyone around you does. You learned to leap from behind the Zhen, and that was good. Now you must learn to think before you leap."

I started to speak but was interrupted by the comms. "Vessel *Something Cool*, you are cleared for departure."

"Acknowledged, control. Undocking now." I took the ship out, syncing up with our escorts, who dropped into place on either side of us as we headed for the jump limit. On the way out, I plotted a jump for a backwater system where I could plan the next move before we headed back to Earth.

Once we reached the limit, I opened comms to thank our escorts, but they didn't respond to hails and just left, continuing on their patrol route. "Plausible deniability," Injala said. "If asked, they never saw your ship during their patrol."

"Won't the Zhen know they're lying?"

She showed her teeth. "But they're not. As ordered, they were on instruments-only the entire patrol. Your ship must have been using a stealth mode, because you never showed up on their plots."

I smiled at the Kelvaki and took the ship into slipspace. Once the weird colors were doing their thing in the viewport, I turned to Injala. "What did you mean, 'set in motion'?"

Her ears quivered in amusement. "Go look in your cargo bay," she said.

★   ★   ★

There was no real need to remain in the cockpit during this jump, which would last a few days. So I unstrapped and headed back. When I entered the cargo bay, I nearly bumped into Liam, who was standing in the doorway staring at a bunch of large metal cargo containers, labeled in Kelvaki with the name of a common shipping conglomerate.

"What's all that?" I asked.

"Don't know," he said. "I was checking out the systems and noticed the cargo doors had been opened for a couple of hours – on *my* code, which I never gave anyone. Thought I'd check it out."

I walked over to the nearest crate and scanned the manifest tag. "'Machine parts,'" I said.

Liam cocked his head to the side. "You know, in a lot of those old movies, 'machine parts' is code for guns." We looked at each other a moment, then scrambled for the crate's release locks.

When we'd got them open, I opened the door to the cargo container and stopped, staring. Liam whistled. There were no guns, but standing before me were four of the combat drones we'd seen demonstrated on Kelvak. Behind them stood ten more ranks of four, all surrounded by shipping materials to keep them upright and secure.

I left the container and counted the others in the bay. "If these are all the same," I said, "that's four hundred and forty of these things."

"Only four hundred," Injala said from behind me. I jumped. "*Kark*, I hate that," I said.

"My apologies." She gestured to the eleven containers. "Ten of them have drones and their weapons; the last container holds armaments, both for humans and for the drones, along with some repair parts."

"Do they come with instructions for repair?" Liam asked.

"Yes," she said, "but a team of Kelvaki repair techs will meet us before we return to Earth. They'll work with you to maintain these drones – and any others my people send to Earth later. I'll give you the coordinates when we leave slipspace."

"Are these from Dierka?" I asked.

"No," she said, her earflaps quivering. "From the Ascendant. In apology that he cannot do more."

"This is," I said, "not inconsiderable."

"Mmm," she said. "It is a beginning. We will talk later." She left us, humming to herself, and I sat on a nearby bench.

"Liam?"

"Yes, O mighty Captain?"

"She," I said, gesturing after Injala, "says I'm reckless." I looked at him. "Am I?"

He took a deep breath, then blew it out slowly as he sat beside me. "Yeah."

"But—"

"Look, you asked me, now listen to the answer." He smiled. "You didn't used to be – you fly like you know exactly what your ship can do, and you can do things with it nobody else I've ever known could. When it comes to battle tactics, you're amazing – or, well, you used to be.

"But ever since we got to Kelvak, something happened to you. I warned you it was a bad idea to go after that assassin on your own. What would you have done had we found hi— her? Before the attack, I mean?"

"I'd have dealt with her."

"Yeah, but how? Quietly? Or would you have shot her in the face and been done with it?"

"I don't know," I said. "Does it matter?"

He sighed. "A year ago – even six months ago – I'd have said you'd be likely to arrest her. But, Tajen, you fired in an enclosed and crowded space, with civilians – children – nearby." He waved off my attempt to speak. "I know we had to catch her, but just about every action you took was reckless. You never stopped to think about what might happen. A lot of people were injured, and we're lucky as hell nobody died."

"They shouldn't have attacked in public!"

Liam's face softened as he looked me in the eye. "The Zhen don't care about bystanders, my love. We need to be better."

"I don't need to be lectured by you, Liam!"

"Then be the man I married!"

I shook my head, frustrated. "I need to think," I said.

He regarded me for several long moments before saying, "I'll be around when you need me. But right now I need to go make sure everything's secure."

I shook my head; he knew already everything was fine, I could tell. Essentially, he was telling me he knew I needed him to leave me alone for a bit. I pulled him close and kissed him softly, then pushed him toward the door.

I closed the crate, and then found my way to the observation lounge – what we called a tiny section of the mess that had a window – where I poured myself a glass of whiskey and sat, staring at the colors of slipspace, considering what Injala and Liam had said. It didn't take me long to reach one inescapable conclusion:

They were right.

But Liam was wrong when he said it began after we came to Kelvak. It had started months ago. When the Zhen began their attrition attacks, I knew Earth was done. I wasn't supposed to admit it, but I knew. We were a tiny group of people with borrowed ships and a dream. Of course we were going to die.

So I started taking chances. I took pilots I never would have cleared for combat into my training program. Worse, I passed them through the program and put them in space, pointed them at the enemy, and sometimes even watched them die, wishing I could take their place.

And that, too, changed me. In all honesty, I've always been an arrogant hotshot pilot, always taking chances I probably shouldn't, just because I could. But now, when I was behind the stick, I was more reckless than I'd ever been. I didn't just take stupid chances, I *looked* for them. I threw myself into combat when everyone around me knew I was unfit to fly.

I couldn't go on like that.

I smiled to myself, stretched, and went to look for my husband. I owed him a hell of an apology.

★   ★   ★

We burst out of slipspace a few clicks away from Shoa'kor Station.

We hadn't originally planned to stop here, but we'd decided to scope out the situation before we arrived at Earth. As Injala had pointed out, it was a long way to go just to get shot down as soon as we entered the system.

"Shoa'kor Station, this is Earth ship *Something Cool*, requesting docking clearance."

"*Something Cool*, Shoa'kor control. Please transmit passenger and cargo manifest."

I smiled as I sent the requested information. "No passengers, three crew, listed. Cargo is not for trade. We're taking it elsewhere."

"Captain Hunt, please dock at berth 17. Stationmaster asks you to visit him at your earliest convenience."

"Understood, Shoa'kor. Hunt out." As I angled for the prescribed docking collar, I chuckled.

"What is it?" Injala asked from behind me.

"The berth they assigned has a straight run from the dock to the jump point," I said. "They know we might have to leave in a hurry."

"Which means they know what's going on," she said.

"Yep."

"Why has the stationmaster asked you to meet with him?"

"Well," I drawled, "ol' Quince and I go way back. We sort of struck up a truce last time I was here. I'm thinking he wants something to maintain that."

"Pity you haven't got much to offer," she said.

"Well, we'll see," I said.

Once the ship was locked down, I asked Liam to see to our supply situation. Injala decided to look around on her own.

"Shoa'kor won't be dangerous for you, I'm sure," I said. "But if you do get into any trouble, just call us on comms. We'll come."

She gave me a wry look. "I am more than capable of surviving a station like this on my own," she said. "But if anyone needs to recklessly shoot their way into a situation, I will call you."

"Ouch," I said. Her face twitched in apology for the jibe and walked off on her own, appearing for all the world like she knew exactly where she was going.

I made my way to the station administration module. I'd been here more than once, but this time the place looked different. It was still seedy, but it didn't appear to be quite the cesspool it had been before. I saw no sign of *shoa'tal*, the enforcers who had worked for the station's controlling crime families the last time I was here. Instead, I saw uniformed station security. I checked some faces against the database in my NeuroNet and realized some of them were the same people, but they were cleaner, more official-looking, than they had been before.

When I got to Jeremy Quince's office, I smiled at the same bureaucrat who'd been Quince's assistant the last time I was here. "Wils!" I said.

"It's *William*," he sniffed. "How can I help you?"

"Stationmaster asked me to come visit at my earliest convenience. I decided this was it."

"One moment," he said, before disappearing into Quince's office. He came back a few moments later. "The stationmaster will see you now, Mr. Hunt," he said.

"It's *Captain*," I sniffed. I considered imitating his walk as well as his demeanor, but I thought it might be overkill, so I contented myself with brushing past the officious ass as I entered. "Quince, hi," I said, then stopped short as I realized we weren't alone. "Oh, I didn't realize you had company."

The occupant of the chair turned silently to face me. "Hello, Captain," she said.

"Seeker – I mean, Jette! You look...."

"Different?" she asked.

That was an understatement. When I'd met her last year, Jette, or

Seeker, as she'd called herself then, had looked hardly a day over sixteen, though I wasn't sure what her chronological age was.

Now, she looked like she'd aged a decade. None of it was bad – she looked good, all things considered. She just looked…older, more in control of her life.

"That's one word for it," I said. "I'm sorry, am I interrupting your business?"

"Not at all," Quince said. He gestured to the other seat, which I took. "We were discussing you, in fact."

"Should I be flattered, or worried?" I asked.

Jette smiled and gestured toward Quince. "Possibly a bit of both, but my business partner has promised to put away his personal issues with you indefinitely."

I looked to Quince. "Listen, I'm grateful for the help you gave me last year, but—"

"Save it," he said. "I did it because I believed in what you're doing. I still do." He grinned. "Like I said last year, I know my faults. I'm sure you know yours. We may never be good friends, but we can be allies. And I've got some information for you."

"What kind of information?"

He flicked a data packet to me. "That's the patrol routes of the Zhen pickets in the Earth system, as best we can figure them from observation. The information's about a week old, so be careful." He flicked another packet at me, and a system plot appeared in my vision. He pointed, and some of the information lit up. "This is what we like to call a nice fat target."

Jette added, "We'd like you to hit it."

I shook my head. "I'm not a hired gun, and I'm not a pirate."

Jette looked pointedly at me. "If you want Earth to succeed, you're either going to need a lot of money, or you're going to need to be a pirate." She gestured toward the graphic. "This is a Zhen weapon shipment. It's headed toward one of the Outer Reach planetary outposts. And it's passing relatively close to here in two days."

"Hit it," Quince said, "and you get a bunch of weapons."

"And the Zhen won't find out about it for months," Jette added.

"What if, once they do know, they track the information leak back here?" I asked.

"Unlikely," Jette said. "The information never came close to Shoa'kor, so far as they know."

I put some pieces together. I liked the shape of the result. "You've got sources in the Zhen hierarchy," I said.

Jette smiled enigmatically. "More or less," she said. "It's better you don't know more than that."

"We'll get you information on shipments like this as much as we can," Quince said. "If you're able to send ships after them, great. If not, the Zhen get them."

"What do you get out of this?" I asked.

"Not a damned thing," he said. "Except maybe a planet to retire to when it's all over."

"You expect me to believe that the stationmaster of what's still, despite some improvement, a back-of-beyond smuggler's port, and the boss of a crime syndicate, are doing this out of the goodness of their hearts?"

"Is that so difficult to believe?" Jette asked.

"Come off it," I said. "What are you getting out of this?"

Jette sighed. "You're not wrong. If you – or your allies – start hitting Zhen shipments, it'll pull patrols off their normal routes. Which opens up new smuggling routes for us. Possibly even some routes we can use to get you supplies."

I thought about it. Earth was still not a completely self-sustaining colony, and given the occupation by the Zhen, it wasn't likely to become so. And having a source of supplies not beholden to the Zhen power structure could be a good thing for us.

"All right," I said. "I've had some ideas in this line already, but it's going to take time to set up. For now, we'll hit this shipment and see how it goes. We'll take the future as it comes. Deal?"

"Deal," they both said.

"Excellent. Now," I said, turning to Jette, "Kiri's here, and would be very upset if she doesn't get to see you."

"I'm free now," she said. "I can brief her on this shipment – as well as just have some time off. I could use it." She lowered her voice. "Cleaning up Shoa'kor has been *such* a pain in the ass. Worth it, but *messy*."

We took our leave of Quince and headed back to the *Something Cool*.

"How's it working out for you, this deal with Quince?" I asked.

"It's been pretty good," she said. "I managed to take over all the remaining Families, and help Quince get rid of a lot of the worst abusers. We still have a lot of criminals hiding out here, of course, and smuggling is our number one industry, but the vices are pretty tamed now. Shoa'kor still isn't 'family friendly', but it's not quite the hellhole it was."

"How'd you manage it?"

"High fines, spaced a few assholes. That sort of thing." She saw my face and laughed. "Remember, I'm cute, but I'm not innocent."

"I'll remember," I said. "Here we are. Go have dinner with my niece. Get her home before we leave, that's all I ask."

"I'll see what I can do," she said, and walked onto the ship.

★   ★   ★

"Okay, what's the target?" Liam asked.

I flicked my hand toward the center of the table, and a schematic came up – a Zhen military transport. "It's a *Ktannic*-class transport," I said. "Minimally armed, but big, and full of good stuff."

"Such as?" Liam asked.

Kiri smiled. "According to the manifest, she's full of pulse weapons, food, and water, all en route to the outpost in the Nikotehn System."

"That's a pretty big ship," Liam said. "There's no way we can get it to Earth without the Zhen stopping us."

"No," I said. "That's where the fun part begins."

"Do tell," Injala said.

"We'll take the ship, and hide it somewhere in the Uncharted Zone." I gestured, and a map showing Earth and a large chunk of the Uncharted Regions appeared between us. I randomly chose a system, marked it, and drew a circuitous route between it and Earth. "We stash some pilots, and some small freighters, with it. And every few weeks, volunteer pilots will smuggle in shipments of food and guns, which we'll distribute through the colony."

"One small point," Injala said. "The pilots who smuggle the shipments to Earth will be putting themselves in great danger. If they're caught, the whole scheme is ruined – the Zhen are very effective at getting information."

"That's true," I said. "But the risk is worth it."

She said nothing. I looked to Liam, and the look he gave me was one of utter trust, but also worry. I realized I was being an ass. I turned back to Injala. "Have you any suggestions?"

"Yes," she said. "Set up a series of stations in the Uncharted Regions. Each one can house a small team of pilots, each of whom knows only two stations. They go back and forth between them with each run. It will be a 'pain in the ass', as you say, to plan and manage, but—"

"If anyone's captured, they can only endanger a few others, and not the whole operation," I finished. "That works for me. Kiri, can I trust you to set the system up?"

"Yes, of course. I'll draw up a list of possible station locations. Setting them up might be difficult, though, with our resources."

Injala raised her hand slightly. "Helping with materiel to do this is within the parameters of my remit from the Ascendant," she said. "I'll help Kiri get it up and running."

"Thank you. Now we just need to hit that shipment," I said.

Liam brought the ship schematic back up and started marking it with red lines and symbols. "These are good infiltration positions," he said. "They have access hatches, but the alarms can be easily bypassed. They're also out of the way and – if the Zhen are operating as normal – rarely crewed. We can get in through a couple of those, meet up and move through the ship to the cockpit."

"How many crew does a freighter like that have?" Kiri asked.

"The ship's huge, but mostly automated," I said. "Usually they've only got four crew members, and they're usually Tradd. The Zhen don't like being assigned to transports. The Tradd do most of the scut work for the Zhen forces."

"And all things being equal, I'd rather fight Tradd any day," Liam added.

"All right," I said. "Liam, work up the infiltration plan. I'll plot an intercept point – we'll hide and hit them when they come out of slipspace."

★   ★   ★

Three days later, we hung in the shadow of an asteroid in the Nikotehn System with all our systems rigged for stealth. The transport was due at any moment; as soon as it entered the system we'd get in position. Hopefully it would follow the flight plan we'd intercepted; this was the most likely entry vector if they did. If they'd deviated, then they might come into the system somewhere else, and we'd have to scramble to get there without giving away our position.

Liam, sitting in the copilot seat beside me, said, "Taj, can I ask you a question?"

"Sure," I said.

"Are you as *karking* bored as I am?"

I glanced at him, the corner of my lips rising. "In pilot training, they do a lot of exercises where we sit and wait – sometimes for hours. So, yes, I'm absolutely karking bored. I'm just really good at hiding it."

"Indeed," he said, deadpan. "I'd never have known it from the way you keep flicking through your console's settings."

"Shut up," I said.

"How's your musing on recklessness going?"

I sighed. "Not really the best time, Liam."

"That's why now's a good time."

I stared daggers at him, and he smiled. I reached over and flicked his ear.

"Hey," he said, "don't flick me!"

"You – and Injala – were right," I conceded.

"Well, yeah. Tell me something I don't know."

"I'm scared."

"Again, tell me some—"

"Never mind," I said, and turned back to the console.

"Ah, *kark*," he said. "I'm sorry, Tajen. Just trying to make you laugh."

"Yeah, well, I'm trying to be serious here," I said.

"Please, go on."

I chewed my lip a moment. "I've known the Zhen were coming soon for months now. And as lucky as we've been, I see no way to beat them."

"We beat them before," Liam pointed out.

"Yeah, and how did we do that?" I asked. "The battle was going pretty damn poorly until I sent the *Dream of Earth* up the flagship's ass." I wasn't being figurative; I'd disengaged my jump drive's safeties, set my ship to jump into the exact coordinates of the Zhen flagship's engineering deck, and abandoned my ship moments before it jumped. In effect, I'd used physics to blow the Zhen flagship out of space. In disarray after the loss of their command structure, the Zhen fleet had fallen apart, become easy pickings for the human fleet. Most had fled the system when they saw the tide turning. According to rumors we'd picked up from new arrivals, several Zhen captains had been executed for cowardice by the Zhen Star Force. "That won't work again. Hell, it shouldn't have worked that once. It was reckless. But that recklessness saved lives that day. I think I've been hoping that doing the reckless moves would keep helping us find a way through."

Liam looked at me for a moment, his face unreadable still. Finally, he drawled out, "Bullshit," and turned back to the viewport.

"What do you mean, 'bullshit'?"

"I mean," he said, "that's bullshit. You're not being reckless because you think it'll help."

"Oh? Then why, O learned sage?"

"You're hoping it'll kill you."

"That's the stupidest thing you've ever said."

"Is it?" He turned back to me. "Tajen, if you live and Earth is lost, then you failed. And it'll be worse than Jiraad."

"You think losing now will be worse than watching millions of humans die on Jiraad was?"

"Yeah," he said.

"How do you figure that?"

"Earth is ours – humanity's – in a way that Jiraad never was. We knew Jiraad was a mistake, and we told the Zhen that. When you failed to save that colony from the Tabrans, it was awful, and it changed your life. But you still had the Empire. If we lose Earth, we're almost certainly going to die – and even if we survive, where will we have to go?" He spread his arms out in a shrug that also weighed the galaxy. "I'm sure the Kelvaki Assembly would take us in, but how many of us do you think will go there? How many would die back on Zhen:da? We'll be a dying people, Tajen. And there is no way in hell you're looking at the possible end of the human race and being okay with living to see that." He sat back.

"That's…." I stopped and marshaled my thoughts. I'd been about to say it was ridiculous, but the truth was, Liam was right. I hadn't put it into words, but once I'd heard it, I had to admit the truth of it.

For one thing, my recklessness in the past had been when I was on my own. I had no relationships but my brother, and I was responsible only for my own ship and life.

But I wasn't alone anymore. Even if I was flying alone, I had a husband, and a niece, and a set of friends who would care if I died. I owed it to them to live, to be reckless only when I had to.

And in a wider sense, I was more a part of the human race than I'd ever been before. I owed them, too, a better Tajen, who wouldn't throw his life away like an idiot.

Of course, I wasn't going to change completely. I'd never stop being a smart-ass, and there was a good chance I was going to risk a Zhen's wrath at least 347 more times before this was over.

But I had to stop trying to get myself killed.

"I think…you might be right," I said.

"Of course I'm right. I know you better than anyone, my very dashing hero of a husband," he said. "And I get it. I do. But if you don't stop trying to get yourself killed, I'm going to get killed trying to stop you. You want that on your shoulders too?"

"*Kark* no," I said.

"Then cut it the hell out, huh?"

I nodded. "Do my best."

"Well, I guess that's all I can ask for," he said, and reached out to me. I took his hand, and our fingers intertwined for a moment before Kiri's voice interrupted us.

"Now that that's settled," she said, "maybe we can pay attention to that ship that just arrived in-system?"

We both turned and looked at her. "How long have you been there?" I asked her.

"Long enough to know what you were discussing," she said. "Now, can we get back to work?"

Liam turned to me. "She is *so* related to you," he said with a chuckle.

"Don't I know it," I said, and turned back to my console. "We still at full stealth?"

"Affirmative," Kiri said.

I feathered the thrusters, which we'd switched earlier to cold-gas to help hide us. The ship's emissions were under strict control, and we'd even shut down the engines to minimize heat. If we were lucky, the heat we couldn't control – like our body heat – would blend in with the background radiation.

I brought the ship in close to the freighter, which had come in pretty close to the vector we'd assumed it would take. We only had a few minutes to do this before the freighter activated their chain drive and begin heading in-system at multiples of *C*, the speed of light.

We snuggled up to a docking port in what should be a little-traveled and forgotten corner of the ship. Thanks to Zhen standardization, our airlocks matched up perfectly. "Locked," Kiri reported from the airlock. Liam and I unstrapped from the bridge then headed to the lock, where we got suited up and armed. "Remember," I said, "if there's any trouble, undock and be ready to run."

"I'm not leaving you," Kiri said, "so try not to get caught."

I shook my head at her. "Do my best," I said.

"Yeah, me too," Liam said.

"Who said anything about you?" She laughed at him and opened the door. "In you go," she said.

Injala walked up and stopped Kiri from closing the door. "If it is permissible, I will go with you," she said to me.

"I don't have time to wait for you to suit up," I said.

In response, Injala merely reached up and touched a spot behind her ear. Armor wrapped around her from behind, enclosing her in a suit of nanite-based armor in seconds. She looked at me, her expression eloquent, and then stepped into the airlock beside me.

"Well, all right, then," I said, and Kiri closed the lock. As we waited for it to cycle, I keyed Injala into the tactical channel Liam and I were using.

The airlock finished cycling, and the outer door opened. Liam immediately got to work on the panel to open the freighter's door. We all swayed slightly when the freighter went to chain drive. "There we go," I said. "We're on the clock now."

"'On the clock'?" Injala asked.

"Old Earth expression," I replied. "It means we've got a limited amount of time before the freighter gets to the outpost."

"How much time?"

"Maybe an hour," I said. "Perhaps more, but I wouldn't bet on it."

Liam got the door open. The cargo bay was in darkness, so as we moved into it, I activated my night vision. The gloom resolved itself into a NeuroNet-generated visual. Cargo was everywhere, but it seemed we were otherwise alone. Good. I made my way to the access hatch to the rest of the ship, and waited for Liam and Injala to take up position. Once they were in place, I opened the door.

My eyes widened, and a moment later I was flying backward as a large green hand slammed into my chest. As I hit the ground, a Zhen warrior entered the room, stalking toward me with murder in his eyes. Liam ran forward to try to take him out, but the Zhen merely swept him aside and kept coming. Suddenly, though, the Zhen stopped, his crest rising to its full height, and then crumpled to his knees before falling onto his side. Injala stood behind him, her own suit having extruded a long blade, now dripping with the Zhen's blood.

"This does not look like a Tradd," she said.

I climbed to my feet. "You're not wrong." I made my way over to Liam. "Anything hurt, Liam?"

"Only in my imagination," he groaned, rolling himself to his feet. "I'm increasingly unhappy with it, if I'm being honest." He gingerly felt his ribs. "I don't think anything's broken, but I should probably avoid any more backhands from large reptilian people from here on out."

"Well, that seems wise." I turned back to Injala. "See any data ports?"

She indicated a wall-mounted console, which I moved to. My NeuroNet connected to the device, and my virtual self quickly flew down the data paths and connected to the various internal sensors of the ship. "Looks like we've got four Tradd, as expected," I said to Injala and Liam, "and an unexpected seven more of these guys –" motioning to the Zhen. "They're all in crew quarters. Question is, why was this guy coming in here in the first place?"

Liam shrugged. "Maybe they detected us docking and coming aboard?"

"No," I said. "If they had, more than one would have come – especially if they knew it was me."

"Ooooh, someone's getting a high opinion of himself," Liam said.

Injala's nostrils closed, and her voice became somewhat nasal as she pointed toward a toilet door and said, "I may have an explanation."

I sniffed. Sure enough, the smell coming off the Zhen was pretty rank, and the toilet was the only thing in here he might have been coming for. But that was a hell of a coincidence. "It can't be that simple," I said.

"Can't it?"

"If it is, it's a first for us," Liam said. "The way our luck's been going, it wouldn't surprise me if they knew we were coming for this ship." He looked at me, suddenly alarmed. "That's not possible, is it?"

"Possible, but unlikely," I said. "This is a standard shipment, on the usual schedule. The only thing unusual is eight Zhen on board." My NeuroNet alerted me and I looked to the door, my eyes wide. "Kark, someone's coming." Liam and Injala bolted for a hiding place, but there was no time to move the body. I put my NeuroNet into stealth mode. It would actively interfere with the vision of any NeuroNet user within sight – say, at least fifty yards, in an enclosed space like a ship – and sort of 'disallow' their neural interface to register me. It was a kind of perception filter, used by Zhen officers of the Imperial security service to move amongst the general population unseen. I'd given myself the ability when I hacked my system last year, during the whole 'Find Earth, kill my old friend Kaaniv' adventure that had started me on this path. I'd wait for him to get close, then stab him – no sense in firing a blaster and alerting everyone else.

The door opened, and a Zhen walked into the room, saying, "Hey, Zhikka, you in there? I wanted to remind you to—" He stopped suddenly, looked down at Zhikka's body, and then snapped his vision to me. His crest flattened, and he backpedaled out the door, yelling "Intruders!" at the top of his voice. He was clearly using his NeuroNet to alert everyone too, because the internal alarms started going off immediately.

I cursed and ran to the door, risking a quick peek outside, and ducked back as he fired at me from the nearest corner. Liam and Injala came up beside me, Liam pulling a stun grenade from his belt. It was a Zhen-made weapon, designed for use on ships without destroying the ship itself. He triggered it, held it for a short count, then rolled it around the door. He followed it seconds later with a second device. Just as he released the second, the first went off, followed by the second.

Liam waited a few tense moments, then poked his gun through the doorway, panning it back and forth. I realized he was using the gun's sensors to check for targets. He nodded, and we went out the door, guns ready, Injala bringing up the rear.

"Well, this changes the situation a bit," Liam said offhandedly, nudging the Zhen who lay sprawled in the intersection.

"You think?" I asked. As we moved, Liam and I kept our eyes moving, clearing each section before moving on to the next. I painted our goal – the ship's bridge – into the heads-up displays projected into our visual fields by our NeuroNets.

As we turned into a new corridor, Liam said, "I thought you were going to go invisible back there."

"Yeah, so did I."

Injala said, "Did you not have time?"

"Oh, I had plenty of time," I said. "In fact, I activated the stealth protocol. But it didn't work. The Zhen must have updated their protocols and somehow locked me out again."

Further conversation was halted by the barricade in our way and the plasma bolts that came from behind it. We turned to retreat back to the last cross-corridor, but as we did, several Zhen stepped into the space and began firing. Trapped between the two, we dove into the nearest doorway, finding ourselves in a small crewman's berth. "Shit," I said, and threw the lock switch. Injala pulled out two small plasma torches and handed one to me. We began to work on jamming the door.

"Here," Liam said, crossing to a small hatch in the wall. "This'll get us into the outer hull service area." He opened the hatch and sent a small probe through. "It's clear."

I finished jamming the door. "It won't hold long, but it will buy us some time."

Injala said, "They will doubtless be coming for us in the hull space."

"Of course they will," Liam said. "But it's not like we're waiting for them. They'll have to find us first."

We entered the space between the inner and outer hulls. As Liam sealed the hatch, I got our bearings. Once the hatch was sealed, we began to make our way toward the bridge.

"This is not as fun as I thought it would be," Liam said as he squeezed between equipment racks mounted to either side of the small space.

"Come on, being hunted through the worst parts of a ship? Seems like you'd be liking it," I said.

"Too dark, too smelly," Liam said. "I do dig the danger, though."

"The two of you," Injala said, "are perfect for each other. I am not sure that is a good thing."

"Tell me about it," came Kiri's voice over our comms. "Sorry it took so long to get through to you guys, but I had a few angry Zhen at the airlock trying to get in."

"Had?" I asked. "What happened to them?"

"Oh, they're dead now," she said. "I locked the airlock down and vented the atmosphere. While we're talking about breathing, are you all wearing your helmets?"

"Uh, no," I said. "Why?"

"Oh, nothing super important," she said. "I was just thinking, that freighter has anti-pirate systems, which I've just activated – and I suppressed the ship's notifications, thank you very much. In five seconds, the whole ship is going to be flooded with vaak gas. So maybe button up your faces."

We didn't waste time speaking, but simply told our suits to raise helmets. All three of us were wearing nano-machine-based suits, so it was only a couple of seconds later that we were all sealed up.

Moments later we heard a crash from somewhere ahead of us. I held out my hand to signal the others to stop and dispatched a probe. A tiny bit of nano-material detached from my suit and floated around the corner. A window opened in my visuals, showing me three Zhen, all unconscious on the floor. Vaak gas was nonlethal, but it affected each species a bit differently. It knocked every species in the Empire – as well as the Kelvaki – out cold. The Tradd would wake up in a couple of hours, but the Zhen would be asleep for longer.

Kiri's voice came back online. "Checking security cameras," she said. "Looks like we got all but one Tradd, who was lucky enough to have a breather nearby. I've locked him in his quarters."

"You're amazing, Kiri," I said.

"I really am," she agreed.

"All right. Let's get moving."

We spent almost two hours moving cargo from one bay and then moving the Zhen and most of the Tradd into it. Then we got the still-conscious one out of his quarters. We tried to march him to the bay, but he decided to fight, so we knocked him out and left him tied up with the others. After securing the bay, we cleared the rest of the ship and went to the bridge.

I checked the boards: a comms signal was coming in. On a whim I flicked the channel open.

"—freighter *Kirrikan*, are you in distress?"

I grinned and began turning the ship back toward the jump limit as Liam input the coordinates for our first jump.

"You have deviated from the flight plan, *Kirrikan*. We are dispatching ships."

"Don't bother," I said. "But do tell the Twenty and the One that Tajen Hunt appreciates the supplies. And if they promise to leave Earth, I might even give them back. Otherwise, I'll be using them in the fight to remove their stench from my planet."

The Zhen hissed in outrage at my insult of the council of red-scaled Zhen:ko who ruled the empire. He recovered quickly, and said, "Stand down, Tajen Hunt! By order of the Empire, you are bound for trial!"

"Oh, please," I said. "How are you planning to get me? I'll be gone before your ships even get here."

"Uh, Tajen?" Kiri's voice broke in. "Check your plot."

I glanced at the tactical plot in my visuals and my breath caught. "You've got to be kidding me."

"What's up?" Liam asked.

I ignored him for the moment. "Kiri, undock and get the hell out of here. We'll meet you at rendezvous point seven." I pointed at Liam. "You got that plot in? We've got a patrol craft practically on top of us. We've got maybe ten minutes."

"Plot's loaded," Liam said. "Where'd he come from?"

Injala said, "Chain drives are fast, but to get here so quickly, he must have been nearby."

"Point is, we need to get to the limit before they get to us," I said. I pushed the throttle to full ahead and transferred power from the ship's systems to the engines, pushing them to their maximum thrust.

"Looks like the Zhen are waking up," Liam said.

"They'll keep," I said. "Those cargo bays are pretty tough. Has Kiri gotten out?"

"Not yet," Liam replied. "She's almost at the limit." A few moments later, he reported, "She's jumped. System patrol craft is almost in weapons range."

"How long until we reach the limit?" Injala asked.

"About two minutes."

"I have bad news: some of the Zhen appear to be trying to hack the doors."

Liam whistled. "Nothing's ever easy," he said.

"I'll handle it," Injala said.

"Can we gas the ship again?"

"No," she said.

"Patrol craft is in range," I said. "Tell me this thing has chaff launchers."

"Yep," Liam said. "Activating now."

The launchers spat out charges that flooded local space with particles that disrupted weapons locks. It wouldn't last long, but it might buy us a few more seconds to get us closer to the jump line.

Hitting a moving target without computer targeting control isn't as easy as games make it out to be unless you're right on top of your target. The system patrol craft wasn't, but we were a large, slow target, and they got lucky with a few hits, shaking the freighter. As the shaking became more and more constant, I began to worry. Evading their fire was impossible. I put our position into my HUD, and my fingers hovered anxiously over the jump controls. The moment we crossed the jump limit, my fingers slammed down onto the controls, sending the ship into slipspace.

"We've got twenty minutes to reversion," I said. "Shall we handle those Zhen?"

"I handled it," Injala said. "There will be no further trouble."

"How'd you do it?" Liam asked.

"I spaced them."

"You did what?" I asked, rounding on her, my fists clenched.

She merely looked at me for several moments, and then said, "May I remind you, Tajen Hunt, that they are your enemy?"

I took a deep breath. "The *Empire* is my enemy," I said. "Not individual Zhen."

Her nostrils flared, a sign of irritation. "If you continue to think like that, Captain, you will *never* regain your world."

"How do you figure?"

"Your best tactic is to make controlling Earth so expensive, so difficult, that it isn't worth the time or lives," she said. "You must be ready to treat anyone working for the Empire as your enemy."

"Any Zhen," I said.

"No. *Anyone*."

"What if it's a human?" Liam asked.

"If a human is working for the Empire, you have two choices," she said. "Suborn them, or kill them."

"And you don't think other humans might think that's a bad idea, and not want to trust me?" I said.

"You must also convince them it is necessary, and therefore convince them not to work for the Zhen."

"That's insane," I said.

"We'll see," she said.

CHAPTER SEVEN

I heard the outer door of the residence open and close. A few moments later, a familiar voice said, "Where's the patient?"

I stayed where I was in the guest room. Liam and Kiri sat across from me, both with guns in their laps. "Hey," the voice said, "what the hell is this?"

"Ben, calm down," another voice said. I stayed where I was, though, despite wanting to run to Ben.

"Calm down, hell," Ben said. "I was told they needed a doctor, not someone to search. What the hell is this about?"

"Found his gun," a new voice said, though one known to me. The voice got louder when she called, "All clear, boss."

I rose from the bed and crossed to the door in two strides. "Hey, Ben."

Ben's face broke into a wide smile and he stepped close, grabbing me in a quick hug before moving on to Liam and Kiri. Then he stepped back, frowned at me, and said, "Took you long enough."

It had taken us weeks to set up the smuggling operation that would be bringing weapons and other supplies to the human resistance on Earth. Once that had been done, we'd had to sneak onto the planet, abandoning our ship out in the wilds and hiking to a nearby farm, one of the many set up by the fledgling colony to keep the inhabitants fed. We'd sent word to Katherine and Ben to come, but not said why, for operational security. I glanced at the redheaded young man who'd searched Ben and nodded. He left us alone, and I smiled at my old friends. "Sorry for the search," I said. "Ryan takes his security very seriously. We got a little information from him, but this place is far enough off the map that they haven't heard much. Why didn't Katherine come with you?"

Ben's face threatened to crumple, and he looked down a moment, then looked back into my eyes and shook his head slightly. Behind me, I heard Kiri burst into tears.

"When?" I asked.

"The night they attacked," he said. "She was leading the defense squadron when her ship was destroyed. We know she was going for her escape pod, but we never picked up the transponder before the Zhen got control of the sky."

I felt gutted. Katherine and I had known each other when we served together briefly, and had met a few times in the years since, but we truly became friends last year when circumstances threw us together, and in the year since, she'd become family. In many ways, we'd adopted each other to help assuage the pain of having lost our own siblings to the Zhen.

Losing Katherine was painful. I wanted to stop everything, take some time to grieve. But I couldn't lose momentum, not now. It would be a betrayal of everything Katherine and I had begun together.

"We'll mourn her properly when we can," I said after a deep breath, "but for now, I need to know: what's the situation in Landing?"

"Pretty bad," Ben said. "The Zhen hit hard that first day."

"Did they take the station?" We'd purposely come in from the opposite side of the planet to hide in Earth's shadow. We'd seen some Zhen ships, but nothing close enough to spot us.

"They tried, but Katherine ordered it scuttled it before they got close. Said we could always build a new one."

"Good plan," I said.

"I'm not so sure. Without a station to occupy, they put most of their forces on the planet – they landed ships at every settlement. They're trying to play the aggrieved party, but most of their energy is being spent keeping things from blowing up."

"Any active resistance?" I asked.

"A little in the beginning, but a few deaths put a stop to that. Diana ordered us to stand down for now."

"Where is she?" Liam asked.

Ben said, "She was arrested at first, but as soon as she ordered the stand-down, they let her go. She's been doing her best to keep the peace in Landing, working with the Occupation forces to minimize force used against us and stave off martial law."

"How closely is she working with them?" Liam asked.

"Only as much as she needs to," Ben said. "She's also given us some information, but she told us to wait before acting on any of it."

"Wait for what?"

Ben looked at his feet for a moment before raising his eyes to me again. "For you," he said. "She told us to wait for you."

I stared at him for a moment, and then said, "Oh, hell no."

"Oh, hell yes."

Kiri looked back and forth between us, then asked, "What?"

"She wants me to lead our forces," I said.

"And? Who else is there?"

"What about Driscoll?"

Ben said, "He won't. Says he's not really qualified to lead on that level." I couldn't disagree. Driscoll was a solid skirmisher, but he'd told me more than once he wasn't great at high-level tactics.

Kiri looked at me. "I think you're it."

She was right, of course. Liam was a good, but not brilliant tactician, and he wasn't nearly as good as I was at long-term campaign planning. I nodded. "Fine," I said. "But before I can come up with a plan, I need more information. Zhen troop deployment, patrol routes and schedules, important locations in Landing."

Ben grinned. "Actually, I think I can help you there." He dug in his pocket for a moment, then held up a small data transfer chip. "I was going to deliver this to Diana as part of my rounds today, but you can give it to her for me. It's got all you need, and probably some you don't."

As I reached for the chip, he pulled it back. "Tajen, I need you to know – I'll help out as I can, but my first priority is my patients. Especially now; the Zhen aren't as nice as they were before. I'm a doctor first, and a Resistance member second."

I nodded as I took the chip. "I understand." I held it to my wrist, where my nanite implant system had a reader. My NeuroNet copied the file to my system, and I gave it a cursory glance. "Good work," I said. "Let's get to it."

★   ★   ★

On a bright and cheerful morning, I walked up to the lone Zhen guard at the gateway of a small warehouse in Landing and, when I was several feet away, said, "Catch!" and tossed him a small object.

He instinctively caught it and, a moment later, fell to the ground as the stun grenade sent a ridiculous amount of electricity cascading through his nervous system, burning out the NeuroNet and causing his body to lock up. Once he was unconscious, I deactivated the device and retrieved it.

Liam and our squad joined me as I crossed the gateway. "Nasty little things," he said, glancing at my hand.

"Not arguing that," I said. "But quieter than blaster fire."

He agreed as we took up positions on either side of the entrance. I checked to make sure the rest of the squad was in position, then used my NeuroNet to open the door. Liam and I each spun into the doorway, surprising the six Zhen guards in the room just as two more of our squad came through the door on the opposite side of the room. "Hands up in the air!" Liam yelled, and we each stepped aside as the rest of our team came in behind us, those on the other door doing the same.

The Zhen weren't wearing their weapons, and we'd taken them by surprise. The squad fanned out into the room, backing the Zhen into a corner, weapons trained on them constantly. "Bailey, come on in," I called, and our last soldier entered with a machine on a grav-cart. She maneuvered the cart into position and activated its anchors. Once the spikes on each corner slammed into the ground, she moved to the machine and aimed it at the Zhen. "Ready," she said.

"Do it," I said, and she activated the machine. It projected a stasis field over the grouped Zhen, locking them into a motionless, timeless state.

"This field will only last about ten minutes," she said.

"Let's hurry, then," I called to the group. "Hitchens, take Watkins and Lee. Bailey, Liam, you're with me."

The redhead from the farm nodded and started issuing his own commands to his group. As they left, Liam, Bailey, and I made our way outside and around the warehouse corner. Liam said, "Out of curiosity?"

"Yeah."

"Why not just kill the Zhen?"

"If it was necessary, I'd do it. But it isn't. Right now I just want them to leave us. If we go around killing indiscriminately, they'll ramp up their responses."

"They've killed enough of us," Bailey said, shaking her head. I winced; Bailey had lost her husband in one of the first attacks after the Battle of Earth.

"Yeah," I said. "And they'll need to answer for that. But we can't just escalate. We're too few, and they're too powerful, to go up against them in a straight on killing fight. We need to be smart."

We made our way to our target, a nondescript building in the depot. It took only seconds to get through the lock, and we slipped inside, threading our way through rows of weapons racks and shelves of ammunition. In the center of the room I nodded to Bailey. She quickly glanced around the room, making calculations. "Setting five should do it," she said.

I set the machine to her specifications. "Anyone want to grab something before we run?"

"Way ahead of you," said Liam, who had just finished stuffing some weapons into his pack. "I grabbed a few things we might need in the next few days. Pity we can't just steal a lot of this and postpone the rest of the operation."

"I know," I said, "but if we did that, the Zhen would crack down before we could spring the rest. Everyone ready?"

Liam gave me a thumbs-up gesture, and Bailey said, "Ready." I signaled the other team and received their 'ready' report. "All right," I said, transmitting the words to the B team, "arm the devices." I armed ours, and a moment later I received the signal from the other device. "Okay, let's go. Bailey, how long have we got on that stasis field?"

"About seven minutes," she said.

"Let's go, everyone. Hunter battalion, converge at our target."

We hurried out of the warehouse, across the warehouse yard and out the gate, meeting up with Hitchens and his team as we crossed the street. The rest of the battalion under my command gathered in short order, coalescing from the side streets and alleys. Together with my own team, as well as Beta and Gamma teams, we numbered one hundred and twenty soldiers, mostly civilians trained in the last year, since the Battle of Earth. We strode up to the doorway of the colony administration office and took up position. I signaled to everyone using my NeuroNet, counted to five, and triggered the devices.

Two large *whoompfs* heralded the destruction of the weapons and ammo the Zhen had stored in the warehouses, as the singularity bombs created microscopic black holes that quickly pulled everything close and then, as the micro-black holes evaporated, released their contained energy outward in all directions.

As the explosions faded, I walked into the admin offices, trailed by my squads. "Ladies and gentlemen," I called out, "this office is being seized by the Terran Provisional Government. All citizens wishing to evacuate, do so now. All Zhen…get the fuck out."

There were no Zhen in the office, but the line got a nervous laugh from a few of the civilians. The clerk behind the front desk nodded to me and reached for the weapon I'd brought for him, then nodded toward the explosions. "You took out their supplies, looks like," he said.

"Let's get this place fortified. Liam, Bailey!" I called out. "Get the force shields up and clear our sight lines. Beta team, we left some Zhen in the armory office. Please escort them to the spaceport." They acknowledged the order and got to work. I motioned to Hitchens for him to follow me, and made my way up the stairs to the roof.

We looked out over the center of Landing. When we'd retaken Earth from the Zhen, we'd used their planetside base as our first colony. Some had tried to convince us to build elsewhere, but there was no point – no matter where we built, the Zhen could find us with orbital scans, so why not use their own infrastructure?

But we weren't stupid either. We'd stripped the place of all Zhen equipment and replaced it all with Kelvaki equivalents so the Zhen couldn't use any back doors in their tech to screw with us. But we'd built our administrative center just outside the spaceport.

In the year since, there'd been several settlements begun in various parts of the planet – we didn't really need everyone in one place, and our flyers and suborbital craft could get us from Landing to anywhere relatively quickly. But Landing was still the preeminent settlement, and it had one of the larger populations on the planet, with just over three million people calling it home. Most of the houses were built outside an exclusion zone that included the spaceport and the administrative complex, which housed our communications tower, the civilian government office, and the planet's only jail.

Right now, teams of soldiers were taking over the administrative complex, from the office I'd just taken to the comms center and the legal offices. Any Zhen were being escorted to the spaceport, where the civilian government would ask them to leave Earth.

I could see from my vantage point all the way to the spaceport, which was already a hive of Zhen activity. "This isn't going to go easy," I said.

"Sir?" Hitchens asked.

I turned and regarded him. Just over twenty, the freckled redhead had been off-planet as crew on a trading vessel when the Zhen had declared martial law on Zhen:da's Virginia Peninsula, where the majority of humans lived. His ship had redirected here and some of the crew, including Hitchens, had decided to stay. "I said this isn't going to go easy," I said. "I want to be wrong, but…there is no way in hell the Zhen will do as we ask."

"Then why give them the offer?" he asked. "I mean, if we're going to go to war, then let's just do it."

I shook my head. "We're already at war – we have been since the Battle of Earth. But even among the Zhen, war has rules. If we break the rules, there's no chance at all the Zhen will observe them. So we do things the right way, until they give us no choice but to do them the messy way." I smiled at him. "Make sense?"

"Yes, sir," he said. "But…."

"Yes?"

"Is it wrong that I'm looking forward to that?"

I sighed. "It isn't wrong," I said. "I know just how you feel – it's exactly how I felt when I was in training for the Space Force. But once the battles start, you're going to change your mind. I guarantee it."

He nodded, but didn't look convinced. I patted him on the shoulder. "For now," I said, "this is your post. Keep an eye on the street and the sky. Let us know if anything's coming in. What kind of NeuroNet have you got?"

"A Jenkat 700," he said, his face turning bright red.

My lips quirked. It was a cheaper model, but not a terrible one. "That'll do," I said. "I assume you've had the Terran update?"

"Of course."

"Good. I'll send someone else up to work with you, but you're in charge here. Got that?"

He snapped to attention. "Yes, sir!" he said with pride. "I won't let you down."

I clapped him on the shoulder as I returned to the doorway. "I know you won't, soldier. Remember – anything coming, let me know. Zhen or not." He affirmed the order and I went back into the stairwell and made my way down.

About halfway, I stopped and smiled up toward the door. He was a good kid, eager to serve, and easy to train.

I hoped he'd make it through.

★ ★ ★

When I came back downstairs, my comms unit signaled me that I had an incoming transmission. "Hunt," I subvocalized. Liam and Kiri, who'd been discussing something in a corner, looked to me, but I waved them off.

"Captain Hunt, we've taken the communications complex," came Diana Adakai's voice. "Rider and Storm battalions report they've met their objectives. How did our hunters do?"

"We've taken the administration complex," I said. "And we took out the Zhen stockpiles. But they'll still have a lot of weapons available. And we're still under the threat of bombardment."

"Orbital bombardment would be a step too far, even for the One," she replied. "Even under Imperial Law, that would be a war crime. Both the Kelvaki and the Talnera would object."

"That won't matter if we're dead," I said.

"Well, let's hope it doesn't come to that," she said. "I'm about to make the announcement. Are your people ready?"

I looked to Liam and said, "Are we up?" At his signal, I replied to Diana, "Yes, we're ready."

"I'll do it shortly, then. Adakai out."

I looked around the room at my command team. "All right, folks. Diana's going to make the announcement shortly. Make sure the local comms don't get jacked, and keep the speakers on."

A few minutes later, I got a priority announcement on my comms from the colonial authority. Diana's face appeared in my visual field. "Good morning," she said, her voice sounding as if we were in the same room, and also playing on the speakers outside, which we'd put up for the benefit of those who didn't have NeuroNets – which mostly meant kids, though we had a small group of humans who didn't use the devices for various reasons.

"My name is Diana Adakai, and I have the honor of being chosen by the humans of Earth to lead the colony we established here. This transmission is going out to everyone on Earth, and to the greater Empire beyond. It is hoped that the Empire allows the message to be freely disseminated, though we have taken measures to compensate if they do not." In fact, the message had been composed and sent out weeks ago via the slipnet; it was far too late for the Empire to squash it. As codes sent out simultaneously with this broadcast were received, the files would begin propagating and playing everywhere.

"In the name of the dead generations of Earth from which we receive our birthright, we, the people of Earth, summon our brothers and sisters to our flag and strike for our freedom.

"We declare the right of the people descended from Earth to the ownership of Earth and to the unfettered control of human destinies, to be sovereign and inalienable. In every generation, humans have asserted our right to freedom and sovereignty; now we have asserted it in arms. We hereby proclaim the Solarian Republic as a sovereign independent state, and we pledge our lives to the cause of its freedom and of its welfare.

"The Solarian Republic is entitled to, and hereby claims, the allegiance of every human who feels the call to join us on our ancestral home. The Republic guarantees equal rights and equal opportunities to all its citizens, and declares its resolve to pursue the happiness and prosperity of its people.

"Until we are able to establish a permanent government, representative of the whole people of Earth and elected by all her people, the Provisional Government, hereby constituted, will administer the civil and military affairs of the Solarian Republic in trust for the people.

"We call upon the Zhen to leave Earth, to recognize the sovereignty of our government and the claim of humans to the soil of our ancestral world, and to permit free travel and emigration to Earth to all peoples of the Empire. We further call upon the Empire to accept our ambassadorial mission and to negotiate a peaceful resolution to our recent disagreements."

When she finished speaking, a scroll of names passed by: the signatures of each of the members of the Earth Council. The message finished, and cheering erupted from my battalion. I motioned my command team – those who had been my crew when we first came to Earth – into a side room.

"Well," I said to the room, "only a question of time, folks. Sleep if you can."

*　　*　　*

We kept waiting for a Zhen response, but by dinnertime, there'd been nothing. "What's taking them so damned long?" Liam asked. We were standing on the rooftop, looking out over the city. Injala was nearby, giving us a moment of privacy as we stood just out of earshot of the gunnery teams manning the rooftop.

"I've no idea," I said. "I expected a counteroffensive hours ago."

"I might have an answer," Kiri said as she stepped up on my other side. She waved her hand, and in my vision a mote of light leaped from her hand to hover in front of my face a moment before unfolding into an audio file with a transcript. "I intercepted this going out on the slipnet. The local garrison leader went back to Zhen:da for some R&R, and the replacement is apparently freaking out. Most of the Zhen on-station were at a *Zhen:saak:arl* tournament."

Liam glanced at the no doubt quite smug expression on my face. "You knew about the tournament. That's why you insisted it had to be today."

I waggled my hand. "I suspected. If I was right, I knew it would give us an edge in the first moves, but I expected the Zhen to recover by now."

"And you didn't tell anyone because...."

"If I was wrong, it would have been harder to get here. I didn't want anyone getting caught unawares and dying because of it." I turned to Kiri. "Anything else?"

"Near as we can tell, the virus I put into the slipnet is doing its job – the orbital weapons platforms are offline."

"Will they stay down long enough for our friend in orbit to do his job?"

"He's already launched. The platforms should be out for good in about –" she paused to check the time, "– thirty seconds."

"You timed that well," I said.

"Thank you." We both looked up and waited. Precisely on time, a series of miniature stars blossomed, visible even in the late afternoon light, flaring for just a few seconds as the fusion cores in the orbital weapon platforms overhead detonated. As they faded, I said, "My compliments to our friend. Hope he gets out of the system in time."

"He did," Injala said. "He communicated with me just before he jumped." She stepped over to join us and looked out over the street. "This quiet will not last."

"Of course not."

"I find myself wondering why you have not deployed the drones."

"I'm keeping them in reserve," I said. "For when the Zhen get serious. The drones are hidden in various places around the city, but I don't want to activate them until we need them. They're our ace in the hole."

Injala stood silent, her eyes blinking, her earflaps opening and closing rhythmically, for several seconds. "I do not understand this phrase," she finally said.

"It means a hidden advantage, kept in reserve until it's needed."

"Ah. A *shalantakka*." Her ears quivered. "Humans use too many words, sometimes."

I stared at her. "It's the exact same number of syllables."

"But four words, when one will do."

I was nonplussed. "I…suppose that's true."

"You are an amusing species." She looked at the setting sun. "I will go in, now," she said. "Be sure to wake me when the Zhen make up their minds what they are going to do."

"Will do," I said. We watched her walk inside, and then Liam and I traded looks. "Just when I think I understand the Kelvaki," I said.

"You know what bothers me?" Liam asked. "I'll probably never find out who won the *Zhen:saak:arl* tournament."

My eyebrows climbed. "You care?"

"Well," he demurred, "not especially. No real competitors here. But I'm always curious."

Zhen:saak:arl was the closest thing to a religion the Zhen had. They had no creator figure, no dogma, except The Struggle. All of life was war, to them – from the beginnings of their species to the attainment of space travel and the series of wars as they built their Empire, it was all an expression of The Struggle – a quest to dominate, to become the strongest.

Even their response to humanity was part of their religion. They couldn't allow us to best them. It was part of why we'd tried to follow, for the last eight hundred years, a policy the first human colonists had called 'political aikido'. We tried to redirect their competitive nature from going against us to other causes, other issues. We'd helped elements within their own culture to turn The Struggle from a mostly outward one to an internal struggle. But it looked like the current leadership, especially the Twenty and the One, had been planning to turn Zhen focus outward again.

And we'd put ourselves right in their path.

★   ★   ★

I was sitting down to have a meal when the call came over the comms system, the voice frantic.

"We surrender! Repeat, we surrender!"

I scrambled from the table toward the map table. "Who is that?"

The watch officer, Shane, said, "It's Billings, sir." He flicked his hand and a graphic popped into view above the table. Billings and his twenty-four men were occupying the offices of the colonial courthouse. The courthouse wasn't tactically important, but it was useful to prevent 'business as usual' from happening, and the Zhen had taken over the legal system of the colony, making it an important symbolic gesture to interrupt their activities on Earth.

Right now, Billings and his group were surrounded by Zhen. Apparently they'd started to get their heads out of their cloacae and had begun their counterinsurgency operations. "Get me a visual," I snapped. Shane's head moved back and forth minutely as he scanned his available feeds from the various airborne drones we'd deployed, then he chose one and flicked a visual up into the air.

We watched as the men and women with Billings filed out of the courthouse and handed their weapons to the Zhen soldiers at the entrance. I counted people. "Where are the rest of them?"

The question was answered shortly, as the Zhen sent Tradd functionaries into the building and, moments later, they emerged with bodies slung between them. "*Shaak*," I said.

"Should we send someone over there?" Liam asked. "Maybe use the drones?"

I thought about it. We could get them out of there, maybe, but we'd lose people or drones to do it. And for only eighteen people? No, it was too dangerous, and for not enough. Billings would have to keep it together in Zhen jail for a while, let the rest of us try to change things.

"No. They've already surrendered." I took a deep breath. "Make sure our defenses are up," I said. "We're going to need them soon."

CHAPTER EIGHT

Katherine Lawson

I came to, my head spinning. "Now I know how Tajen feels," I moaned, tried to open my eyes, and squeezed them shut again at the first hint of light. "Simmons, can you reach the medkit? I need a painkiller." There was no response. "Simmons?"

It was then that I realized I wasn't in the pod's seat, but lying on a floor. Keeping my eyes pointed to the ground, I opened them slowly, acclimating to the light before raising my head.

I was lying alone in a white cube, about three meters to a side. The ceiling was translucent, giving off a small amount of light. There were no features anywhere, the surfaces smooth and seamless. The moment I sat up, though, a small slot in the door opened, and a tray slid through. Once the door it came through shut, the seams disappeared. "Nice trick," I said. The tray held a cup of water, a covered plate, and an analgesic from my pack. So whoever had me, they were paying attention.

I dipped a finger into the water, the tiny sensor embedded under my fingernail sampling it. The word SAFE appeared in my vision for a moment. I touched the sensor to the pill and got the same result, so I took it. I idly uncovered the plate and blinked at it. "Holy shit," I said. I tested the food too, and when my system reported it was safe, I took a bite. "Damn." It was chili, an ancient recipe my brother had found in one of the books in the *Far Star*'s database and adapted to use with Zhen spices and produce. I'd had this dish hundreds of times; I'd even taught Tajen how to make it, but nobody made it like Takeshi. And it tasted *exactly* like Takeshi's.

When I was done, I sat back and waited for the drug to work. "You know, this floor is karking hard," I said into the air. "You guys may like the whole 'stone and sand' thing, but humans need a bed." I started when a part of the wall slid out, revealing a human-sized bed. "Okay. That's new." I levered myself up and sat on the bed. It was pretty comfortable, which was confusing.

I'd been in Zhen cells before, when I was a soldier and pissed off my CO. This was nothing like it. For one thing, the beds there were made of stone, not this amazingly soft…whatever it was. Apparently they'd stepped up their prisoner facilities.

"Hello?" I said. "You guys plan on interrogating me or something? Or am I just going to sit here forever?" My voice completely failed to echo in the chamber, as if the walls just sucked all the sound into them. I could hear the sounds I made, but nothing else.

I turned my head, straining to hear a sound from outside. Nothing. I couldn't even hear the engine hum and vibration that was a constant in every spaceship I'd ever known. I checked my internal chronometer and found I'd only been unconscious for about an hour.

I gave up and closed my eyes. If I wasn't going to be interrogated right away, I might as well get some rest and prepare for it. I ran over the anti-interrogation techniques I'd been taught in the Space Force, breathing deeply and deliberately. Before long, I fell asleep.

★   ★   ★

When I came to, I was floating in the cube. I tried to reach for one of the walls, but I was unable to move, held by some sort of forcefield. Trying to move felt like pressing a strong magnet against another with the poles reversed. I couldn't feel any surface, but the pure force pressing against me kept me in place. But I didn't feel as if I was resting on anything; I might as well have been in zero-G.

Unlike earlier, the cube's walls weren't white – they now pulsed in various colors, none of them staying put for more than a few seconds.

"Where is the one who failed?" came a voice. It wasn't a Zhen voice, but sounded as if it might have been processed somehow.

I frowned and tried to turn my head to look around, but the forcefield held me motionless. "What the hell are you talking about? Failed at what?"

The room disappeared, and in its place I was suddenly floating in space. I instinctively panicked, thrashing my arms and legs – trying to, anyway – but came to my senses a couple of moments later, when I realized it wasn't cold, and a vacuum wasn't trying to kill me.

In the middle distance, I saw a fleet of Zhen ships. It didn't take me long to figure out what I was looking at. Every human in the Empire, and probably most of the Zhen, too, had seen this. It was Tajen's fleet, over Jiraad.

The scene played out, but there was no sound. Graphics in an unknown language occasionally appeared and highlighted one of the Zhen ships, as if I was watching an alien recording. "Where is the one who failed here?" said the voice.

"What?" I had a feeling I knew what they wanted, but I wasn't giving it to them.

The picture zoomed in on the *Shir'kaan*, Tajen's ship, actually going through the walls onto the bridge. The camera continued to approach one man, turning around him and rotating to keep him in view. I found myself staring at a younger Tajen Hunt.

"Where is he?" came the voice.

"I don't know," I lied. The room turned yellow for a moment, shot through with green.

"You are lying. You are his associate. He spoke to you often. You know where he went."

"He's my friend," I said.

"Yes. Friend. Where is your friend?"

"Why the hell would I tell you where he went?" I snarled. "We're trying to stop you bastards from taking over our planet. I'm not helping you."

"We do not want your world. We are not Zhen."

What?

It made sense. This cell was nothing like a Zhen cell, and Zhen interrogations were usually more the sit-you-in-a-chair-and-browbeat-you kind, if not the rake-you-with-claws kind. They knew torture wasn't actually useful, but they still did it, the bastards. Well. Some of them did.

But if these weren't Zhen, then who the hell were they? The voice wasn't Tradd, and it wasn't Tchakk. And it sure as hell wasn't Kelvaki or Hun. There was only one other known race, and that was the Tabrans.

But nobody had heard anything out of the Tabrans since the end of the last Tabran War, after the Jiraad incident.

I raised my voice. "Tajen didn't fail at Jiraad," I said. "You did."

There was no response for nearly a minute. Then, "How do you define our failure?"

"You killed millions of people rather than find another way."

"We warned the Zhen what would happen."

"But you didn't kill Zhen. You killed humans who didn't know what was coming. They died in pain and fear because of your actions. It wasn't the Zhen who dropped kinetic warheads on Jiraad, that was you. Millions of humans died that day, because of you."

There was no reply, but I was suddenly lying on the bed again. I sat up, checking my NeuroNet, and realized I'd been in a virtuality, an unreal space where my perceptions were controlled by external forces. "Don't do that!" I snapped. "My mind is mine. Stay out of it! You ask permission before immersing me in your illusions!" I was breathing hard; I absolutely *hated* being forced into virtualities.

"Stand by for visitor," the voice said. I tensed, got up from the bed and stood in a corner, ready to fight – though I knew that if they had planned to hurt me, they wouldn't have announced their arrival.

It's just that nobody in the Empire I'd ever heard of had ever seen a Tabran. We'd heard them over comms, speaking in Zhen. And now, apparently, I'd heard them speaking English. But nobody had ever seen one. The Empire sent ships, both openly and in secret, to their homeworld, but the ones sent openly were forced to dock at stations where all negotiations were held from behind screens, and the secret ships had never returned. So I had no idea what I'd see.

Urban legends claimed all sorts of scary appearances for them. Some said they had to be nightmarish, or else they'd have shown themselves openly millennia ago. Others said they hid their appearance because they must be tiny and weak, and didn't want the Zhen to know it.

So I was ready for anything – anything, that is, except what came through the door when it opened.

"Simmons?" I said dumbly.

"My true name is much longer, and human vocal assemblies are unsuited to the sounds, so 'Simmons' is as good a name as any," he said. "If you prefer, you could call me by my function."

"Which is?"

"I am a proctor."

"What?"

"It is my task to decide if humans are ready."

"Ready for what?"

"To meet the Tabrans."

I frowned. "So you've seen them?"

"Indeed, I have worked quite closely with them."

"What are they like?" I asked.

He paused and smiled. "Let us not get ahead of ourselves," he said. "Are you ready to begin?"

"Begin what?"

"The test."

"No."

"Very well," he said. "I will return later, when you have—"

"No."

He frowned a moment, and regarded me. "What do you mean, Captain Lawson?"

"I refuse to be tested."

"You cannot refuse," he said. "The test is necessary."

"Horseshit," I said. "If the Tabrans want to talk to me, or any other human, they know where we are. And they've been watching us for what, eight hundred years now? If they don't know if we're 'ready' for their bullshit by now, they never will be."

Simmons regarded me silently for some time, then said, "Come."

"I told you, I'm not doing your damn test!"

"The test is concluded," he said. He waited a beat, and then added, "You passed."

"You're kidding me," I said, looking at him.

"I am not," he said. "We have known for some time that humans are ready in a general sense. But we needed to know if *you* were. It appears that you are."

"Ready how?" I said, rising to my feet.

He beckoned me to follow him and left the room. I followed him out, down a corridor that looked much like my cell. "It is hard to explain in human terms," he said. "Tabran thought processes are nothing like ours, which is why they need me and others like me."

"To translate?"

"Not language. The Tabrans can translate the language easily enough without help. But concepts are slippery. They are difficult. Human and Tabran thought are worlds apart in many ways."

We entered a large room with a huge window along one wall, one of the biggest I'd ever seen on a starship. The view right now was a planet. It was night on the side facing us, and I saw a few cities glowing with blue light. "What planet is that?" I asked.

Simmons didn't even glance at it. "That is Tabra," he said. He chose a seat at the long table that sat below the window. "Please, be seated."

I lingered at the window. "Am I the first human to see this?" I asked.

"Of course not," he said. "I have seen it many times."

I turned back to him. "You're human?"

He looked at his hands, turning them over to inspect them. "Do I not appear so?"

I looked at him. While he was a little odd-looking, it wasn't anything outside the realm of human norms. "Humans don't live on Tabra," I said.

"Some do. Not many. But some."

"How?"

He motioned me to a seat, and I decided to take it.

"I was a crewman on a cargo freighter called the *Heavy Lifter*, about ten years ago. We were smugglers, using legitimate business as a cover for more illicit cargo. One day, we were interdicted by a Zhen cruiser. They shot our engines out and left us to die.

"We drifted for weeks, scrounging and rationing supplies in an attempt to keep as many of us alive as we could. More than half of us died. We were down to only three of us when another ship arrived. Rather than finish us off, they rescued us." He looked around. "It was a ship very like this one. After some time, I was approached by one of the crew."

"Where are the crew?" The corridors we'd come through had been empty, and the ship, based on what I had seen, had to have too many crewmembers for empty corridors to be a thing.

"The crew have stayed out of sight until you are ready to meet them," he said. "They are…sometimes unsettling to look at."

"Tabrans are ugly?"

"No. Far from it. But most of the crew are not actually Tabran."

"Now I'm confused."

He stopped, holding a hand up for silence. After a moment, he lowered his hand. "Your confusion is about to end, Captain Lawson." He stood.

"Allow me to introduce our hosts," he said, indicating the opening door.

I stared at the being on the other side for a few seconds, then turned to Simmons.

"You have *got* to be kidding."

★　　★　　★

We walked down a corridor, Simmons on one side, the Tchakk-that-wasn't-a-Tchakk on the other. I stopped walking, shaking my head.

"Let me see if I can wrap my head around this," I said. I pointed at Simmons. "You're human, but with augmentations courtesy of the Tabrans."

"Yes."

"Okay then." I pointed at the Tchakk. She looked mostly like every Tchakk I'd ever seen, excessively tall and spindly, gray, with long arms and extensive bony ridges covering her scalp; but unlike those Tchakk, her eyes glowed, and there were faint lines, suggesting subdermal circuitry, under her skin. But that stuff doesn't usually glow. And her voice held that same overly processed sound I'd heard before in the virtuality. "And you're two beings in one body?"

"Essentially correct, but flawed," said the Tchakk.

"Can you explain that? One more time?" I asked her.

"I was born Tchakk," she said. "I ran the plains of the Tchakk home, under the sun and sky. But the Many That Are One came, the ones you call Tabrans. Many of them offered to join with me, to make me different than I was before. I said yes. Now we are many, and two, and one."

I turned to Simmons. "So what the hell is an actual Tabran like?"

He pursed his lips. "Tabrans – the beings who began the war against the Zhen – have been gone for centuries now."

"What killed them?"

He spread his arms wide. "We're not entirely sure," he said. "Our best guess is that the Many were created originally as a weapon of war, and there was an accident that wiped out the original, biological Tabrans. The Many did not become what we now know as Tabrans until centuries later. Once they awakened, they tried to reach out, to say hello to other species in the Empire, as well as the Kelvaki. But in their natural form, they are difficult to perceive, and some perceived them only as the weapon their makers had intended them to be.

"Eventually, they realized they needed better ways to interact with the galaxy." He escorted me to a niche in the hallway, which contained what looked like a spacesuit designed for exploration. It was vaguely humanoid, but the arms and legs were too long, and the head was an odd shape, as if it was designed for a creature with a snout. "These 'encounter suits' were the first attempt. They are basically a robotic platform, designed to look more or less like a biological Tabran." A hologram flickered into life above his hand, showing me what the Tabrans had looked like. They did indeed have long snouts, ending in large nostrils and a flat mouth with tusks protruding from their lips. "The suits gave those they met something to focus on, but it didn't help these new Tabrans interact with 'messy biological life'."

"The mechanical constructs did not work," the Tabran/Tchakk said. "So we attempted to create biological constructs. But biological life is complex beyond the engineering. You have emotions. They inform and cloud your judgment in equal measure. We did not have the experience necessary to understand. We needed aid. So we sought others." She looked down, her eyes closing momentarily. When she opened them again, she looked to Simmons.

He continued the 'historical tour'. "They considered raising cloned – or genetically engineered – replicants, but after some debate, they decided this would be unethical, as it would give the biological form no choice in the matter. So they began to seek out those willing to join with them."

"Join with what, exactly?" I asked him. "I get that the Tabrans aren't biological, but what are they, exactly? Implanted AI?"

"More or less," he said. He stopped at an empty niche, and waved his hand over it. A hologram took shape, depicting a shifting cloud of silver. "This is the natural form of a modern Tabran. It is a fully sentient nanite swarm."

"A what?" I said, incredulous. "Nobody has ever managed to create nanobots that are sentient. They simply can't run code that well. They do what they're told, when they're told. They can't make decisions, or question their existence, or debate morality."

"True," he said. "But I did not say they are nanites. They are nanite *swarms*."

"Even swarms need a controller unit to do anything useful. They just don't have the bandwidth to--" A flash of insight went through my brain. "You mean they exist as a gestalt," I said.

"Exactly so. As a swarm, they are sentient and sapient. They can divide themselves into smaller still-sapient swarms, to a point. But in that form, they have no emotion. So, some of them – not all – find biologicals who wish to join, and they 'incarnate', as they put it, into that being."

"For how long?"

"For life," he said. "The biological's life, anyway, which is greatly extended by the incarnation process. The nanites grant great strength and regenerative abilities to the biological lifeform. They cannot extend life indefinitely, but they can give their host a life much longer than what they would have lived otherwise."

"What about when the body dies?"

"Most often, the Tabran embodied in the swarm will spin off a piece of itself to develop into a new nanite swarm, and then join the queue for another volunteer."

"The queue?"

"There are more Tabrans than there are willing beings to incarnate in," he said. "The Tabrans seek those who are lost, who have nothing else to live for – people like myself, dying in space – but not all are willing to become hosts. Some volunteer to act as interpreters and advisors. Others wish to live on Tabra, free of the ongoing war. Some of their children volunteer, some do not." He shrugged.

"What's it like on Tabra?"

"Quite beautiful," he said. "But sometimes melancholy, when you remember you are walking in hallways originally built by people long since turned to dust."

I turned to the Tchakk/Tabran. "What's your name?"

She bowed her head, folding her long arms against her thin body. "I am The Sunset After a Storm," she said.

I looked at Simmons. "They all have names like that?"

"Yes," he said. "Most are longer."

"What about the part of you that was Tchakk?"

"Her name translated as Sunset," she said. "Our names always incorporate the meaning of the original being's name into the Tabran descriptor."

"Okay, then. Your full name is a bit of a mouthful. Can I call you Sunset?"

"You may," she said.

"Can I talk to her, without you?"

"No," she said. "Once joined, we are one being."

"But the host survives?"

"Of course," she said.

"Can you leave her?"

Sunset looked at Simmons. "Yes. But it rarely happens."

I looked to Simmons. "Why?"

"I have never been joined," he said, "so I'm not entirely sure. But I spoke to a Kelvaki who had been joined once. He said that it had been an amazing life. He only asked to be disincarnated because he had reached the age where the Tabran could not grant him much more time, and he wished to die on his own, and not force the swarm to remember the moment of death."

"Wow," I said. "So why haven't you volunteered to be incarnated?"

"I did," he said. "But they needed me for something else." He indicated Sunset's glowing eyes and skin. "It is not possible to hide the effect of having been joined. I was tasked with going to Earth, meeting you, and learning what I could of your people's new colony there."

"Why?"

"Because it's time for the Tabrans to make penance for their mistakes."

"You mean Jiraad?"

"Among other things."

"Such as?"

Sunset interrupted. "It is time to help the Zhen," she said.

CHAPTER NINE

Tajen Hunt

The sounds of gunfire and yelling woke me. Seconds after I rolled out of my makeshift bed, my comms activated. "Tajen!" came Liam's voice, "Any chance you could get your ass out of bed and get up here?"

"On my way," I said. I ducked by several medics in the hallway I'd used to catch some sleep and took the stairs to the rooftop three at a time. I rushed to Liam's position on the north face, looking up the main street toward the starport. About a mile out, I could see Zhen forces advancing down the street, mobile barricades moving slowly ahead of them.

"*Shaak*," I said. "When did they get here?"

"About two minutes ago," Liam said.

I scanned the soldiers I could see. "They look to have a lot of equipment and personnel that wasn't in the reports I got."

He nodded. "Sure looks like it. And there are more soldiers out there than we expected. They hit the outer perimeter of the taken zone. They took the comms tower back right away."

"Did Diana escape?"

"Yeah. She's on her way here."

As we watched, the Zhen's mobile barricades slammed down, anchoring themselves at a cross street. Once anchored, the barricades deployed overhead force shields, protecting the Zhen soldiers from overhead fire.

I activated my comms. "Hitchens, get me a bird's-eye view of this crap."

"I've got a drone overhead, sir. Here's the view." It blossomed in my vision.

I took in the sight for a moment, then cursed and shut down the connection. "They're setting up a siege," I said.

Moments after I said it, my NeuroNet registered an incoming message from 'Zhen Imperial Earth Command'. We'd long ago propagated a patch that removed the Zhen ability to override our 'Nets, but we could still choose to see the message. I allowed it to proceed.

"Citizens of Earth," the Zhen commander said, "take note that as of now, martial law is in effect. Humans may go about their business outside the central zone. However, all humans must be inside their homes at sundown. Anyone caught outside after sunset will be shot on sight.

"Those humans who have unlawfully occupied the administration zone are in violation of Zhen law and are commanded to surrender to Zhen authority immediately. Those who surrender will not be harmed."

The message cut out, and Liam shook his head. "Martial law, just like we expected."

"It's what I would do in their place," Injala said, joining us. Diana Adakai was right behind her.

"Diana," I said. I indicated the Zhen line. "They've got more soldiers and gear than we had in our projections." I realized she looked harried and exhausted. "Glad you made it out. Are you all right?"

"We lost half the soldiers we had at the tower. Do I look all right to you?"

I stared at her. Sixty men and women, gone, and there was something in her expression I didn't like. "Orders, ma'am?"

"Why do you think the Zhen opted for this standoff?"

I thought about it a moment. "They could crush us pretty easily," I said. "So the fact they're going for a siege means they're worried."

"About?"

I pursed my lips. "If I had to guess, it's the political situation. Even if the people back home accepted us as criminals, if the Zhen crush us they're worried we'll become martyrs. If they try to take us using conventional assault, the tactical situation is bad for both of us, but worse for them – we've got the buildings, and if they push past that perimeter, we can rain hell down on them. They can take us, but it would be costly.

"The only way they can take us easily is orbital bombardment or artillery; we took out the possibility of the former, and the latter would look bad back home, to both humans and the rest of the Zhen. So they're going to sit there and wait."

"Wait for what?" Diana was a canny leader, but war was nothing she'd ever taken part in.

"For us to give up. We haven't got the supplies, in food or materiel, for a long-term siege. Even if we did, the supplies wouldn't last forever. So they'll wait for us to give up, and then they can just arrest us and be done with it."

Her shoulders settled, as if releasing tension.

I motioned her away from the soldiers manning the gun emplacements, to a quiet area near the door to the building's interior. I lowered my voice. "That's what you – the council – really wanted, isn't it?"

She looked away, opened her mouth, then closed it, her lips forming a flat line. "Yes," she said.

"Son of a bitch," I breathed. "You knew what they really had. You didn't give me all the information."

She paused before answering. "We needed you to plan the operation – if we'd done it, it would have failed to even get off the ground. But the point was made that if you knew all the details, you would try to talk us out of this."

I was shaking with anger. "Is this offensive even expected to succeed?"

She met my eyes. "No," she whispered. "We knew it couldn't. We knew people would die. But that's the only way to get the people on Zhen:da to hear us."

I stared at her, and tightened my mouth into a tiny point to avoid screaming at her. "All command staff," I said, my eyes not leaving hers, "meet in the command room immediately." I pointed her toward the stairs. "Let's go." I marched her downstairs and into the office I'd taken as the command room.

Once Liam, Kiri, Hitchens, and Bailey were assembled, I shut the door and activated my scrambler just in case anyone was trying to listen in. I made sure the office glass was tuned to opaque, then turned to Diana.

"Talk."

She shook her head. "Tajen, this is high-level—"

"They are my team," I said, my voice low and quiet. "Talk."

She took a breath. "The council never expected to even last until you got back. We know it's only a matter of time before the Zhen quietly lock us all up and make us into criminals in the minds of our people. The best we could hope for was visibility back home, to the Zhen as well as to humanity. If they see what's going on, then maybe they can put pressure on the government."

"When you asked me to lead our militia, you said nothing about this."

"We thought—"

"I'm not finished," I snapped. "You maneuvered me into leading these people straight into the Zhen's claws. Did you even think about what the Empire would do to them when it was over?"

"Arrests and prison time," she said. "What they always do when we demonstrate against their—" She seemed to become aware of the expressions of my team. She stopped talking and looked back to me. Her demeanor shifted in an instant to fear. "What didn't we see?"

I sagged against the wall behind me. "Everything," I said.

She waited.

"This isn't the same Zhen Empire we've been dealing with for the last eight hundred years, Diana. This is an empire on the brink of interstellar war with the Kelvaki, an empire that has seen humans finally stand up and tell it to go to hell. We took this planet in a military operation. We declared it ours, set up a colony. In their minds, we *stole* it. Haven't you been listening to me for the past year? The old rules are gone. They're going to go further than they used to, and the thoughts of the Zhen back home are going to matter much, much less than before.

"And that's even if the Zhen back home get the truth. How do we know any of this is on the newsfeeds in the Empire? For all we know, our asses are hanging all alone out here." I sighed. "And even if most of it is getting out, we're going to be portrayed as the bad guys. And you know as well as I do how many of our own species will believe that, let alone the Zhen."

"What can we do?"

I shook my head, not sure whether to laugh, cry, or shoot her. "Nothing. We're in this until the end, because the only way out—" I stopped, thought a moment, and rose to my feet. "Hitchens!" I snapped.

"Yes, sir?"

"Find me an exit. Some way – a *hidden* way – to get as many people out of the administrative zone as we can. Go under the Zhen, over them, whatever you have to do. But find me a way." I turned to Liam and Bailey. "I've got a plan," I said, unable to stop myself from grinning at them.

They looked at each other, and then said in perfect unison, "Oh, shit."

★   ★   ★

Later that night, I was standing on the roof once more, watching the Zhen line, when I heard a series of odd tones.

"What the hell was that?" I asked the gunner next to me.

"Sir?"

"Those tones. Any idea what they were?"

He looked nervous. "I didn't hear anything, sir."

I shook off the feeling. "Carry on," I said, and went inside. I was starting to think I was just tired and should get some sleep for a few hours when I heard a distinctly non-human voice speaking. I couldn't understand the language; it didn't sound like anything I'd ever heard before. But then it changed, and my blood ran cold.

I'd distinctly heard English. It had said, "No, not yet," before switching back to the unknown tongue.

"Right, then," I said, and changed my course. I found Kiri tinkering with a drone. "Busy?" I asked.

"Sort of," she said. "I'm modifying this drone to help Ryan find that passage out you asked for." She finished tightening something, stepped back, and checked the display on her desk. "Damn," she muttered. "So much for that idea. Anyway, I need a break from *this* project. What can I do for you?"

"I'd like you to check my NeuroNet."

"Sure, what's wrong?" she asked, gesturing me to a seat. She settled a diagnostic tool over my head and picked up her display.

"Not sure. I was on the roof and heard some weird tones, then down here I heard a language I've never heard before, and then the words 'No, not yet.' Could I be picking up an entertainment channel?"

"Not likely," she said. "The Zhen shut down the entertainment feeds. All that's playing now is news updates from 'Zhen Colonial Command'. How long ago was this?"

"Just a couple of minutes," I said.

She tapped something on her screen and said, "Well, whatever you heard, it didn't come from your NeuroNet. I'm not reading any incoming transmission in the last two hours."

I frowned. "I know what I heard, Kiri. And the guy next to me didn't hear it."

She spread her hands wide. "I'm not saying you're wrong, but there's nothing in the record."

I thought a moment. "Could my NeuroNet be failing?"

"You mean a cascade failure?"

"Yeah."

"There's no sign of it on the scan," she said. "A cascade failure would show a fault somewhere."

"What about on Kelvak, when my stealth field didn't work? It happened again when we took that freighter."

She frowned. "Liam mentioned wondering why you didn't use it."

"I did," I said. "Only it didn't work."

She frowned, then said, "I'd need a Zhen system to check to be sure, but it sounds like they must have patched the assassin's 'Net. They probably did a system-wide patch."

"So instead of accepting my own 'Net's commands to ignore me and delete me from her vision, it just ignored the instruction and let her see me." I sighed. "I'm kind of embarrassed I didn't even think about them doing that. Dammit. I was all pleased with myself, and they probably patched their systems as soon as they figured out that's how I killed Kaaniv."

"Well, it's not like you've had a chance to use it since then. And we patched human systems to remove that vulnerability. Stands to reason they'd at least lock *you* out of their systems."

"So much for Tajen Hunt, the invisible avenger."

"Meh. You're better off visible as Tajen Hunt, rebel leader, in my opinion." She looked closer at me, and her expression softened. "Have you slept?"

"Not much," I admitted.

"Tajen, shit," she said. "No wonder. You've been up and working for way too long. Go sleep. You've got good people in place while you're down. Take some time out."

"Take your own advice, kid."

"Yes, yes," she said. "I'm immune to your habit of turning all advice on the giver, Uncle. Go. Sleep."

"Yes ma'am," I said. "Right away, ma'am."

I tried. I went to my cot, I laid myself down, closed my eyes, and tried to sleep. But it wouldn't come, which frustrated the hell out of me.

I'd been a soldier for a good chunk of my life, and an independent ship operator after that. I was used to getting sleep whenever and wherever I could. But I was also a worrier, and I had always had a hard time sleeping when something was bugging me, good or bad.

After two hours of tossing and turning, I decided sleep wasn't going to come, so I might as well give up trying. I gathered my gear and began wandering the building, checking in with our forces.

I found Bailey berating a junior on the ground floor. "...and if I see you pulling that shit again, I'll personally nail your ass to the wall, do you understand me?"

"Yes, sir."

She turned and stomped away from the soldier. She didn't notice me, and I followed her around the corner, where I found her slumped against the wall. "You okay, Bailey?" I asked.

She started, realized it was me, and relaxed. "I'm fine, sir."

I jerked my head back toward the soldier she'd just reamed. "What's with Sad-sack back there?"

She sighed. "I caught him targeting Zhen soldiers with active pings, and the safeties off."

"Son of a *kark*," I said. "Did the Zhen react?"

"No, we got lucky there," she said. "Either they thought we were trying to provoke them into doing something stupid, or, more likely, they have better officers over there keeping their men clear-headed." She shook her head, disgusted. "I'm sorry, sir. It shouldn't have happened. I should have been checking on them more often."

"Don't be too hard on yourself," I said. "Almost nobody in this 'army' is a professionally trained soldier. People like you and me, we're a minority. But I put you on my command team for a reason."

"I know, sir. My electronic warfare skills are—"

"Not at all why I picked you," I interrupted. I looked her in the eyes a moment, and said, "Do you really not know why I wanted you on my team?"

She looked nervous. "Elkari, right?"

"Yep. When I met you, I had a feeling I knew you. It didn't take me long to remember you were the woman who helped me at Elkari. If you hadn't been there to back me up, I doubt the Zhen on board would have listened to me. And if you hadn't been on the ECM, we never would have gotten close enough to that cruiser to take her out." I touched the place on my belt where my ten:shal, the ceremonial dagger of a Hero of the Empire, used to hang. "You deserved the honor as much as I did," I said. "I tried to tell them, but they shut me down. I guess they were only willing to name one human to the rolls."

"And look how that worked out for them," she said, her eyes twinkling. "Don't worry about it, sir. I didn't help you to get honors, and you were the rightful commander and you had the plan. You did the heavy lifting."

"Still, they should have honored you."

She waved that off dismissively. "I'd rather get honored by my own people. Remember that when this is over."

I clapped her on the shoulder. "Carry on, Bailey." I left her behind and continued. As I climbed the stairs to the second story, I heard those alien words again, and stopped, trying to focus on them. It was like trying to grab a grelkin, though – slippery as hell, and moving faster than seems possible. I could only focus on a syllable here and there, and the rest just faded out as soon as it was over. Suddenly the voice started to sound panicked, and then there was an earsplitting tone that dropped me to my knees on the stairs.

As suddenly as it began, it was over. I rose to my feet, my face wrinkling in a frown. Even though Kiri hadn't found a problem, there had to be a reason for these things, and I still thought my NeuroNet failing was probably the most likely cause.

Even if it was, though, there wasn't anything we could do about it right now. Even if we weren't in the middle of an insurgency, Earth's colony was still in its infancy, relatively speaking, and our medical clinic didn't have the equipment to remove a NeuroNet and install a new one, even if I could get to the clinic in the first place. And it wasn't like I could go to the Empire and get it done – or even the Kelvaki Assembly, at least not until this was over.

No, I was going to have to keep going and just try to get used to these hallucinatory episodes. I'd get the NeuroNet looked at when I had the time, but until then, I was just going to have to deal with it.

*　　*　　*

I was in the 'command room' discussing plans with Liam when Bailey stuck her head in. "Sir, the Zhen are moving their line forward."

"What?" I rose and looked at my video feed from the front, and sure enough, a large group of Zhen were moving cautiously forward down First Street, named that because it was the first road built in the new colony, leading from the captured Zhen starport to the colonial administration building – the building we were in.

"*Skalk*," I said. "They're coming for us."

"I thought their plan was to wait us out," Liam said.

I thought a moment. "Either we were wrong, or someone's looking for some glory," I said. Zhen military doctrine was usually to follow orders exactly, but some ranks – both military and social – had some leeway. If whoever ordered this succeeded, they'd raise their stature in the Zhen military machine, maybe even get named to the roll of Heroes of the Empire. If they failed, they'd either die in the attempt or their superiors would make sure they died afterward. It was better to die in the attempt; the disgrace of being executed for failure would almost certainly ensure some sanction on their family, if the family had any importance at all that could be taken. Normally, all this kept the military in check, but there was always someone who was thinking about what they could get for themselves. Hell, I'd done it myself; it's how I became the Hero of Elkari.

I was not going to let whoever was behind this get that glory. "All gunners," I said on the tactical comms line, "prepare for battle but do not fire until ordered." I beckoned Liam to follow me. "Time to spring our trap."

We went up to the rooftop overlooking the street. As I exited the building I held my armor package against my chest and triggered it, waiting a moment for the nanite-based armor to spread around my body, forming itself into a ground-battle configuration. Once it finished, I stepped up to the rampart we'd erected on the roof's edge. I hooked into TacComm and said quietly, "Stand by, drone handlers." A series of acknowledgements came over the comms.

We watched the Zhen battalion come slowly up First Street. They were being careful, checking the street for mines and other traps. They found a few, marking and avoiding them rather than wait to defuse them – they were probably afraid we'd fire if they stopped to do that. It was almost amusing watching them flow around the marked areas like water;

I thought it was very nice of them to leave themselves vulnerable like that – though stupid. Whoever was leading this group wasn't the sharpest claw in the fist.

As the battalion's foremost units reached the halfway mark between their line and our position, I activated TacComm. "Drone units, engage. Roof gunners, suppression fire. Keep them from moving forward."

Even as the gunners beside me opened fire on the Zhen, the buildings to either side of them practically exploded as the drones we'd hidden inside burst out, firing plasma rifles into the Zhen position.

The first volley killed dozens of Zhen in short order. The Zhen, to their credit, recovered from the surprise quickly and began to fire back, but they were in an exposed position – their forcefields had all been concentrated on the front line and above, to prevent gunners from higher positions picking them off. And now the gunners were raining fire down on those shields, making it impossible for the Zhen to shift them without getting cut to pieces by our plasma bolts.

Several Zhen, in trying to move back, set off the mines they hadn't bothered to defuse, creating even more chaos in their ranks as more of them fell. It began a chain reaction: Zhen forces trying to avoid one mine inadvertently pushed their comrades into another mine's detection field.

The Zhen fell back, defending themselves as best they could. I stopped firing, but my gunners kept up until the Zhen had withdrawn completely. "Drone units," I said, "take up posts around my position. You're front line now. Handlers, you're now on frontline support. Trade off as needed. I want someone on-station at all times." The drones were largely autonomous, but had to be given objectives and occasional instructions. The drone handlers were stationed away from the actual fighting, connected to their units through their NeuroNets. Injala had drilled them incessantly while we prepared for the rebellion; her reputation among them wasn't good, but they respected her. Relations were improving between them, finally: she'd told me she was pleased with their progress, which word I'd gotten to them myself. Most humans weren't able to understand Kelvaki attitudes well enough to see through her demeanor to the praise she was giving them.

I took a breath and looked at Liam, who'd been firing on the Zhen beside me. "Well, that was bracing," I said.

"That was too easy," he said.

"You're not wrong. Someone was being tested, and I don't think it was their commander." I looked out over the battleground for a moment. "Pretty sure he's dead, though."

"How many did we take out?"

I scanned the street, and my implants counted bodies. "Looks like... at least two hundred. Probably more. Some of them are piled together."

"Think they'll attack again?"

I shook my head. "Not like that. Even with the drones no longer hidden, they know a frontal assault is too dangerous." I looked skyward. "If they can get orbital weapons platforms in place again, we're doomed. Our forcefields aren't good enough to repel firepower of that intensity. But I'm betting on air power."

"Bombers?"

"Bombers."

"Will our shields hold?"

"For a while," I said. "But not forever." I surveyed the buildings between us and the front line. "Signal our gunners on those rooftops to start filtering back to this position. I have a feeling they're not going to be secure over there much longer. Pull the shields from those buildings and use them to reinforce our own."

"Got it," he said.

I smiled and clapped him on the shoulder. "Don't worry, we'll get through this."

"I know." He clearly didn't believe me. I didn't mind the lie.

I didn't believe me, either.

★　　★　　★

I'd been right.

Two days after the Zhen's disastrous sortie, I was on the roofline checking in with the troops when I heard the distinctive sound of *Sik*-class bombers headed our way.

I immediately activated the TacComm and snapped, "Incoming bombers. All teams, take cover! Full power to shield emplacements! All gunners, weapons free!" I raced down the stairs, headed for the command center. Behind me I heard the guns cycling up to full power, and a few of them started firing. I didn't have a lot of hope, though – those bombers have some of the best shields and armor in the Zhen fleet; they're designed to withstand the firepower of Tabran guns. Nothing the Zhen or the Kelvaki have is quite that powerful, and we were using mostly Zhen weapons.

My command team, plus Diana Adakai, gathered there. I waved at the holotank, and a miniature representation of the area appeared in the center of the room. I expanded the image area, shrinking the buildings, until the red dots of the approaching bombers appeared.

"Seven of the shitmongers," Liam said. "It's gonna be bad."

"Ten seconds," Kiri said.

"Everyone brace yourselves," I said. "Our shields should hold, but it's going to be a rough ride."

"Five seconds," Kiri said.

"Kiri?" Liam asked.

"Yeah?"

"Shut up."

She was about to reply when the first bomb hit. It didn't hit us, but one of the outlying buildings between us and the Zhen line. But the bombs continued to fall. We felt the shockwaves of the other explosions, which built and intensified, the sound a blanket of thunder that rolled over us. The building around us shook as if a giant had grabbed it and given it a mighty shake. It was all we could do to keep our feet in the constant rolling and bucking of the world. The Zhen had unleashed hell on the center of the colony.

Even as I was trying to keep my feet, I was musing on the waste. The Zhen could have destroyed the buildings around us with demolition charges. They had a whole arsenal of weapons that could easily have leveled the buildings. But they'd chosen bombers.

This was only partially meant to clear the battlefield of obstructions. It was mostly to demoralize us. I knew that even if this building survived, it would be all that was left of the administrative center.

I was glad we'd evacuated the area. But there were going to be a few people left, people who didn't listen when we told them to leave. Now they'd be yet more of Earth's dead, more victims of the Zhen war machine.

I was so very tired of this shit.

When the thunderous noise abated, I took stock of the room. "Everyone okay? Liam, you hurt?"

"No," he said. "But I'm going to have trouble hearing for a while."

"Yeah, me too," I said. "Let's go up top."

Liam and I made our way to the roof; the rest of my team split off as we moved, helping recovery and cleanup. When we got to the rooftop, the gunners had already retaken their positions.

Our building was the only one left standing.

Everything else, from the colonial admin building all the way to First Street, seven blocks away, had been reduced to rubble. I turned, and I felt the blood drain from my face as I saw the total of the devastation the Zhen had brought. There were a few walls standing, here and there, but the city had been flattened in a seven-block radius around us. The entire center of the colony had been reduced to scrap.

"Dammit," I said. "I thought they'd focus on the buildings in front of us." Outside the blast zone, I could see civilians gathering, checking the damage and also making sure their own homes were safe. "I didn't expect them to go so far."

"They used thermobarics," Liam said. "Anyone who wasn't behind the shields here is dead." He sighed. "At least we evacuated the civilians before this. But...."

"Liam."

"Yeah?"

"We're not going to get through this."

He turned to me in alarm, took my elbow, and pulled me away from the gunners. "Hey, hey, hey," he said. "Don't let them hear you say that shit. You are Tajen Hunt, and you are going to get them through this."

I wanted to roll my eyes, but I simply closed them for a moment. "I'm just a guy, Liam. I'm not a genius, and I'm not a savior. And I don't see any way to win this. Hell, the council didn't expect us to win in the first place. Don't you get it? This is all symbolic, and those assholes in charge think we're going to surrender and be put in jail for a while, and everyone back on Zhen:da is going to suddenly agree with us and come to our aid." I switched on my TacComm and said, "Hitchens. You there?" When I got an affirmative, I said, "Bring Diana Adakai up to the roof."

When Hitchens arrived with Diana in tow, I turned in a circle, my arms wide, as if to encompass the devastation. "Happy?" I snapped. "I just pinged our forces. We've lost over seven hundred soldiers in that bombing. You know what that means?"

Her face paled. "How many have we lost, total?"

Liam said quietly, "One thousand, three hundred and fifty."

Diana crumpled into the nearest chair. "We were so certain," she said, her voice shaking. "The Zhen have always been heavy-handed, but they've never done anything like this." She was lost in thought, trying to comprehend something she'd never quite allowed herself to believe: that the Zhen were no longer our benevolent overlords, if they ever had been. She was going through the same thing I had a year ago – finally seeing the truth of our oppressors.

I wanted to give her time to process, but we just didn't have the luxury. "Diana," I said. "You need to talk to the council. Tell us what you want us to do."

She stared at me for a moment, her face betraying her shock and fear. After a moment, though, she steeled herself, her face hardening with resolve. "You're with me, Tajen. I'll call the council to meet." She rose with Liam's help and said, "Ten minutes, conference room." I nodded and she left, going through the door and down the stairs deliberately.

Hitchens moved to follow, but I grabbed him. "You find me that exit yet?"

His face reddened. "I'm so sorry, sir. In the chaos, I forgot—"

"It's all right," I said. "It's probably moot now, anyway."

"No, sir!" he said. "You don't understand – I didn't forget to look, I just forgot to tell you. We found a passage underneath – it originally linked the starport with the admin center, but it's been extended in the other direction."

"Who extended it?" Liam said.

"Near as I can tell, it was a project made by Mr. McShane, sir. He felt it might be necessary if the Zhen came back. He actually built in bulkheads to block the starport – they're closed now – and the exit is about six blocks past the edge of the admin zone, in the middle of a residential block."

I smiled. "Well done, Ryan." The redheaded soldier beamed. "I want you nearby – I'll have orders for you soon."

"Yes, sir!" He snapped to attention.

I clapped him on the shoulder. "Go," I said. As he scurried off, I turned to the gunners. "You lot! Be ready! Orders are to maintain vigilance until further notice." I turned to Liam. "Stay here; keep them focused. I'll let you know what's going on as soon as I know."

He acknowledged the order and leaned in for a kiss. It was against protocol, but...what the hell. As our lips met, the air filled with catcalls from the soldiers around us, and we both started laughing. "Get back to work!" I called, and went down to meet with the council.

★   ★   ★

The moment I entered the conference room, my smile faded.

Diana sat at the head of the table, with the surviving council members filling out the rest of the table. Kiri was no longer a member of the council, having resigned her position to go with me to Kelvak, but otherwise the faces remained the same, though perhaps a little less sure of themselves, courtesy of the last few days.

Diana looked around the table. "I'll get right to it," she said. "Two minutes ago, the Zhen commander contacted me. They have demanded our surrender, or they will level this building – and the rest of the city."

The council members looked back and forth, shocked. Driscoll spoke first. "They can't be serious," he said. "That goes against all the rules of—"

"They don't care about the rules," I said. "As I said to Diana earlier, these aren't the Zhen we're used to. This is the true face of the Zhen we're seeing now."

"So you think we should surrender?" Eliana Pearse said.

"No," I said. "I think we should escape."

"Escape how?" asked Patrick Clarke. "They've leveled everything for blocks. There's no way we could get out unseen."

"Not exactly true," Neil McShane said, and I pointed at him. "I set up an escape hatch months ago. It runs under this building."

"And you didn't say anything about it until now?" asked Connie Plunkett.

"Diana knew," he said. "And Tajen's people discovered it."

Clarke bristled. "But we could have gotten out—"

He stopped when Diana held up a hand. "Arguing about this is pointless," she said. "Tajen, what do you propose?"

"Stall the Zhen," I said. "Evacuate our personnel here through Neil's tunnel. When they come out in the residential block, they can disperse from there. I'd bet at least some of the civvies will help them."

Connie Plunkett spoke up. "I can send some of my people to prepare the way," she said.

"What's the point of escaping if the Zhen will just destroy the city?" Neil asked. "Don't hear me wrong, it's not like I would prefer to put myself in their hands, but escape means nothing if we die soon afterward. We'd never get out of the city before they leveled it."

"Not to mention the rest of the people in the city," Diana said. "No, clearly it's not possible for everyone to escape. I negotiated a solution." She waited until she had everyone's attention, and said, "The council will surrender. Everyone else will be allowed to leave, provided they turn over their weapons."

"I don't buy it," I said.

"Why not?" she asked. "Their commander says they are interested only in a cessation of this rebellion. They haven't the facilities to imprison everyone."

"They just killed seven hundred people without even thinking about it," I said. "You really think they're going to let everyone else go?"

Driscoll nodded. "He's right," he said. "I wouldn't trust the Zhen as far as I could throw one."

Pearse leaned forward. "We lead the colony. If our imprisonment can save our people, I'm for it." She looked at me. "But I'm not an idiot. We shouldn't trust them. We council leaders can surrender. The rest should escape through Neil's tunnel."

Diana considered this. "I see no problem with that plan. Those in favor?"

For perhaps the first time since we took Earth, the entire council agreed. Diana pursed her lips, considering, then turned to me. "Make it happen. I'll sell it to the Zhen."

I rose from the table. "Command team, on me." I made my way back to the command post, where most of my team was waiting. Liam joined us a moment later. He opened his mouth to speak, saw my expression, and simply closed his mouth and waited.

I closed my eyes, took a deep breath, held it, and let it go slowly. I opened my eyes and said, "We're surrendering."

Nobody said anything for several long moments. Finally, Liam said, "Well, shit." He rubbed his face. "I assume we're handing over weapons?"

"You're not handing over anything," I said. "The council will surrender, guaranteed imprisonment. The rest of us will flee through the escape tunnel and filter out through the neighborhoods."

"Are we sure we can trust the Zhen?" Liam asked.

"Of course we're not," I said. "So keep operational security in mind."

"Got it," he said.

We began planning for the withdrawal, deciding who would go in what order, dividing the forces we had left into groups. About twenty minutes into our planning, Diana sent a message asking to speak with me privately. I created a virtuality, linking the two of us into a VR conference. We could see the others around me, but in the real world, I was just sitting there while the others couldn't hear or see my side of our conversation.

"Tajen," Diana said, "the Zhen have agreed to our plan – with one change."

"Which is?" I asked, trying to ignore a sinking feeling I already knew.

"They want you to surrender alongside the rest of us. A year in prison for all of us."

"Bullshit. They'll kill me as soon as I'm in their power."

"I did raise that point. The commander says pressure from the civilians on Zhen:da has maneuvered the Twenty and the One into a compromise. They're afraid of martyring you."

"This isn't going to go well when I tell my team," I said. "Or my husband."

"So you'll go along with it?"

I scoffed at her. "Like I have a choice," I said. "You didn't say it, but I'm pretty sure if I refuse, the whole deal is off."

"Yes," she said.

"Then it's time for me to play my part."

I dropped the virtuality conference and watched my team work. Liam, Kiri, and Bailey were discussing which teams would be better together.

I wasn't at all certain I believed the Zhen's promise of imprisonment over execution. Even if they lived up to their word, I could probably expect constant attempts on my life while imprisoned. But I didn't see a choice. If the alternative to everyone on Earth dying was five years in prison – or my death, if it came to that – then I'd suffer it.

Bailey would be okay. We were friends, sure, but she'd had bigger losses. I couldn't help but smile; I knew that if I told her that, she'd pin my ears back. But she'd know I was right in the end. She was strong, stronger than any of us, and she'd get through.

Kiri would be harder hit, of course. It had only been a year since we'd reconnected. Five years away would be bearable, but if I died, she'd be the last of our family, all alone in a universe where human life was balanced on a knifepoint.

But Liam...Liam would suffer every bit as much as I would. We'd so intertwined our lives over the last year, he'd find it harder than anyone to get through it. I hated to do it to him, but...as I'd said to the Kelvaki council, I would play the hand I was dealt.

I stood. "Bailey, Kiri...Liam. All three of you need to get out together, through the back entrance before the surrender kicks off."

"No fucking way," Liam said. I should have known he'd figure it out.

"Wait, what?" Kiri asked.

"Change of plans. The Zhen require everyone on the council to surrender. They know me, they know I'm here. I have to surrender with the rest of the council, or the deal's off. You three are going with the escapees."

"No!" Kiri said.

"You're insane if you think we'll go along with this," Bailey said.

I sighed. "Look. I don't like it either, but this is what's happening."

Liam drew himself up. "If you think I'm leaving you behind—"

"Liam!" I said. "The alternative is the entire city bombed. I can't live with that. I need to do this. And I can't do it if I'm worried about you."

"Tajen," he said, his voice cracking, "you can't trust them!"

"I know," I said. "Believe me, I know. It's why I want you three to escape. Take Hitchens with you. Injala too."

"Why go along with this?" he asked. "Why don't you come with us?"

I gestured outward, to the rest of the city. "Because there are children out there."

He wanted to argue, but he knew as well as I did what I had to do. He stared at me, then said, "How long will you be gone?"

"A year," I replied. "Unless they manage to kill me in that time."

He stared at me for several long moments. Suddenly he stepped closer to me, his hands rising to grip each side of my face. "Don't you even say that," he said. "They are not going to get to you, my love. Do. Not. Let.

Them. Whatever – *whoever* – they throw at you, you fight. Fight and come back to me. Promise me."

"I promise," I said. "Just make sure you get away. I can't fight if I'm worried about you. Stay safe." I kissed him, not the tender smooch of a normal leave-taking, but hard, passionately. It was the last kiss I'd have until I got out; I was damned sure it was going to be a good one.

I broke from him. "That goes for all of you," I said through the lump in my throat. "Take care of each other." I hugged Kiri to me. "I love you."

She held on to me, clinging like she had when she was two years old. "I don't want you to go," she said, her voice catching.

"I don't want to go, either," I said. "But we have to do what's best for everyone." She let go of me. She stood there, uncertain for a moment. Liam reached out to her, and pulled her into his arms. I smiled at the two of them.

Bailey said nothing, but as I turned to leave, she called my name. I turned to look at her, and she snapped me a perfect salute. I smiled, returned it, and went to join Diana and the others.

On the way out, I ran into Hitchens. "Ryan," I said, "I want you to stick with Liam, Bailey, and Kiri. You go where they go, got it?"

"Yes, sir."

"Good man," I said. I clapped him on the shoulder and continued.

Two hours later, at the appointed time, I filed outside the building with Diana and her staff, as well as the remaining council members, and a quarter of our fighters, men and women who had volunteered to go with us, to face imprisonment with us. The fighters took up ranked positions outside the admin building we'd occupied. The rest of our forces had already filtered out over the last couple of hours and fled into the city. So far, there was no sign anyone had been caught.

The Zhen commander surveyed the ranked fighters before stalking back to Diana. He towered over her, leaning forward as he asked, "This is all you had?"

Diana faced him, resolute. "We had more; your bombs killed them."

He grunted and turned to his underling. "Get me a count," he said. The underling sent him the information with a flick of his fingers. The commander turned to address the ranked prisoners. "Human rebels," he said. "I am Commander Grevink of the Zhen Imperial Space Force.

You have chosen to surrender yourselves to Zhen authority. To the vast majority of you, the Twenty and the One extend the mercy of the Zhen Empire to its people. You will be allowed to return to your homes, without your weapons. Your colony, which is now recognized by the Imperial government, will be allowed to remain on your ancestral world. Your taxes will be increased to pay the past year's taxes due, with penalties, and to pay for the damage done to the colony in this and previous illegal actions."

He paused, and many of us looked at each other. This was not what we had expected to hear. I glanced at Diana beside me. Her face was a mask of confusion – and dismay. "This isn't what we agreed to," she said quietly. I started to respond, but the Zhen commander had begun speaking again.

"Some of you, however. Some of you must pay for these actions." He gestured to an underling, who called out the names.

"Diana Adakai, Jim Gould, Eliana Pearse, Patrick Clarke, Constance Plunkett, Neil McShane, Driscoll."

Commander Grevink gestured toward us as he spoke to the rest of the prisoners. "You placed your faith in these people," he said. "That faith was rewarded with illegal actions that led you to this." He gestured at the destruction around us. "Someone must pay for the mercy given to the Terran colony."

On his last word, everyone on the council but me fell to the ground, and something wet hit me in the side of my face. I looked down at Diana and froze. Her head was simply gone, and the something that had hit me was all that remained of it. I was too stunned to say or do anything. I simply stood there, wondering why I was still standing. I dimly heard the crowd of prisoners roaring in outrage. There were shots fired, and I shook off my sudden paralysis and turned to see some of the prisoners were down, shot when they tried to charge the Zhen.

Grevink simply stood, watching me. Some part of me noticed his claws were beginning to poke out of the sheaths on his fingertips. I knew, in that moment, he wanted to kill me himself. He wanted it to be personal, painful. I just stood and stared at him, waiting for the attack I knew would come. I hoped Kiri and Liam had made it to safety, and I wished we'd had more time to say goodbye.

Eventually, Grevink relaxed, his claws sliding back into their sheaths. "You want to know why, I imagine," he said calmly, almost gently. "But you know why. If we allowed your leaders to live, they would only plot and plan for another rebellion. Now, the head of your rebellion is dead. The body will wither and die."

I looked at him slowly. "Why aren't I dead?" Even to my own ears, I sounded like I was pleading to die with them.

He gestured toward Diana's body. "She claimed you were not part of the decision-making body behind this action." His expression turned sour. "And you have too many friends in the Talnera to kill you now. It would cause 'unnecessary internal friction', I am told." He made a gesture that indicated an action distasteful but necessary. "So we must allow you to live."

"I was to be arrested. Imprisoned."

He shook his head. "Rebellions always grow in prisons. I will not give you a place to recruit more to your cause. I agreed to the deal she offered to get you here, to show you the folly of your path."

I realized this was personal. "To humiliate me," I said.

His expression answered that I was right.

"Why?"

He pointedly ignored the question. "You are beaten, Tajen Hunt. Go rot in a hole and die, or better yet…do something that destroys your support back home, so I may kill you openly, in sight of all." He waved a hand, and the Zhen forces began to pull back. He simply turned and walked away, leaving me standing next to the corpses of my leaders, and the dream we'd shared.

CHAPTER TEN

I woke up in the cabin I'd built – well, I'd programmed the machines that built it – and walked outside and down the path to the lake. Liam and I had discovered this place early in the colony's existence, and I'd decided it was going to be our home. We'd built the cabin and stocked it, but we didn't spend much time here, as it was several hours' flight away from Landing, and we had jobs to do there. When the Rising had failed, Liam had brought me here to rest and recuperate. But I hadn't left for months now. In the aftermath of the Rising's failure, I'd assumed that I'd come back to the fight eventually. I told Liam I needed a few weeks.

Weeks became months. In that time, the Zhen had re-established their control over the planet quickly, from the orbital surveillance and strike satellites to their garrison in Landing. They'd found the perfect way to keep us down: by helping us rebuild the city center and bringing in much-needed supplies.

Liam continued to work back in Landing, and joined me every few days, but I was done fighting. The Zhen had destroyed us, and they held all the cards now. Injala had tried to talk me into fighting again, but when she failed, she left me, simply walking off one day. I had no idea where she was, now.

As I sat in the chair I'd placed under a tree on the lakeshore, I noticed a small animal at the water's edge, drinking. I was watching it when I heard the drone of a shuttle approaching. The little creature bolted for some nearby foliage, and I stood and watched the shuttle come in on its antigrav and settle softly to the ground in the landing area we'd ringed with stones.

I smiled and approached as the door opened and Liam stepped out, followed by Bailey and Kiri. My smile got even wider, and I gave them each a hug. "Anyone hungry?" I said.

"I am always hungry, you know that," Liam said. Bailey and Kiri both indicated they were hungry. I turned and led them to the cabin,

Kiri and Liam taking up station on either side of me. "How's Landing?" I asked Kiri.

"I haven't been there in a couple of months," she said. "Once the Zhen pushed us all out to the villages, there wasn't much point. I've been working with some guys in Hotty."

"Wait, what?"

"Well, we call it 'Hotty', but officially it's named 'Hotcrap'."

"Really?"

"Yep. The villages were settled by people like you. What can I say? It's hot, it's crappy." She waved a hand. "At any rate, we're trying to find a way to re-enable the stealth protocols so we can use them against the Zhen." She sat at the table.

"Any luck?" I asked, as I began to prepare a tray of various foods from the pantry.

"No," she said. "Nothing we've tried has worked." She looked troubled.

"What happened?" I asked.

She took a deep breath. "We lost someone."

I turned slowly toward her. "Wait. Are you telling me you're still working with the Resistance?"

She stared at me a moment. "Of course I am. Who did you think I was just talking about?"

"We all are," Bailey said.

I turned to look at Liam, who raised his hands placatingly. "I know you've been trying to stay out of it, Tajen, but not everyone has that luxury." I bristled, and he continued, "The Zhen aren't benevolent overlords now any more than they were last year. They're fucking with our planet and our people, and we have to fight them."

I put the tray on the table and took a seat. As Liam and Bailey sat, I shook my head. "What's the point?" I asked. "The Zhen run the planet. They've done everything right. What's the ratio of original colonists to newcomers now? How many Zhen live on Earth?"

Kiri reached across the table to cover my hand with her own. "Tajen, you remember Ryan Hitchens?"

"Of course I do. How is he?"

"He was caught in an alley the other night, after curfew. The Zhen beat him senseless. He's all right," she hastened to add, "but he was beaten badly — far beyond what's legal, but of course nothing will get done about it."

"And he's not the only one," Bailey said. "Things aren't any better now than they were when we began this whole thing. It's getting worse here, in fact."

"How's Ben?" I asked, trying to change the subject.

"He's fine," Liam said.

Bailey tossed her head. "If by 'fine' you mean 'barely scraping by'. He's had to reinvent a ton of herbal remedies to make do, because the Zhen won't give him as many nano-pods or even all the meds he needs."

I shook my head. "This will pass," I said. "Things will improve."

"Damn it, Tajen!" Liam exploded at me. "I love you, but this has gone on long enough. I know they hurt you. They hurt all of us. Diana and the others weren't the first or the last people they've killed."

Kiri held up a restraining hand to Liam, then turned to me. "Tajen, I know it hit you hard. But you can't let them win."

"Why not?" I asked, though even to me, the question was stupid.

"My father," she said. "This planet. Billions of humans who died here, because of the Zhen."

"That's not fair!" I said.

"No, it's not." Her gaze hardened. "But it's also not fair to leave the fight when we need you."

I sat back and took a deep breath. "I know you're right," I said. "All of you. But…." I put my head in my hands. "I was so close to death that day. It shook me, in a way nothing else ever has. I've tried to pick up my blaster, but I have a hard time even aiming at rocks. Every time I pick it up, I feel Diana's…." I waved off that image. "I'm scared. Plain as that."

Liam said, "But you've faced death before. What was different this time?"

I shook my head. "For you, ground battles are normal. But I'm a stick-jock," I said. "In space, death is always possible, but it's…it's almost clean. Your ship goes to pieces, and you're either consumed in the fire, or you die in space. Your brains don't get splattered all over your friends, you don't…." I sat back again. "No, that's bullshit."

"What do you mean?" Kiri asked.

"I can justify it all I want, but the truth is, I was starting to buy into my own legend." I raised my hands in the air. "The great Tajen Hunt. Right up until Diana told me the truth, I'd thought we were just days from getting what we wanted. And then the Zhen said I'd go to jail, and I was okay with that. I thought I could use that. But then they killed Diana, and the others. And I suddenly came face to face with the reality that I'm just a guy who's been incredibly lucky." I looked at my friends, and my lover, and I asked them, "How long before my luck runs out? I just started to live again, to have friends and family. Why should I risk that?"

Liam leaned forward. "Because living isn't enough, my love. You also have to be who you are. And Tajen Hunt is not a man ruled by his fear."

Kiri had to join in. "Nope. He's a badass, in a ship or on the ground."

"Let's not get ridiculous," I said.

"Who's getting ridiculous? You *are* a badass."

"It's why I fell in love with you," Liam said.

"No it isn't."

He tossed his head. "Well, no. But it's part of the attraction." He gave me his best 'you love me' look, and I laughed.

"You're right," I said. "You're all right."

"Does that mean you're back in the fight?" Bailey asked.

I took a deep breath, considering what I should say. In the end, I settled for, "Yeah. I'm back in."

Liam whooped. "All right, let's talk about—"

"No," I said. His face fell, and I smiled at him. "First, let's eat and enjoy the day. Then we'll talk shop."

★　　★　　★

Later that day, I dropped a book onto the table. "That's our guide," I said.

Liam picked it up and read the cover. "Kelvaki. On the Application of Force in Non-Conventional Arenas," he read. "Where did you even get this?"

"Injala left it behind for me."

"Where is she, anyway?"

"I was hoping you knew. She got fed up with me and left a few months back."

Kiri said, "She's in Hotty, advising us. I thought you knew."

"Well, good," I said. "Do me a favor, let her know what's going on?"

"Sure." She got a distant look in her eyes for a moment. "It's done."

"Thanks. So. Who's running the Resistance, right now?"

"Ha!" Liam barked. "We tried, but we couldn't hold them all together. 'The Resistance' is a myth. It's more like a bunch of tiny independent cells operating more or less randomly, without any real communication or cooperation." He shook his head. "We tried to take the lead, but…." He sighed. "We're not real popular right now. Too many of them see us as the idiots who lost the Rising."

I considered that for a moment. "Well, the first thing is to knock that bullshit out of their heads. Second is the lack of communication. I take it there still aren't slipnet capabilities outside Landing?"

"Not much," Kiri said. "We've managed a few small nodes here and there, but nothing comprehensive."

"So we need a reliable method of communication," I said. "But not Resistance-wide. We need to set up cells of operatives. Each operative will have a way to contact one other cell, but if possible they'll know only one person in that cell. That way we minimize the ability of the Zhen to find us all easily. And we make sure all the contacts form a web across the settled areas. Nobody should be more than two hours outside the web."

"That'll help," Liam said, "but what about operational security?" He sketched shooting motions with his hands. "When we're operating, the Zhen can use our NeuroNets to find us. After Ryan got hit…I don't think we can count on our evasion routines anymore." To my questioning look, he said, "I think they followed Ryan specifically. They located him via his 'Net's ID tag."

"*Skalk*," I cursed. "Can we shut them off?" I asked Kiri.

"The ID tags? No, I've tried. They're hardcoded into the system."

"How about turning off the NeuroNets themselves?"

"I've heard it can be done," she said, "but it's not supposed to be easy. I'll look into it."

"Good. Liam, I need access to the slipnet. Know anywhere I can do that without triggering the Zhen threat-analysis routines?"

"No, but I can take you to someone who does. He's a few hours' flight from here. Gotta warn you, though – he's a character."

"Dangerous?"

"Not to us," he said with a laugh. "Except maybe your patience."

"Sounds fun. Let's go there now, please. There's some things I need to check."

He stood and bowed. "Your wish is my command, my love."

Bailey stood as well. "It's my flyer. You're not leaving without me."

"Okay. Kiri, we'll be—"

"Nope," she said. "I gave you your space, my dear uncle, but that's over now. Where you go, I go." She gave me the sweetest smile she was capable of. "Now that the team's back together, we are not splitting up again." She stepped closer to me. "Got it?" She gave me the look her dad and I had always called her 'angry teddy bear' face – a perfect mixture of fierce and adorable.

"Got it," I said.

★　　★　　★

As the shuttle lifted off the cabin's pad, Bailey took up the comms. "Colonial control, this is shuttle *Crappy Racer* lifting from destination. Headed to grid Arkan-7-Fent-6. That'll be the end of flying for the day."

"Destination logged, *Crappy Racer*," came a human voice. "Be aware there is a police action over Settlement 27, local name 'Sitonit:da'." There was the barest hint of a smile in the unknown man's voice over the name, a clear insult to the Zhen, and more specifically to the Zhen:ko, who ruled the Empire. "Best to maintain course and stay out of their exclusion zone. Run transponder addition Delta-8 to signal permission to pass has been given."

"Understood," Bailey said. "*Crappy Racer* out." She closed down comms, and I leaned forward.

"How far out is Sitonit:da?"

"If it isn't over by the time we get near enough to see, it'll be about ten klicks out, seventy degrees off our bow to start. We'll be in visual range in about an hour."

"Are 'police actions' becoming more common?"

"There've been three in the last week alone. All of them rounding up former or current members of the Resistance. That village is the HQ for a pretty active Resistance group, but I don't know that I know anyone there."

I looked to Kiri. "How about you?"

She checked her records, her hands fluttering in what seemed to me to be empty air, before she grabbed at something and flicked it to me.

It became visible and floated in front of me, and I groaned as I read the name. "Charlie Hughes," I said. He'd been one of the unit commanders during the Rising. "I don't suppose there's any chance we can help?"

Liam shook his head. "Not if it's anything like the last one. We're not armed well enough, and this ship isn't named *Crappy Racer* because she's fast." He tapped the bulkhead near him. "No offense," he said to the ship.

About an hour later, we began to see a buzz of Zhen flyers over Sitonit:da. Or, rather, we saw a buzz of flyers over the raging inferno where Sitonit:da used to be. The flyers circled the inferno, keeping their weapons armed at the settlement. From time to time, one of the flyers would fire briefly at something on the ground. "Gods above and below," I said.

Liam, looking over my shoulder, said only, "Dammit."

"Is this happening often?" I asked. "Why hasn't anyone told me?"

Bailey shook her head. "Not common," she said. "This is only the second time I've heard of. But I'm not surprised."

I sat back, staring out the window at the burning village. "How many people?" I asked.

Liam shrugged. "Probably a couple of hundred, all Resistance. No telling how many were captured, and how many were killed." He sighed. "Tomorrow there'll be some bullshit on the slipnet about how the village was destroyed by the Resistance to prevent the happy settlers from strengthening their ties with the Zhen."

"How many children?" I said, but the question was rhetorical. "If you hadn't already convinced me to come back –" I pointed with my chin toward the glow on the horizon, "– that would've done it."

Bailey began to argue in Zhen with someone on the other end of a comms line. "We are not approaching Settlement 27," she said. "We are en route to Settlement 17." She paused. "Delivering new residents." Another pause. "Clearance code 7-4-3-Kamtak'a. Understood." She waved the comms off. "Asshole."

"Trouble?" I asked.

"A little, but nothing a little preemptive bribery couldn't fix," she said. "I got hold of the same algorithm that decides code rotations. It gives me a new clearance every time I need one."

"Wow," I said. "Who'd you have to bribe for that?"

"A human, fortunately," she said. "It cost me a dinner date and a lot of transport favors. Just call me Taxi Jane." She shook her head. "Least he's cute."

The rest of the flight was without incident. As we circled around to the landing pad at Settlement 17, I asked, "What's this place called? I can't remember."

Liam said, "Originally it was Linden's Landing, but it's been renamed. Now they call it Anna's Rest, after Anna Hutchins." He looked toward the center of town. "They buried her in the town square."

Hutchins had been one of the first colonists to join us on Earth, a grandmother of three who wanted her family to join her. Some had, some were still on Terra. "So where's this hacker?"

"This way," Liam said. We followed him through several streets and alleys, until we found ourselves finally in a dark alleyway that ended in a dark, empty courtyard. Liam stalked up to a dark doorway and pounded on it. He dropped into his faux Scottish brogue, copied from entertainment files salvaged from the files our colonist ancestors had taken with them to the stars. "Open up!" he called. "Delivery for ye!"

The door opened, and a lone human stood silhouetted. "Knock that crap off, mate," the man said. He peered out at the rest of us. "Holy shit, izzat Tajen Hunt? Get in 'ere, mate!"

The accent was similar to the one Liam and I sometimes affected, though not quite the same. Even before the Zhen takeover, many of the younger Earth colonists had begun affecting accents they found and absorbed by watching Old Earth entertainments, but whereas most of them chose what we assumed to have been fairly common regional accents, a few chose some pretty out-there ones. This one was thick as neutronium, and barely understandable. I walked closer to the guy and held out my hand. "Hi," I said. "I need your help."

He grabbed my hand and clasped it happily. "Not a problem, my bra!" he said. "Why I'm here, innit? Come in, come in!"

We entered, and he took a quick look around before shutting the door and locking it. He took a moment to verify we hadn't been seen on several monitors. "Can't be too careful, eh? Right, looks good, let's go." He led us down a long corridor that ended in a narrow spot we had to squeeze through, then opened into a large room, a combination bedroom and workspace. "Have a seat," he said. "Right, what can I do for the great Tajen Hunt?"

"First, you can stop calling me that. Just 'Tajen' will do. Second, I need you to get me access to the slipnet – but without certain, ah—"

"'Imperial entanglements', right?"

"Exactly," I said.

He pursed his lips. "Yeah, boss man, I could do that," he said. "Question is, what's in it for me?"

"Excuse me?" I looked at Liam. "Who is this guy?"

"Tajen, meet Aleph. Not his real name, but he won't tell me that. He's one of the best hackers I've ever known, though, so I let him get away with it."

"You running from something?" I asked him.

"Nah," he said. "Just don't like the name my parents gave me."

"So what is it you want, Aleph? Money?"

"I don't need money."

"No?"

"No. I got enough money before all this started. Walked away from it to come to Earth. You know why?"

"Enlighten me," I said.

"You."

I blinked at him. "Me."

"Yeah. That speech you gave, when you told us all what the Zhen had done? Bruva, it gave me *shivers*. And I knew I wanted to be a part of it. So I hied off to Earth with the rest of them as was inspired by you. But when I get here, I'm told you don't need someone like me in the militia. I was helping set up the colony's infrastructure, but then the Zhen take over, and it's 'Your services is no longer required', innit? So I's been out here, doing odd jobs, fixing people's broken electronics. I'm *bored*, man. I want to do summat that matters, you know?"

I thought about what he'd said. "How about joining my team?" I said.

"Depends. What you doin'?"

"We're starting the fight up again."

His face fell. "Yeah, that's stupid. Got yer ass kicked when ya tried that, didn't ya?"

"Yeah. But we're not doing it that way again. The council tried to make a statement by losing. That's stupid, it was doomed. This time we're going to be sneaky. We're not taking over Landing again. That'd never work. Instead, we're going to make Earth so dangerous for the Zhen, they won't want it anymore."

"And how you stop them from nuking us all from orbit?" he said, folding his arms.

"Leave that to me," a new voice said, and we all jumped. Those of us who were armed pulled our blasters as we rose and turned toward the voice. Injala stepped through the gap into the room and smiled. "The Kelvaki will make sure the Zhen don't just destroy you all," she said. "I'll make sure of that."

I stared at her. "How'd you find us?" I asked.

"Tajen, please," she said. "You are not the only one with a brain. This was your only possible goal once you came back to the fight." She smiled at Liam. "And I knew you would, eventually."

I glanced at Liam. "That smile mean something?"

He sighed. "I owe her credits," he said.

"Do I want to know how many?"

"Not really," he said airily. I knew enough to drop it there.

Aleph wasn't so sanguine about an alien waltzing right into his lair. "Right, how'd you get through my door?" he asked.

"I'll tell you later. And I will help you revise your security to make it more effective than wet paper. Later – right now you have work to do," she said, looking pointedly to me.

"Riiiight," Aleph said before turning to regard me. "Okay, boss man. I'm not totally convinced you're not going to get me killed, but it's better than being bored. Let's get started." He waved to an access terminal on his desk. "Get hooked into that thing, and I'll weave the magic to get you to the slipnet." He leaned back and closed his eyes, connecting to his system. I did the same.

Connection was simple, as always when accessing the slipnet. Whatever Aleph was doing, it was invisible to me. I was able to access the feed, getting a sort of 'god's-eye view' of what had been going on while I was wallowing in my self-imposed exile.

While the Zhen had apparently found a way to prevent my stealth ability from working on their operatives, they'd failed to find a way to curtail my ability to surf their systems. I had the same levels of access I'd had after rebooting my NeuroNet last year, and my probes breezed through their security buffers.

They'd been busy.

I'd known that the Zhen opened Earth up to human colonists soon after the Rising's failure. Some Zhen came, as well, but the majority of the incoming settlers were humans, given land and equipment with which to establish businesses on the new colony. What I hadn't known, because I hadn't let Liam tell me, was that many of these humans were fully pro-Zhen and quite wealthy by human standards; their mindset seemed to be that while the Zhen owed humanity for 'the mistakes of the past', that we shouldn't hold the present Zhen accountable for that. Arguments using the One's comments to me from the battle last year about her plan to engineer us into their image did little to sway opinions; people tend to believe that which bolsters their own preconceptions, after all.

This had been boosted by a set of decrees called the Punitive Laws, which forbade humans who had taken part in the Rising from owning land, voting in colonial elections, or holding any kind of publicly elected office. Thanks to high rents and home prices, Landing was now nearly entirely the domain of the pro-Zhen humans, who were quickly becoming the aristocracy of Earth, while the vast majority of humanity lived in satellite villages. Any weapon designed for more than hunting was forbidden to humans in the villages, and all weapons were forbidden in Landing itself. The few Kelvaki drones remaining after the Rising had been scrapped.

A few months into the new settlement wave, the crops in Landing's agricultural fields began to fail due to some kind of mold. The organism turned out to be resistant to most methods of control we knew. Eventually a cure was found, but in the meantime many in the settlements outside Landing were devastated, their entire crops lost. But humans form communities, and even the residents of Landing helped to keep people in the villages fed. Still, the financial damage was great, and some farmers had no choice but to take out loans to survive – loans with incredibly onerous terms.

I crafted some messages to people on Zhen:da I thought I might be able to count on, both human and Zhen. When I was done, I withdrew from the system and blinked for a few moments. "All right," I said. "Let's get started rebuilding our network."

CHAPTER ELEVEN

It took me four months to get what I called the Terran Intelligence Service set up, recruiting each individual operative carefully, after observing them clandestinely and making sure they were fully committed to the human cause. The name 'Terran Intelligence Service' was entirely unofficial, of course, but the work they did wasn't.

A clerk working in the Zhen military offices slipped us information on Zhen operations, especially raids on villages. A minor office functionary supplied me with information on counterinsurgency plans and the residences of both Zhen and humans working for the Empire.

But my best informant was someone I had no intention of even trying to recruit. I'd met him purely by accident. I was standing in a market square just outside the central zone of Landing, shouting to the crowd.

"The fact that the Zhen occupy our planet should not be taken as defeat!" I shouted. "They can jail us! They can shoot us!" I pointed to the Zhen soldiers who were beginning to gather at the edges of the crowd. "But we have a power they will never understand and can never have! We have the power to refuse to bow down to any government not our own. To refuse to cooperate with any institution not our own. We are humans, and we demand human rule over our own!" The crowd roared in approval, and I eyed the Zhen. "The Zhen would like to shut me up. To jail me, or maybe even shoot me. But they need to know that if they silence me, they've only silenced one of us! Individuals are easy to kill, but we're not individuals. We are the people of Earth!" I raised my voice to a shout. "If I fall, who among you will stand and take my place?"

The crowd roared and raised their fists in the air. The Zhen began to move into the crowd, and the crowd surged against them, refusing them entry. I felt a hand grab my elbow and pull me off the platform I'd been standing on. "Time to go," Liam said. He dragged me through the crowd, not letting go of my elbow until we'd broken out of the crowd and were running down an alleyway.

We turned a corner and ran smack into a Zhen in the harness of a police commander. We turned to go down a nearby alley, and he held out a hand. "Stop!" he said. "There's an ambush that way."

I noticed his gun was still holstered. "What's going on?" I asked him. "You don't seem like the normal kind of cop I'm used to."

He shrugged. "You're persuasive," he said. "And I'm not liking what I'm being asked to do lately." He held out a small chip. "Information here. Probably useful to you. If you think so, I can get more."

I quickly scanned the chip for any kind of location tag; there was none. "How will we contact you?" I asked.

"Instructions are on the chip," he said. "But for now? Go this way." He indicated a basement door behind him. "The tunnel in there will take you outside Landing. Comes out about a half-klick from your flyer."

"You found our flyer?"

"I did," he said, emphasizing the pronoun. "The Zhen Empire did not."

"If this all pans out…thanks."

"Good luck. Now get out of here before we're seen."

Liam and I ducked into the basement, which turned out to be a laundry room for the building above, and a tunnel. As we made our way down the tunnel, Liam asked me, "Do you trust him?"

I thought about it for a moment. "I want to, but I'm not stupid. In addition to checking out what he gave us, put a watch on him. I want to know what he's doing every day, from breakfast to sleep."

"Got it," Liam said.

We made it to the flyer and took off, angling for the edge of the city. Once we were in the air, Liam said, "Do you really think you should be taunting the Zhen like you were back there?"

"What do you mean?"

"Tajen, you practically dared them to take you out."

"Is that what you think I was doing?"

"Am I wrong?"

"Yeah," I said. "I mean, mostly. I know you're worried about me, but I assure you I'm not being reckless. I wasn't daring them to take me down. I was warning them not to. When Grevink killed the council and left me, he as much as told me the Zhen back home are worried about martyring me. This speech was to show them they're right. If they take me out, I become far more powerful as a symbol than I am as a lone man."

"But that's the thing," he said. "You're not a lone man. You're the leader of a movement. They already took out the heads of one. Why not do it again?"

"They could. But killing our leaders didn't stop us last time. Whatever the Zhen are, they're not stupid. And they know there's a critical mass on atrocity. They do it again, it might be too late. Then they have a full-blown uprising on their hands."

"At what point do they just say 'to hell with this' and bomb Earth to the bedrock again? It would be a lot easier to wipe us out now that we're basically rebels."

"Well, yeah. That's the thing that keeps me awake at night," I admitted. "But the truth is, they need us alive here, or they lose the public."

"Thing is, Tajen, I got a message from Zhen:da recently. They're not seeing anything about Earth on the official Zhen channels."

"You're kidding," I said.

"I wish I was. Nearly a total media blackout since the Rising. As far as anyone back on Zhen:da is concerned, Earth's peaceful and everything is going swimmingly now."

"Well," I said. "Then I guess I know what we need to do."

*　　*　　*

"And how exactly am I meant to do that?" Aleph asked.

"I'll help," Kiri said. "It shouldn't be too hard to set up a link with the slipnet. We can bounce it off—"

"The Zhen satellites and like, I know," Aleph said. "It's not the tech stuff I need help with, though, innit?" He pointed at his own face. "I'm not exactly a good writer and talker, am I?"

Kiri gave him what we called the 'Hunt Deathstare'. "You and I both know you're better at it than you want to seem," she said. "But I get you. I'll be the public face." She turned to me. "All right, go away. We'll get the Voices of Earth set up and running." She thought a moment. "Better yet, I'll recruit several speakers. That way it won't look like it's all coming from one source. And it makes it harder for the Zhen to shut us down."

"Make sure it's not just an anti-government mouthpiece," I said. "If we screw up, that needs to be shown too."

"Got it," Kiri said. To Aleph, she said, "First thing, let's figure out who we need. I think Jinny Thomas would be good for analysis. She's got a great mind for that."

"Oh, right," Aleph said. "You know how to find her?"

"Sure, she's...."

I turned away from their conversation and tuned it out. "Liam, take a look at this," I said, flicking a map into his awareness. "I've spoken in about half these settlements. What do you notice in the days following?"

He frowned at the map. "More arrests."

"Which means?"

"The Zhen are cracking down."

"Sure," I said, "but check the reasons. It's not stuff that was already going on. Every time I speak out about the Zhen ruling over us, and tell people we need to rule ourselves, there's an uptick in refusals to cooperate with Zhen forces or rules."

"People are getting fed up with them."

"Right. And that gives us an opening."

"Okay. But we still have the problem of arms. No weapons in Landing, and very few out here."

"Let's find Injala," I said. We retired to a corner away from the others in the room and I sent a message to Injala's NeuroNet, inviting her to a conference.

"Yes?" she said, seeming to appear beside us.

I waved my hand, converting our real-life space into a virtuality conference. "We need to start moving weapons into Landing," I said. "Any ideas?"

"Of course," she said. "First, what kinds?"

"Everything we can," I said. "But emphasis for now should be on small, easily concealable weapons. Pistols, knives, grenades. That sort of thing."

"I can get such things to Earth, of course – we've already got the pipeline up and running," she said. "But dispersing them throughout the colony will be your job."

"How can you get them here?" I asked.

She smiled. "Your draka has arranged for a Kelvaki courier to remain in-system at all times. We speak at prearranged intervals. If I ask for shipments, they will be provided. All we need to do is pick them up and disperse them."

"Dierka's keeping an eye on us, huh?"

"He is keeping an eye on *me*," she said. "*I* am keeping an eye on *you*, as it were."

I narrowed my eyes at her. "You're more than his retainer, aren't you?"

She inclined her head.

"And your position is?"

"That…would be telling," she said. "Far more fun to watch you try to figure it out."

"Well, have fun, then. But please, request what you can. We'll work on the distribution." A thought occurred to me. "Where are you right now, anyway?"

"I am making arrangements," she said. "Don't ask what for. It's better you don't know until and unless you need them. I will make the requests. Anything else?"

"No," I said. "I'll contact you again if I come up with anything."

"Very well," she said, and cut the feed.

Liam and I dropped the virtuality and found ourselves alone, a note sitting on my lap. It said, *We're out doing thy bidding, Uncle. Make some lunch for us. Kiri.*

"Same old story," I muttered. "No respect for her elders."

"She learned it by watching you," Liam said, and I threw a pillow at him.

★   ★   ★

A few weeks later, Liam and I sat on the lowered cargo ramp of a small delivery flyer in the middle of the desert. We both wore jackets against the cold, as the flyer was powered completely down and we couldn't risk a fire. The circuits of the jackets' heat elements kept us warm as we stared at the sky.

"People on Zhen:da don't get it," Liam said.

"What do you mean?"

"How beautiful the sky is at night. There are only a few places on the whole of Zhen:da where you can see the sky like this."

"I've read it was the same on Old Earth," I said. "Cities were so bright it blotted out all but a few stars. By the time the *Far Star* left, there were probably only a few places on Earth a person could see the sky like this, too."

"Crazy. Did you ever see anything like this when you were on Zhen:da?"

"No," I said. "How about on Terra?"

"A few," he said, "but Terra's still mostly wilderness. A few more decades, it'll be like Zhen:da. Or the majority will move here, and ruin this view."

I chewed the corner of my lip as I thought about this land covered in cities. "We have to do better."

"What do you mean?"

I took a deep breath. "If Earth does grow, we need to do better by it than we did the first time. I've read the archives. Earth was a mess by the time the Zhen came. We'd nearly destroyed our ecosystem. In some ways, the Zhen bombing our civilization into dust was good for the planet. We can't let it get that bad again."

"How could we?" Liam asked. "The problem back then was fuels we don't use, and mining we don't need. We can get everything we need from the asteroid belts, I'd bet."

"But we need to make sure we don't screw that up, either."

"I see your point, but I think that's a bit outside our mandate here," Liam said.

"Yeah."

"Let's free the planet, then worry about the environment, okay?"

I smiled and put my arms around him. As he relaxed back into me, I held him tight. "You have good ideas," I said.

"I know," he murmured. "I'm brilliant."

I gently turned him around in my arms and kissed him, my lips brushing his. He returned the kiss, leaning into me. As our lips parted, a loud beep interrupted us and we broke apart, Liam rising to his feet. "Damn," he said. "Incoming."

We both tuned our implants to the prearranged frequency and followed an object down through the sky.

The crate, about half the size of our flyer, hit the ground, the old-fashioned parachute falling down around it. Liam and I hurried to it. I found the release and triggered it, and the pod's cover silently rose to reveal the contents.

Inside, packed in crash-foam, was a collection of weapons, mostly blaster rifles and pistols, with grenades and extra power packs, along with a few nano-armor packs, taking up the remaining space.

This was only one pod of many dropped tonight across the planet by our Kelvaki allies. Each pod would be met by a team of Resistance volunteers, who would unpack the crate and get it to a dispersal point, where the weapons would be repackaged and smuggled throughout the colony's settlements. The Zhen might get one of the pods and recovery teams, but the odds of them getting them all were slim.

I'd asked Injala why the Kelvaki were helping us, when they'd made it very clear they couldn't do so. She'd looked at me, seeming vaguely disappointed. "The Zhen demanded your arrest before we finished our meeting, you'll recall. If they had not, you'd have been informed that while the Assembly cannot openly move against the Zhen, the opportunity for undermining their war machine is too advantageous to be ignored. We cannot allow the Zhen to see us as taking an official position in this war, but weapons? Covert intelligence sharing? These we can and will do. Unless..." she looked quizzically at me, "...you don't want our assistance?"

I wasn't going to refuse that, now was I?

I smiled as I picked up a rifle, and Liam said, "It makes you that happy?"

"Just remembering a conversation with Injala."

"Are you okay, because, I mean...she's not funny."

"Sure she is, if you understand Kelvaki humor."

"You understand Kelvaki humor?"

I chuckled. "Not in the least," I said. "But Dierka said she's got a great sense of humor."

"Well, she'd have to, working with us," he said. "I get the feeling she's always several steps ahead of us."

"I think she works very hard to maintain that image," I said.

We put the last of the rifles in the flyer. "I'll trigger the destruct," I said, and went back to the crate.

Each crate was composed of an alloy that could withstand the stresses of atmospheric reentry. The Kelvaki scouts dropped them from low-Earth orbit, with carefully planned trajectories to take them as close to the planned landing site as possible. The crates had a maneuvering suite of thrusters with limited guidance control by an onboard computer, but mostly they were falling bricks filled with goodies. To avoid any Zhen sightings, though, we had to make sure they couldn't find any trace. So each crate also had a specially programmed package of nanites, designed to destroy the crates and, if not opened properly, their equipment.

I activated the nanites, and watched as they literally ate the crate, reducing it to a fine powder that blew away on the wind.

"That gives me the creeps," Liam said. "Imagine if they ran away and ate everything."

I flicked a readout to his visual field. "They're dead," I said. "Confirmed. Besides, Injala told me they only have enough power to destroy the crate and parachute before they go inert. They lack the programming to do anything else."

"I hope so," he said.

We got the flyer airborne and flew back toward home, trusting the forged clearances to keep us out of trouble. When we landed, volunteers quickly unloaded the flyer while another team filled it with vegetables and other supplies. When the switch was done, another team of pilots flew the craft on its usual rounds of the villages, delivering supplies and goods and picking up goods meant for our own. Along the way, they'd also clandestinely collect messages for the Resistance.

Liam and I, meanwhile, got some much-needed sleep, and then spent a few hours with Injala, planning the next day's activities.

It would be a hell of a day.

CHAPTER TWELVE

"I hate fighting in gravity wells," I said. "And I *really* hate being stuck in tiny rooms." I looked up at the ceiling and tried to imagine the scene in orbit. "Give me space combat any day."

Injala's ears quivered with her amusement. "Of course," she said. "We need only liberate your planet again, then you can build your space defenses and prepare for the Zhen to attack yet again."

"I hate you," I said.

"Do you really?"

I held my hand up, my finger and thumb mere millimeters apart. "Little bit.".

After a moment, she said, "Isn't a spaceship basically a tiny room?"

"Your point?"

"I just do not see how being stuck in a tiny room is any different just because the room can move. If *this* room were to suffer a loss of structural integrity, you wouldn't die – at least not immediately. It would seem better than a spaceship, at least in that regard."

"It's different."

"Is it?"

"Yes."

She narrowed her eyes at me and turned away to scan the street. "They're coming," she said. "Any moment now."

I used my 'Net to access the camera I'd set up outside. A Zhen patrol was coming down the street, an antigrav transport with soldiers clinging to the sides and back. I kept a careful eye on the transport's position relative to the buildings. "Steady," I said, my finger hovering over the COMMIT button on my remote. "Almost there…." I resisted the urge to tell my people to ready themselves; we were in a self-imposed comms blackout until I hit the switch. "Now!" My finger stabbed the button.

Below us in the street, the antigrav transport suddenly slammed down, the grav-nodes whining in protest. The driver tried to get the vehicle up again, but the Kelvaki gravity mine we'd set up kept it solidly grounded – and made it difficult for the Zhen to move, as well.

One of the Zhen tried to reach for his weapon, but the motion unbalanced him and he fell from the transport. He was still stuck in the mine's field, though, and could do nothing when a human rose from the roofline and put a plasma bolt into him. Scarcely a moment later, the air filled with the sounds of plasma fire as the rooftops on both sides of the street erupted, the plasma bolts crisscrossing the street and slamming into the soldiers on the transport.

The mine expired as it ran out of power, and the transport rose up again, so violently it tossed some of the soldiers from the top and sides. It began to move, sluggishly at first, then gained speed quickly – and slammed into the building at the end of the street.

We didn't wait around, but ran for the exits. Every volunteer had a carefully designed path to get away, which each of us had memorized. Injala and I took the alleyway behind the building, climbing the short fence at the end and crossing the next street. We could hear Zhen klaxons blaring as emergency teams converged on the ambush site.

As we ran, locals occasionally flashed a sign identifying themselves as allies and pointed away from Zhen soldiers. Eventually, we found ourselves in much calmer areas, and slowed to a walk. "We should get you off the street," I said.

"My disguise is holding," Injala said.

I looked at her, and she was right – all I saw was a human. "That holo is weirdly convincing," I said, "but we both know it isn't perfect. The less risk, the better."

"True," she said. "Do you have any ideas?"

"Yes," I said, stopping next to a delivery van. "Your ride, madam," I said as I opened the door. Injala stepped into it, and I followed, closing the door behind me. "Drop us at South-47," I said, and the driver, who had previously been reading his book while munching on a pastry, slipped the book into his pocket, dropped the pastry onto the seat next to him, and got the van moving.

"Did it go well, sir?" he asked.

"Objective met," I said. "And I'm sure your sister got away clean." He nodded and kept his eyes on the road as Injala and I sat in the back on the van's metal floor.

"I take it 'South-47' is code, but we are going east?" Injala said.

"The directions have no relation at all to where the stops are," I said. "We figured it would be easier to keep the Zhen guessing that way. North-12, for example, is at the extreme western border of Landing's admin area."

"Clever. And may I assume North-13 is the other end of town?"

"You may assume," I said, "but don't expect to be correct."

After several minutes of silence, she said, "Come on, Tajen."

"North-13 isn't even in Landing." I pointed a finger at her. "And that's all I'm going to tell you."

"You don't trust me?"

I waved that off. "No no no, not that. I just don't want to risk it – you never know if we've been compromised." I flicked the file at her. "Most of our operatives know only some of the drops, but a few know them all. Might as well trust you, but…not your government?" I made a rocking motion with my hand. "Just in case."

She nodded approvingly. "We'll make a Kelvaki spy out of you yet," she said. When the van pulled into a small village an hour out of Landing, we were met by Liam and Bailey. "How'd it go?" I asked Liam. "Anyone not make it back?"

"Everyone's back," he said, and I took a deep breath with relief. "There's nothing on the Zhen news channels, but we managed to grab some choice comments from the Zhen TacNet. Kiri and Aleph are about to send it out on the VOE."

The Voices of Earth was Kiri's project, as we'd agreed. She'd been broadcasting my speeches and essays on the Zhen Empire out to the rest of the – well, the Empire. So far the Zhen had found themselves unable to block or delete her broadcasts over the slipnet. Just in case, though, the same broadcasts were being copied to the Kelvaki, who were using their own spy network to insert the broadcasts into the Imperial slipnet feeds. I'm sure the One was apoplectic, but I couldn't find it in myself to care.

The broadcasts were definitely bringing us more volunteers, but the real goal was to make the Zhen back on all the Imperial worlds, and the humans on Zhen:da and Terra, understand what was going on out here.

We'd gotten a few smuggled reports from the Kelvaki spynet that humans were incensed at the way the Zhen were operating on Earth. That martial law had not been rescinded in the first days after the Rising was one thing, but that it was still in effect eight months later was another. The Punitive Laws were another topic of dissent in both the human communities of the Empire and the Talnera itself, the ruling body of the Zhen Empire.

The Twenty and the One might hold the real power, but the Talnera had the power to sponsor and refuse legislation, and the only tactic they had was to stall the legislative process. The Talnera was now deadlocked on everything, from minor issues to major appropriations, and it was slowing the Zhen war machine down.

"I bet the Twenty and the One are pissed as hell they ever created the Talnera," Bailey said. "It probably seemed like a good idea back when they did it, but now they're stuck with it."

"Good," I said. "I hope they choke on it."

★　　★　　★

Liam and I were in the middle of planning our next raid when there was a knock on the door. We froze for a moment, looking at each other. "We expecting anyone?" Liam asked.

"No, but the lookouts didn't sound an alarm," I said. "So we're probably okay."

"Unless they're dead," he said. His eyes lost focus for a moment, then widened. "Oh." He moved toward the door. He wasn't going for a weapon, so I started to relax. When he opened the door, Kiri was standing there, literally bouncing on her toes.

"We did it!" she squealed.

"Did what?" I asked.

"We beat them!" She calmed down, and said, "Well, kind of. Look!" She flicked her wrist, sending information to the room's holoprojector. The hologram appeared in the middle of the room: a Zhen in uniform.

"His Most Excellent Governor, Commander Grevink, announces that the Zhen Empire has benevolently decided to allow the humans of Earth to elect their own representatives to the Talnera, with the proviso that all human guerrilla attacks must cease. The elected representatives will be welcome to take seats in the Talnera on Zhen:da, to be a voice for Earth in the steering of the Empire's policies.

"The election will be held in one month. Any human may put their name forward." He frowned, as if the words he was about to say tasted bad in his mouth. "All humans currently living on Earth may vote. To ensure fairness, humans will handle all aspects of the election, and all candidates may send observers. Message ends."

The hologram faded, and we stood staring at the space it had occupied for several long moments. Finally, Liam looked at me. "Are they serious?"

"Either that, or it's a trap," I said. "If the Zhen want to find out who the most human-minded colonists are, add their names to a list…maybe even take them out?"

"What do we do?"

I thought about it. What *could* we do? I paced, thinking furiously. When Liam tried to say something, I held up my hand, demanding silence. Finally, I turned to them again and said, "It doesn't matter." I shook my head. "If they're lying, we won't know until it's too late. If they're not, it's a chance we can't pass up. We just need to find someone who wants to run."

"Why not you?" Kiri asked.

"Oh, *hell* no," I said.

"I agree with him," Liam said.

I pouted at Liam. "You don't think I could do it?"

He licked his lips. "Look, Tajen. I think you'd do your best – and it wouldn't be awful, but it wouldn't be great, either. You're a military leader, not a civilian one. But mostly I just think the target on your back is big enough as it is. For you to go to Zhen:da would be insanity."

"Any ideas?"

"Maybe," he said. "Let me look into it."

"No," I said. "If we have to put someone up, we can, but let's see how it develops organically first."

Kiri said, "I should put this out on the VOE, though, yeah?"

"Of course," I said. As she left excitedly to do just that, I smiled at Liam. "Maybe we're getting somewhere. Send the word through the network. No more attacks until further notice."

★   ★   ★

Three days later, there was a knock on our door again. I opened it to find a silver-haired woman in long flowing robes that gave her an otherworldly aspect. I recognized her immediately: her face had been all over the news channels, both Zhen and human. "Talvikki Suzuki," I said. "Come in."

"Thank you," said the leader of the Free Earth Party. She glided across my living room and sat on my couch. "I'll get right to the point. I want you to stop."

I looked around my room, pretending to be confused. "Stop…?"

"Come now, Mr. Hunt," she said. "We both know you're leading the rebellion." Her stern look warned me not to lie to her, and honestly, I didn't really want to.

"All right," I said. "I've already ceased all attacks, at least until we figure out if the Zhen are being honest with us." I frowned. "I'm sorry, but I was under the impression from the news that you're on our side."

"I am on the side of human independence from the Zhen. That is not the same thing as being on the side of your war."

"Granted," I said. "But as I said, I've stopped."

"I have been many things in my life, Tajen Hunt, but stupid was never one of them. You may not be actively attacking them, but your activities are not entirely confined to direct attacks, are they? I'm fine with your 'Voices of Earth' continuing, but I want you to cease the operations designed to annoy the Zhen, as well. And I want you to do something for me." She looked primly around the room. "Is there any chance of a cup of tea?" she asked.

I barely suppressed a laugh and rose to make the tea. "Of course," I said. There was already water on the stove for my own tea, which she'd no doubt noticed. I fussed about with preparation and placed the finished pot on a tray with two cups. I took it to the table, poured her tea, and then sat across from her again. "So what is it, precisely, you want me to do?"

"Well, two things," she said. "The first is to endorse me and my party for the election."

"Easily agreed to," I said. "I'd already decided to vote for you. I have no problem giving you my support. And the other?"

"I want you to run for office."

"That's…not a good idea," I said.

"Nonsense," she replied. "You are Tajen Hunt. There isn't a single candidate standing you couldn't beat." She set down her cup. "The candidate for this neighborhood is Linis Terrell. Have you met him?"

"No, I don't believe I've had the pleasure," I said. Internally, I was asking myself why I was suddenly talking like this. Something about her brought it out in me.

"It wouldn't be a pleasure," she said. "He's a dreadful little man, totally in agreement with the Zhen on every issue."

"You're kidding," I said. "How does that even happen?"

She spread her arms wide. "He's done well under the Zhen," she said. "Not every human cares that they destroyed our people. It's...." She visibly searched for the right word.

"It's monstrous," I said.

"Yes, that works," she said drily. She picked up her tea and sipped it before continuing. "The thing you'll find about people, Tajen – I assume I may call you that – is that they can be so entirely self-focused that the suffering of others who are already dead might as well have never happened. It's distasteful, even monstrous." She tipped her cup to me. "But it's human nature. Be that as it may, our problem is that we need your support – and we need your voice."

"My voice?"

"Yes. I know you don't think of yourself as a politician. And truth be told, you're not – but I don't need you as a politician. I need the hero you've become to our people. Like it or not, they'll vote for you, because they trust you. Your support could mean the difference between Earth's putative leader being a Zhen toady, or a boardroom-hardened old bitch like me." She smiled sweetly. "You really want the latter, I promise you."

"If I do this, the Zhen won't be pleased."

"No," she said. "Which is even more reason to do it."

"What if they withdraw their support for the election?"

"They wouldn't dare," she said. "Even their client races are supporting it, and the Kelvaki have demanded the right to send observers to make sure the election occurs without meddling. If they were to drop the election, it would make them look afraid – and the Zhen cannot ever risk that, as you well know."

What she was asking was absurd, and yet it also made sense. My voice, added to hers, would sway a fairly high percentage of voters. On the other hand, as Liam had suggested, it would increase the size of the target I was already wearing.

"I'll need to talk to my husband about it," I said. "I can't agree without his approval."

"Of course," she said, standing. "Only don't take too long," she added as she moved to the door. "The deadline for declaring your candidacy is in three days."

"Look, Ms. Suzuki, don't hold your breath – my husband isn't likely to agree to anything that means I have to go to Zhen:da."

"Oh, didn't I mention?" she said with an impish grin. "If my party wins, there's no way *any* of us will be going to Zhen:da. Mind you, we're not going to tell anyone that before the election." She winked.

I saw her out the door, then shut it behind her, leaned against it for a moment, and sighed. "Nothing's ever easy," I muttered.

★　　★　　★

I stood on the stage, my voice broadcast from my NeuroNet through the PA system. "My opponent would have you believe that living as part of the Empire is a necessity," I said. "That we don't have a choice, so we should just bow to the inevitable and try to 'make the best of it'." I licked my lips. "Well, that's easy for him to say. The Empire has been very good to him. He's made a fortune in service to the Empire. He could afford to live anywhere, do anything, in comfort.

"But what about the rest of us?" I paused as the crowd roared. "What about the people who have suffered under Zhen prejudice? What about the people of Jiraad, sacrificed in the Zhen's chess game with the Tabrans? Oh, wait – we can't ask them," I said, lowering my voice. "They're all dead. The Tabrans claimed the world, but the Zhen settled us there anyway. And you know how that ended – three million humans on Jiraad wiped out, and the Zhen wring their hands, pretending we can't see their claws.

"My opponent wants things to continue as they have been – he wants to walk the path of capitulation, of sacrifice. But what he really wants us to do is surrender to an enemy who killed our civilization and then tried to make up for it by treating us like hell for eight hundred years. They say they gave us a home – but they lied to us first. They say they've protected us – but they harmed us first. They say they want the best for us – but they keep us second-class, and even when their actions are made public, they continue to claim they have the high ground." I stopped speaking and looked around the stage, at the thousands of humans gathered to hear the speeches today, the last day of campaigning before the election tomorrow.

"Well, as our ancestors said, *fuck that*! Fuck their patronage. Fuck their arrogance. Fuck their Empire! Vote for the Free Earth Party. Vote for humans to control their own destiny!" I smiled as I remembered the line Liam had given me last night. He'd gotten it from an old pre-Destruction vid, and I had no idea if it would work, but why the hell not? "No surrender, no retreat!" I shouted.

The crowd lost their minds. I waved, exited the stage, and ran right into my opponent, Linis Terrell. He sneered at me. "Nice speech, Captain, but it won't do you any good."

"We'll see," I said, and went to brush past him, but he stepped into my path.

"Do you really believe all that nonsense?" he asked.

"I believe you're going to lose," I said. "That's all I need say to you. Good evening." I brushed him aside, greeting Talvikki, who simply stared at Terrell until he backed down and walked on stage.

"Let's get out of here," she said, "before we have to listen to that idiot's speech." As we left, a chorus of booing reached our ears. "Let's hope that's a good sign."

"Let's hope tomorrow ends with anything other than a Zhen crackdown," I replied.

"Yes. Quite."

★　　★　　★

No campaigning was allowed on election day, but that didn't mean we just sat around waiting.

Worried about any tampering with the election, I had Aleph keep a close watch on things. Voting happened through the NeuroNet, with some paper ballots cast by people who didn't have 'Nets installed – a tiny minority of humans.

When a citizen went to their nearest polling place, they linked their NeuroNet to the computer and registered their vote. Each vote was checked against the NeuroNet's unique identifier codes, and then tallied by the colony's central computer. It wasn't foolproof, but it was the way voting happened in the Empire.

We'd argued for a purely paper ballot, but the prep time that would have needed would have been silly, and in the end we'd conceded the need to do things the traditional way – but we insisted on having access to verify votes for all campaign teams, as well as the Kelvaki observers.

Injala had assured me that the observers were professionals, and they spent the entire day linked into the system, running checks. I'm sure the Zhen were nervous as hell, allowing that, and so they had their own users linked in. In the end, the honesty of the election was guaranteed by the rampant paranoia of all sides.

"How are we doing?" I asked. I was in the Free Earth Party headquarters, sitting with Talvikki Suzuki and one of the other regional candidates, Mbaku Oleyuo.

"Well in some places, not so well in others," Talvikki said. "Mbaku here is winning, as are you."

"But?" I prompted.

"But we're losing in the central Landing districts."

"Well, we expected that, didn't we?"

"Of course, but the material point is that if we lose too many, we'll need to make compromises we probably don't want to make."

We watched the returns come in right up to the last minute. When the last tallies were checked and verified, I sat back and looked at the graphic floating over the table. The Zhen-backed candidates had taken several districts in Landing itself, but the Free Earth Party had won the majority of available seats by a landslide. "Great gods of ancient skies," I said, "we did it." I looked around the table. "Now what?"

"Well, first thing," Talvikki said, "is we all go make acceptance speeches. Promise that we will represent our people to the best of our ability."

"And when shall we go to Zhen:da and take our seats?" Mbaku asked.

"We don't," she said. "In a few days, we will announce that the elected representatives of the Free Earth Party will *not* go to Zhen:da and take our seats in the Talnera." She looked around the room. "We will instead declare ourselves the first Parliament of Earth and form a new government here."

Some of us had known this, but it took a few others by surprise. Steven Dahl, a slightly pudgy man who'd been a grocer back home, laughed. "Well, that's going to put a fly in the ointment."

"Just one?" Talvikki asked.

"Talvikki," he said, "you know that's not going to go over well."

"I know," she said. "But eventually one has to take a stand, and this is ours. Anyone disagree?"

I looked around the room, one eyebrow raised. A couple of people looked nervous, but nobody dissented with the plan.

"Right, then. We'll carry on. Now, cabinet assignments." Talvikki kept the momentum going, and it became obvious she'd been thinking about this all along. She handed out governmental jobs to her selected core of newly elected ministers, and rewarded some of the less favored with important positions.

Me, she made chief of intelligence. It was my job, she said, to safeguard the rest. It was a sensible job to give me, as I already had informants placed throughout the colony.

"Now, go placate our 'masters'," she said. "We'll start the real job in a couple of days."

Two days after the election, the new parliament, with the exception of the Imperial Unionist Party members, gathered for a public announcement. "We, the elected representatives of Earth, with some exceptions, have decided not to travel to Zhen:da to take our seats in the Talnera. It makes little sense to us to travel so far for so long to become minor voices in the affairs of a larger Empire that does not serve our interests.

"We instead will remain on Earth, where we will form a new government. We, the assembled representatives of the humans of Earth, do, in the name of the peoples of Earth, ratify the establishment of the Solarian Republic and pledge ourselves and our people to make this declaration effective by every means at our command.

"We solemnly declare any foreign government on Earth to be an invasion of our rights that we will never tolerate, and we therefore demand the evacuation of our world by the Zhen garrison currently stationed here."

The crowd before us roared. Some of the cries were boos and jeers, but the majority were roaring with approval. Fists were raised in the air. I glanced at the Zhen security officers, who lined the edges of the crowd. Most of them looked nervous, but some were looking at us in murderous rage. They knew they'd shortly get an order to arrest us.

Fortunately for us, we also knew this, and in a well coordinated and planned series of maneuvers, we scattered, each of us taking a different route to get away.

Liam and I had found and furnished a new home. It wasn't as nice as the one we'd started with, but this one was hidden, and right now that was important.

But hopefully, it wouldn't be necessary much longer.

★　★　★

I was headed home with some groceries when I realized I was being followed. I sighed and turned into an alleyway. It was covered, and full of refuse. I quickly ducked back into a dark corner behind a stack of crates.

I waited several long minutes, but nobody came into the alley. I shook my head at myself. Clearly I was jumping at shadows. I stepped back out and froze when I saw the Zhen standing relaxed in the alley's mouth.

"That was terrible, Tajen Hunt," the Zhen said. I realized, as he stepped closer, that he was the one who'd let Liam and me escape recently. "I am not an amateur. You are, I take it?"

"We're on the ground," I said. "If we were in space, you'd never find me." His mouth dropped open in a Zhen expression of amusement, and I couldn't help but return it. "So, what do you want?" I asked.

"Only to give you some information," he said. "You are all in danger."

"Tell me something I don't know," I said.

"I am trying to."

"It's an expression," I said. "It means—"

"I get it. I am here to tell you that the Zhen command has the names and addresses of the entire Solarian Republic leadership. They—"

"Will get nothing," I said. "Those addresses are all fake."

His hand moved as if tossing something to me, and a hologram flew from his hand to hover in front of my face. It had the address for Talvikki Suzuki – the real address where she was staying, not the fake one we'd set up to fool the Zhen. "Shit," I said.

"Indeed." He flicked his hands a few times, and the addresses changed to show others. "They are planning to move on them tonight," he said. "Act accordingly."

I frowned at him. "Why are you helping me?" I asked.

He sighed, a growling deep in his throat. "Not all of us are corrupted by the actions of our government, Captain Hunt. Some of us think we should leave humans to their own destiny and planet."

I stepped closer to him. "Then help us."

"I am doing so."

I shook my head. "Not this. I mean, thanks, but we need more."

He gestured *resignation*. "I do what I can, when I can. I can do no more than that." He tilted his head. "We have families too. And the :ko," he said, using the shorthand for the ruling caste popular among his own, "cast a shadow over us all." He waved in farewell, and turned to walk away.

"Hey," I said. He turned back. "You have a name?"

"Zekan," he said.

"Thanks, Zekan."

He said nothing, but sent me his comms code before walking away.

I watched him go. That was the damnedest thing, I said to myself. I continued home, but you better believe I paid much better attention on the way.

★　　★　　★

As soon as I got home, I called an emergency meeting of the cabinet. Fortunately, we didn't actually need to gather anywhere; thanks to Kiri and Aleph, we'd set up a secure network with which we could meet in virtual spaces. I logged into the space and waited as the others logged in.

Once they were all there, I said, "Thank you for coming. I—"

"Hold on," said Nicola Tynes. "Last I checked, you're the minister of intelligence, not the president." The titles had been dredged from Old Earth records, and we were all still getting used to them. We'd flirted with using the Zhen terms we were all familiar with, but that seemed stupid when we were trying to break free of their Empire.

"Yes," I said. I tried to continue, but Tynes talked right over me.

"Then first of all, why did you call a meeting? You're exceeding your authority."

I suppressed my urge to throw something at her. "I called the meeting as minister of intelligence, because it's an emergency. I didn't have time to follow the niceties of procedure – we're all in danger." Now I had their attention. "The Zhen know where we all live – our true addresses, not the blinds we officially filed. And they're going to raid each and every one of us tonight and arrest us for treason."

Voices erupted in chaos as each of the ministers began talking at once –

all but Talvikki, who simply watched me from the other end of the table. After several moments, she said quietly but with force, "Quiet, please." As the hubbub died down, she said, "How do we know this, Tajen?"

"I was given the information from an informant in the Zhen hierarchy."

"Not your Kelvaki friend?"

"No."

"Then whom? I find it difficult to imagine this information being entrusted to humans."

I sighed. "I was contacted by a Zhen officer."

The table erupted again, but Talvikki calmed things down once more. "And you trust him?"

I hesitated. "He claimed to be part of a Zhen faction that supports what we're doing. Even if that's true, I wouldn't say I entirely trust him, no. But he gave me the proof that they know where we live, and he seemed to be telling the truth." I spread my hands as if weighing things. "Look, if he's lying, what's the goal? Either he's telling the truth or he isn't – but the outcome of each of those possibilities is vastly different. My recommendation is that nobody sleeps at home tonight. Find another place to lay low for a few days – my network can help with that."

"What if that's what they want?" Tynes said. "We all shuffle around to new places, and they find us that way?"

"They already know where we are," I said, enunciating each word carefully.

"So you say," she said, enunciating mockingly. "*I* say, we stay home. If Tajen is right, then we become symbols of everything that is going on here. The uproar from the people and Tajen's Kelvaki friends will get us out in short order. If Tajen's information is wrong, then we'll all be fine."

"That might be the stupidest thing you've ever said," I replied.

"Tajen!" Talvikki snapped. I held my hands up in apology and sat back. Talvikki regarded everyone and said, "I cannot instruct you in this. You're all adults and should make up your own mind. For myself, I will not be home tonight. Now, if there is any other business?" She looked around the virtual table. "No? Very well then. Be safe, all." As they began dropping out of the conference, she called to me. "Stay, Tajen."

When they'd all gone, she asked, "Is it possible I stay with you and yours?"

"Well, we'll need to find a new place to hide, but yes," I said.

"Very well. Where shall I meet you?"

"We'll pick you up. Give me an hour."

"Very well." She smiled, and was gone from the conference.

I dropped out and called Kiri and Liam. "Our place," I said. "Now."

★   ★   ★

Later that night, Talvikki, Liam, and I were hiding in a darkened apartment across the street from Talvikki's own apartment. I'd argued that we should be far away, but Talvikki wanted to see what the Zhen did, if anything. So I'd found a volunteer who lived nearby, and he'd allowed us to use his home for the night. Injala was nearby with a fire team, ready to intervene if we were compromised.

The Zhen moved in just after 0100, when most everyone would be assumed to be deep asleep. They pulled up in a truck with antigrav turrets as escorts. We pulled back from the window but kept watch through sensors we'd placed earlier as the Zhen calmly walked to Talvikki's apartment, getting through the building's secured entrance with a wave of their leader's hand. They walked right into the locked apartment and searched it efficiently. When they didn't find her, they searched the place for clues. Finding none, they apparently decided to trash the place, and shot just about all of her furniture to splinters.

"So that's what a frustrated Zhen looks like," Talvikki murmured.

Their job thwarted, the Zhen moved on. About an hour later, I got a call from one of my watchers. When I disconnected, I turned to Talvikki. "They got Tynes and four others," I said.

"What about the other five?"

"They're safe."

"What do you think they'll do now?"

"The Zhen? Probably put them on trial."

I was wrong.

The next morning, the Zhen sent a broadcast to all citizens. Grevink stood with the four captured ministers in what appeared to be a prison yard. Each of them was cuffed with their hands behind them, a Zhen soldier holding each one securely.

"People of Earth. The Twenty and the One who rule our great Empire added seats to the Talnera reserved for your people, despite years of tradition that those seats are opened only when a client period ends. It was hoped that this could heal the breach between our peoples.

"Rather than work toward their goals in the correct way, they have seen fit to declare war on the Empire! In accordance with the law, we arrested these members of the so-called Solarian Republic. These fools," he said, gesturing to the prisoners, "chose to commit treason. Their guilt is obvious – we have them on record as declaring Earth's independence. Their sentence is, as prescribed by Zhen Imperial Law, death. The sentence is to be carried out immediately." Behind him, the Zhen soldiers fired blasters point-blank into the backs of the prisoners. As they let go, the bodies fell like sacks of rocks.

Grevink spoke again. "Others of this Solarian movement, including the traitors Tajen Hunt and Talvikki Suzuki, have fled, and are even now being sought." Our names and faces began scrolling across the screen. "Until they are all found, the colony is once again under martial law. Human police forces are suspended until further notice. All humans will submit to Zhen authority.

"A reward of 100,000 Zhen credits is offered for information leading to the arrest of each of the fugitives." He glanced at the bodies meaningfully. "Anyone aiding the fugitives will be arrested and charged with crimes against the Empire."

"You know, I'd heard Grevink was bloodthirsty," Talvikki said. "But I didn't think he was foolish."

I looked at her. "I don't understand."

"He has just made a catastrophic error," she said. "Do you recall when I said that I wanted you to stop the war and try my way?"

"Of course."

"I hereby rescind that. Go to war, Tajen. Show the Zhen how costly we can make it for them to remain here."

"Yes, ma'am." I started to turn away, but stopped. "You know it will get bad," I said. "They're not going to run away after a raid or two. It could be the Rising all over again."

"I know," she said. "But the people voted for us knowing what we wanted. I must believe that means they want it too."

CHAPTER THIRTEEN

Katherine Lawson

I looked at Sunset as if she'd grown extra heads and started singing in three-part harmony about the Glory of the One. "Help the Zhen?" I said. I turned to Simmons. "Is this a translation error?"

"No."

I made a frustrated sound at his non-answer and turned to Sunset. "What do you mean, help the Zhen?"

"A mistake was made, Captain Lawson," she said. "We made things worse than they were. You must understand. May I show you?"

I gestured down the hall, toward the room with the screens.

"No," she said, touching my head gently. "Inside."

I sighed. "You want to share the memory?"

"Yes."

"Fine," I said, "Let's—" I stopped talking when I realized she'd already started.

I was standing amidst wreckage. A Tabran floated beside me. It was unincarnated, a shifting silver cloud. It spoke to me. Though I could not hear it out loud, I knew what it was saying.

"It is this way." It led me around the wreckage. Judging by the tech, I recognized the wreckage as Zhen, but that became obvious when we found a Zhen:ko. Her body was pinned by a large section of machine. Judging by the severity of the wounds, she didn't have much time left.

The cloud settled over the unconscious Zhen, fluttering over it, flashes of energy igniting in the cloud. Finally it rose. "It can be saved," it said.

"We have never incarnated with a Zhen," I said. "Why now?"

"The war has gone on too long. Our originators intended us as a weapon to destroy the Zhen. That intention destroyed them. We shall end the war another way."

"She has not volunteered," I said. "It is unethical."

The cloud pulsed for a few seconds. "I have run the simulations," it said. "This one is of the ruling caste. The ethical compromise is justified." The cloud settled over the Zhen:ko once more, and over the course of several seconds, filtered into the body.

As it did, I lifted the wreckage off the Zhen's body. Her legs had been mangled, but the nanites of my Tabran companion would be able to repair that. I straightened them, ignoring the grunt of pain from the unconscious reptilian.

A short time later, the body woke. "Contact has been made," it said. "Assimilation is in progress. Repairing injuries."

Once the reptilian's injuries had been fixed, it stood. "Ready to depart," it said. "Zhen ships are incoming. We must move quickly."

The memory ended, but I was still in the virtuality. Sunset stood beside me. "I don't understand," I said.

"That was the beginning," she said. "This came later."

I was standing on the bridge of the *Seeker in Strange Places*. We were on a tour of the outer systems, patrolling our borders, when an alarm blared. Fierce Warrior in Battle checked his scopes and called out, "Zhen vessels approaching. They have locked targeting sensors on us."

Seconds later, the ship was fired upon. As the rocking subsided, Fierce Warrior activated his comms. "We are under attack by Zhen. Keeper of Broken Promises, report to the bridge."

There was no response. Fierce Warrior turned to me. "Find Keeper of Broken Promises," he said. "We need her expertise."

As I ran through the ship's corridors toward the location where the computer said Keeper of Broken Promises was, I began to smell burning plastic. Black smoke filled the corridors the deeper I got into the ship's interior.

I turned the final corner and found Keeper of Broken Promises. Her scales glistened red over her flexing arms as she ripped her claws through Embrace of a Summer Night's throat. The dark blue blood of the Tradd host's body spilled across the white surfaces of the corridor. I recoiled. "Keeper of Broken Promises, what are you doing?"

Her skin and eyes did not show the glow of most incarnates. She was raging, her body heaving, as she stood over several lifeforms. I glanced over them, my sensor nets probing, and was horrified to see they were all dead. Of course, I knew that only the biological host was dead, but violent deaths wreak havoc on the incarnated swarm within. It sometimes takes hours for the nanites to re-establish their gestalt and act again.

The Zhen incarnate turned and stalked toward me. "My name," she growled, "is Zornaav." She struck at me, and only my swarm-boosted reflexes kept me alive as her claws raked across the place my neck had been. "I am Zhen. Whatever you have done to me will be repaid," she said, "by your death."

I quickly backpedalled. "We sought only to bring peace to our peoples!" I said. "The war is a remnant of the past! There is no reason for us to fight!"

She moved faster than I did, slamming me against a wall. Her face inches from mine, she snarled, "War is its own reason!" She drew back her hand for a killing blow – and recoiled as the hand disintegrated in a burst of plasma.

Behind me, the human volunteer called Simmons stood with a plasma rifle aimed at Keeper – I mean, Zornaav. Beside him was another volunteer, also aiming at her. Simmons fired again, hitting her in the chest, and kept firing, his companion joining in. Zornaav staggered back from me. Under the sustained plasma fire, she turned and fled.

Simmons immediately raised a communicator. "Simmons to O'Neill. The Zhen incarnate is headed your way."

I was standing in front of Sunset and Simmons once more. "Wait. That was decades ago. How do you still look the same?"

Simmons said, "The technology of the Tabrans is very good. As I said earlier, they cannot extend human lives indefinitely, but they can slow the aging process, even for those of us who are not incarnated."

"Okay," I said. "I recognized that Zhen."

"I thought you might," he said.

"How did she return to her people?"

Sunset said, "She made her way to an airlock and escaped the ship. Her symbiotic swarm kept her alive."

"I thought she rejected the swarm."

"No," Simmons said. "For some reason, she was able to suppress it. The Tabran swarm is part of her, but it is not an amalgamation, as it is with most incarnates. She is dominant. It does as she wills."

I considered that for a moment. "The Zhen:ko choose the Twenty, and the Twenty choose the One," I said. "So somehow she used her swarm to give herself an advantage, and get chosen. And now she runs everything." I started to laugh.

"What is funny about this?" Sunset asked.

"The Zhen Empire is ruled by a Tabran," I said. "That's funny."

"It is *not*," Sunset declared.

"But—"

"The Zhen Empire is run by a Zhen, who has usurped control of a Tabran," said Simmons, gently interposing himself. "I knew Keeper of Broken Promises. It would not have done the things it has done as Zornaav."

"Okay," I said. "So what is it you want to do? Invade the Zhen Empire?"

"Not exactly," he said. He looked to Sunset.

She smiled. "We need Tajen Hunt," she said.

I blinked. "Then why not get him? Why bring me here? He's on Kelvak."

"Well, no," Simmons said. "It has—" he began, and stopped. "It has been longer than you realize, since we left Earth. The journey to Tabra was long."

"How long?" I asked, my guts sinking.

"Two months," he said. "We have kept tabs on him. He is on Earth. However, given what we know, he won't be there much longer."

"Come," Sunset said. "We must prepare you."

"Prepare me how?"

"You must learn."

CHAPTER FOURTEEN

Tajen Hunt

The execution of the elected human representatives did not have the effect the Zhen had assumed.

Back on Zhen:da and Terra, demonstrations rose from grassroots campaigns demanding the Zhen leave Earth. The government didn't allow media to go out over the slipnet, but we got reports from our Kelvaki allies, including video.

It didn't take long for demonstrations to become riots. I watched all night as what had begun as a march ended in blood and death. We never did get an accurate accounting of the death toll, but it was easily in the thousands.

The next day, the Zhen Empire declared a state of martial law on both Zhen:da and Terra. On both worlds the proclamation was worldwide, but on Zhen:da the harshest measures came down on the human enclave of the Virginia Peninsula.

The night after we received word of the riots, I woke in the middle of the night. I glanced at the clock and groaned when I saw it was still hours before dawn. We'd been asleep for some time, but I knew Liam's breathing, and I could tell he was awake.

"I'm scared," I said.

"What? Please tell me what in known space scares the Hero of Elkari?"

I swatted him. "I'm serious," I said.

He rolled onto his side, one hand supporting his head while the other came to rest on my chest. "I am too," he said. "I've seen you face down raging Zhen. If you're *scared*, I'm *fucking terrified*."

"And yet you can still crack jokes."

"It's who I am. What can I do to help?"

"Not sure there is anything," I said. "You're here for me—"

"Always."

I smiled and leaned in to give him a kiss. "Which I appreciate, more than I let on most of the time. But my fear isn't something anyone can fix. I'm not afraid for me alone, or for you, or even Earth. I think...." I stopped, flustered and unable to talk. "I think I might go down as the man who got the human race killed."

"Well," he said, "the good news is that, if that happens, there won't be any humans around to care." My face folded, and he leaned over and put his arms around me. "Hey, I'm sorry. Sometimes the jokes aren't well thought out." He sighed. "It's a risk, but let me ask the obvious question. If we don't do this, what happens?"

"The Zhen get their way."

"Which means they kill as many of the Resistance as they can catch, and then start their social engineering project up again. In another few centuries, our culture is much more intertwined with theirs and we're sycophantic bootlickers."

"Yes."

He was silent a moment, and then said, "Well, fuck that."

I couldn't help but laugh. "But do we have the right to make that choice for all of humanity?"

"Does it matter? Tajen, like everyone else, we make the choices we have to make to be able to live with ourselves."

"I guess so," I said. "Go back to sleep, love." I rolled over, staring into space. A few moments later, Liam's arms wrapped around me. A few moments later I could hear his snore. I smiled, pulled his arms closer around myself, and went back to sleep.

For the next few weeks, we hit the Zhen whenever and wherever we could. Some of the operations went off without a hitch, others not so well. Tonight was our biggest operation yet, and Liam, Injala, and I found ourselves at the edge of the Zhen base's airfield. I checked my harness, making sure all my gear was secure.

"Remind me why we're not using drones to do this?" Liam said.

Injala said, "The drones are too loud, and not precise enough."

"Right," he said. "Still, this is going to suck if we get caught."

"That's true. I have a suggestion. Don't get caught."

He looked at her, nonplussed, then chuckled. "Copy that."

"Ready," I said.

Liam finished checking his own gear. "Ready." He looked at Injala. "I don't have to ask."

"No," she said.

As we approached the field, Injala activated the electronic units strapped to our chests. Liam and I stopped outside the forcefield fence, apprehensive. Injala gave us a long-suffering look and simply walked through the forcefield. I followed, Liam right behind me.

We crept out onto the field. Our NeuroNets were slaved to a drone hovering high above, marking sentry and patrol positions. In the dark of the moonless night, the airfield's lights illuminated only a few small areas.

Crouching beneath a troop transport, I took one of the explosive packs off my harness and attached it to the transport. When I'd placed and activated it, I moved on to the next transport. I was on my back, in the middle of placing a pack, when I heard a Zhen voice very close, stalking quietly between the parked vehicles.

I held as still as I could, checking the map overplayed on my vision. The guard was right next to me, not more than six feet away, but his tracker wasn't showing up on the drone's sensors. The son of a bitch had forgotten his tracker – or, more likely, had purposely left it behind. It appeared he was stalking an animal not far away.

I stayed motionless, the explosive pack held above my chest inches from the transport hull. If I attached it, the Zhen would definitely hear it. If I put it down, he'd hear that. All I could do was hope he left quickly – and that I didn't breathe too loudly. I took shallow, slow breaths, trying to sync up with his own breathing as he hunted something between the transports.

My head was turned toward him, and I saw an insect inches away from me. The tiny little eight-legged beast had a tail with a stinger we'd learned to hate. The venom of these little bastards was quite painful, and though we had developed a counteragent, I wasn't in any mood to get stung, especially not in my face. I stared at the little insect, thinking furiously at it to go away and bother someone else. Something spooked it and it ran off in another direction. I was about to sigh in relief when I realized the Zhen was crouched down, staring at me. Both of us opened our mouths to speak, but his voice was stopped by the sudden appearance of a spike spearing through his head and into the ground. A moment later, Injala's whispered voice came to me. "Are you going to lie there forever, or are you ready to move on?"

I quickly placed the explosive and readied it, then crawled out from under the transport. Still crouched in its shadow, I thanked her. "Think there's any more untracked guards out here?"

"Unlikely," she said. "But possible. Keep an eye out. And let's hurry, shall we?"

Slowly, methodically, we crept across the field, placing explosives on every transport and fighter until we ran out. Then we exited the field as stealthily as we'd entered. Once far enough away that we could watch without immediately being seen, we stopped.

"Ready?" Liam asked.

"Go for it."

"You do the honors," he said, holding out the detonator to me.

"No," I said, "go ahead."

"No no, I insist."

Injala grabbed the detonator. "For Siharen's sake!" she said, and hit the detonator.

Instantly, every aircraft on the field exploded. The noise and pressure of the explosions, and the base alarms, washed over us. "Nicely done," I said.

The next morning, I was starting to compose a new message to the Zhen when I heard the sound of ground vehicles approaching at speed. I leaned over to look out the window and saw several ground transports slide to a halt in front of the building. Zhen poured out of the vehicles and formed up. "Raid!" I shouted.

My people evacuated the office quickly; we'd practiced for this sort of thing. As the last person out the door, I sent a code from my own NeuroNet to the charges installed in the walls, computers, and desks. They weren't explosive, but instead sprayed an intensely flammable goo over everything in their area of effect – then ignited the goo.

Flames spread, hot enough to melt plastics and even some of the metal in the office. I didn't stay to watch, but ran for the rooftop. Once there, I grabbed an infiltrator gun and aimed it for the rooftop across the way. I fired and the harpoon grabbed on to the wall. I set the gun into the wall of my building and activated the anchor.

I attached a device to the line and slid down to the other side. As

I ran toward the other side of the building, shots hit the ground near me, spurring me on. When I got to the other side, I grabbed a handle hanging off the edge and leaped, allowing the line's automatic tension to slow me down before I hit the ground.

Once on the ground, I ran to a nearby flyer and jumped into the saddle. I started the machine and took off at speed. As I turned a corner, I saw a Zhen blockade ahead. "Shit!" I said, pulling back on the control yoke. The flyer rose, and I could feel impacts, as if the bottom was being hit by blasters. I flashed over the barricade and continued on, hunching down to avoid taking a blaster bolt to the back of the head. I yanked the controls, turning once more. "Control!" I called. "I need nav help! Get me out of here!"

"No need to shout," Kiri's voice came back. "I got ya. Turn right, then immediately left, then right again. That should get you to the canal."

I followed her directions and reached the canal and the road beside it. I slammed the accelerator all the way forward, moving the flyer over the canal to avoid the crowds on Canal Street. "Now what?" I said.

"You might want to lose the guy on your tail," she said.

I glanced over my shoulder and cursed. I couldn't get much more speed out of this thing, but it was a damned sight more maneuverable than the military vehicle chasing me. I pulled it in a hard right, onto a side street, the flyer's bottom scraping against the building on the left side of the street. My pursuer couldn't make the turn, and flashed by.

I zigzagged through the neighborhood, narrowly avoiding a crash with another pursuer. Kiri sent me a route, and I led the two vehicles toward a choke point. As I flashed through the space, I realized a trap had been set. Fortunately, neither of the pursuing Zhen pilots noticed. The first was hit by an anti-tank round fired at exactly the right moment. As it was rocked by internal explosions, the second tried to avoid a collision and instead impacted the side of the building. I spared a thought for the people within, hoping no one was seriously hurt.

"All right, Kiri, I'm clear," I said. "I'm headed back to the canal – where do I go from there?"

"Turn left on Denali," she said. "We've got a fresh flyer waiting for you there." It was highlighted in my visual as soon as I saw it, and I slammed down next to it none too gently. I hopped out, took the assigned flyer, and rose smoothly up into the traffic stream.

I got home without incident, and found Liam waiting for me. He grabbed me in a hug. "So glad you got away," he said.

"I'm glad you weren't there," I said. "Anyone caught on the way out?"

"No, you were the last to check in. How'd they find us?"

"Not sure," I said. "But I'm worried. I need to talk to Zekan." I sent a message to his comms code, requesting a meeting. A few minutes later, I got a set of coordinates and a time.

"You're not going alone," Liam said.

"Yes, I am," I said. "But you'll be on overwatch."

*   *   *

Liam and I arrived at the coordinates a couple of hours early. I wanted time to check the place out and make sure it wasn't a trap. The coordinates Zekan had sent me led to one of the few remaining structures on Earth. It had been part of a city once, but now all that remained was crumbling buildings overgrown with plant life. The Zhen had scoured much of the Earth bare, but here and there one could find recognizable bits, usually filled with wildlife. We'd scanned the place from above and found no evidence of Zhen or anything else other than animals nesting in the remnants of the old world.

I waited at the foot of what we assumed had been a monument of some kind; there had been more to it once, but it had long ago fallen, the shattered pieces now long since reclaimed by vegetation.

There was nobody around. Liam took up position above in the remnants of the ancient tower, keeping watch. At the appointed time, a small civilian-model flyer arrived, landing just outside the ruins. I took shelter behind a large lump of rubble, waiting. A few moments later, Zekan appeared, walking calmly to the center of the ruin.

He waited patiently, even though he had to have seen our flyer and knew we were here. Just as his body language started to reveal his irritation, I stepped out of my shelter. "How'd they find us?" I called.

He turned, his arm twitching toward the blaster on his hip, but he relaxed when he saw me. He said nothing, however, until I joined him. "Greetings, Tajen," he said. "I am glad to see you escaped the raid."

"Yeah, thanks," I said. "How many civilians were hurt in my escape?"

He sighed. "Nobody died, but thirteen people are being treated for their injuries."

"Shit," I said. I knew I'd need to consider our actions better in future, but right now there were other things I had to know. "How did they even find us? We'd only been in that location a week. Are they watching us that closely?"

"Of course they are," he said. "But it is worse than that. I was glad to get your request to meet. I needed to find you anyway. To warn you."

"What's going on?"

"Your actions have embarrassed Grevink," he said. "He is getting desperate. If he does not bring your rebellion to heel quickly, he risks being recalled to Zhen:da. That will not end well for him."

"My heart bleeds for him."

"I'm sure it does," he said. "But his desperation is placing your people in greater danger. Up to now, his response has been measured, following standard doctrine. But he has increased the leeway he is giving his forces."

"I've noticed," I said. "I saw an old man being searched on the street the other day. He asked why him, and got slammed into a wall so hard he was bleeding from his skull. He wasn't even one of us!"

"Yes, I have seen similar things. But they are about to get worse. Grevink has called in a new force. They arrived this morning."

"What's so special about them?"

"They are not the best of the Zhen people, Tajen. They were recruited from prisons and stockades, and every one of them is an anti-human bigot. Their brief is to do whatever it takes to find you and end your rebellion. Grevink calls them the *Ten'sekt*, but the rest of us refer to them as *shenkat*. They wear the symbol on their uniforms. You'll see."

Ten'sekt meant 'secret dagger', but *shenkat* meant 'dirty knife'. I couldn't help but chuckle at the way the nickname betrayed the feelings of the regulars toward these new soldiers. "I need names. Faces."

"I'll do what I can. But they are not engaging much with the rest of us. And there is more. I do not know how to say this, but there are Imperial spies among you."

"What?" I couldn't believe it. "I know there are humans who've informed. We try to prevent it, but the lure of credits is—"

"That is not what I mean," he said. "I do not speak of informers. These are human agents, loyal to the Empire, who are here to infiltrate your movement and destroy it from the inside. And they are already among you. They have been for some time."

My blood ran cold at the very thought. And yet...we had been suffering some setbacks, recently. The raid, on an office we'd only just established. Operations that hadn't gone smoothly, volunteers who'd died. "You're telling me," I said, "that there are humans among my organization, working for the Zhen?"

"Yes."

My voice was shaking with rage. "I want names."

"I don't have them. That information is sequestered, far above my station."

"Who has it?"

He thought a moment. "Grevink. Perhaps one or two others in the hierarchy."

"I'll arrange a way to hack into the system. We'll need your help."

He looked nervous. "Tajen," he said. "Giving you information I have is one thing. But I never signed up for this."

"You never 'signed up' for this?'" I shook my head. "Look around you," I snapped. "The people who lived here never signed up for your people to arrive in orbit and bomb them into oblivion." I pointed across the water to the jungle on the other side. "How many people died there, Zekan?" He started to speak, but I spoke over him. "Millions. Men, women, and children, all going about their lives. Until one day the 'mighty Zhen fleet' appeared and systematically wiped them out." I held my arms out, pointing to the buildings around us. "This is just one city. But there used to be cities all over this planet. Multiply the millions who died here by the number of cities that used to exist. Your people killed *billions* of us! And then you more or less enslaved generations of survivors for eight...hundred...years. And you're going to tell me you 'didn't sign up' to help us? Then what the fuck are you doing, talking to me right now?"

"Risking my life," he said, his voice taking on an edge.

"Well, boohoo," I said. "I'm risking my *species*."

He seethed and then his anger seemed to suddenly deflate. "Very well," he said. "I'll do what I can."

"Thank you," I said. "Truly." I waited a beat. "I know this is dangerous for you too. I'll do what I can to minimize your risk as well."

"I will await your contact," he said. "Until then, be safe."

"Yeah," I said. "You too. I mean it, Zekan – don't go getting caught on me. I need you."

He gave me a 'no shit' look, then got back into his flyer and took off.

When Liam rejoined me, he had a questioning look on his face. "You really think there are humans working for the Zhen?"

"I hate to say it, but it's the only explanation I can think of for some of our setbacks recently."

"Shit."

"Yeah. Let's go. I need to talk to Kiri."

★   ★   ★

"I can design a remote data probe for that, no problem," Kiri said. "But how will you get it into their datanet?" The Zhen had been careful to keep their datanets sequestered from the planetary slipnet, which made it difficult to hack their systems and steal information. So far, we'd had no luck, but now I finally had an in.

"It's handled," I said. "Better I say no more."

She glared at me. "Don't tell me you suspect me."

"Not a chance. But the more people know who my contact is, the greater danger he's in. This is one bit of intel I need to keep to myself. Forgive me?"

"Eh. I guess so," she said with a grin.

"Thanks. Call me when the probe is ready."

"Will do."

I left her to build her probe and went to find Liam. I found him sitting with Bailey and Ben, each with a glass in hand. "Ben!" I said. "I haven't seen you in months!"

"I've been busy," he said. "There are only so many medics who will work on members of the Resistance." He took a drink from his cup, and added sourly, "Especially now."

"That doesn't sound good. What's changed?"

"New directive from the lizards," he said. "Any doctor caught treating a Resistance member's wounds will be charged with treason." He sighed. "And when I say 'charged', I mean 'summarily executed'."

"Jaysus," Liam said.

We all sat in troubled silence for a while before I spoke up again. "Things are going to get very bad once Grevink's new friends get rolling. This cannot stand."

"So what do we do about it?"

"Two things," I said. "First, it's open season on the DK."

Kiri frowned. "DK?"

"Dirty Knives," I said. "It's what the Zhen who support us are calling them."

"How many Zhen?" Bailey asked.

"Not enough," I replied with a shrug. "I only know the one, but he says there are others." Nobody mentioned how I'd neglected to tell anyone his name.

"So, open season – meaning the volunteers should feel free to attack them whenever?"

"Not just 'feel free', though – they should feel *obligated* to. Attacks of opportunity on any DK, anywhere. They should take precautions – try not to harm innocents, and try not to get caught or killed. Otherwise, harry those assholes as much as possible. Destroy their vehicles, shoot at them, anything to disrupt their operations and make their lives harder. And not only when they're on duty. As long as positive ID can be made, they are priority targets."

"And the second thing?"

"Once we get the IDs on the human agents, we send them a message."

"Which is?" Kiri asked.

"Get me the names, first."

★   ★   ★

I handed Zekan the chip. "Slot this into any access port. It'll let you know when it's done."

He rumbled in his chest, a sign of nervousness, as he took the chip. "I'll contact you when ready," he said. "Try to be patient. I may not be able to get away the moment your probe finishes."

"I understand," I said, and he left.

I waited a few minutes before leaving. I walked down the street toward the market, where I bought an ice treat and found a seat where I could sit and watch the people of Landing go by.

In some ways, it didn't look significantly different than it did before the Occupation began. People shopped, people ate, people lived. I watched a little girl playing catch with her dad, and a family having a picnic in the shade. Shoppers haggled with merchants, their voices rising and falling in a chorus of good-natured ribbing and a lot of laughter. Humans were living their lives.

But if you looked closer, you could see the shadows over everything. There were Zhen guards here and there in the market, and humans tended to give them a wide berth, many keeping their eyes averted from the guards and doing their best to appear small and insignificant.

And there was good reason to try. A young man who made eye contact for a few moments too long with a Zhen guard found himself slammed hard against a wall. A woman with two young children had to stand by as a Zhen guard searched her bags for contraband, trying to calm her children, who were utterly convinced the Zhen were going to kill them. She tried to reassure them, but it was futile. Not only were the Zhen huge and scary, but every guard was armed with a pulse rifle and wearing heavy armor.

It was, on reflection, a perfect summation of the relationship between humans and Zhen. On the surface, things were fine. Humans went about their business, living their lives, and the Zhen watched over everyone. But their vigilance was rooted, not in parental love and a desire to protect, but in fear and a desire to control. They didn't trust us, because we were too human, too wrapped in our own desires, to be good little clients. And rather than let us go – rather than admit that maybe they'd erred all those centuries ago – they increased their hold, going from oversight to a stranglehold on our planet.

My eye was caught by a flash of sunlight on armor, and I looked up to see a Zhen in an unfamiliar uniform. Where most Zhen soldiers wore harnesses that held their equipment and rank insignia, these two were clad neck to toe in armor and carrying weapons far better than anything the regular soldiers had. And on the shoulder of each of them there was a representation of a bloody dagger.

The Dirty Knives.

Whereas Zhen soldiers always walked as if they owned the place, these guys walked as if they were the most important thing in the universe, expecting others to get out of their way. It didn't matter if it was human or Zhen: they expected everyone else to move. Several people were slammed aside when they got too close.

The humans they spoke to seemed to defer to them even more than usual, and given what we'd seen and heard of them, I couldn't blame them. But I also couldn't let this lot go unchallenged.

I'd said it myself: open season on the DK. And here was a brace of the bastards. What better way to send a message to Grevink than with the new force he expected to change everything for him?

"Is this a good idea?" I murmured to myself. "Ah, fuck it. Gotta die of something." As the DK approached me, I stayed seated. I couldn't wear my favorite blaster openly, as such weapons were forbidden to humans, especially in Landing. But I had two hold-out pistols up my sleeves. Each of them was good for four shots before they'd be completely drained, but mine had been modified by Injala for 'dirty tricks'. As the DK walked by me, the pistols slid into my hands, and I rose and followed the two. I adopted a stagger, as if drunk, and stumbled my way between them, 'falling' to my knees after bodychecking the one on the left.

"Watch it!" one of them yelled, kicking me. I felt a rib crack, and I cringed away from the Zhen, being sure to keep my face averted. I adopted a rough voice and hacked my way through, "Sorry, sirs. Won't happen again!" as I backed away from them.

Once I was far enough away, I stood up and grabbed a fuzzy fruit from a nearby stand. "Hey, assholes!" I said, throwing one at the nearest DK. They turned to me, grabbing for their guns, and I gave them the rudest gesture a Zhen could give. "Bye!" I said, and sent a command to the pistols I'd secreted on each of them. Both pistols, which had been charging up since I placed them, overloaded, the small explosions enough to blow rather large holes in the DKs' torsos.

I didn't wait around to see what happened after that, but started running immediately. One of the ordinary guards chased me, which I discovered when the shot he fired missed and hit a doorway to my right. I cut into an alleyway, calling up my NeuroNet's map of the area. I ran as fast as I could, but the burning in my side made it harder than usual, and I was beginning to flag.

The Zhen behind me wasn't letting up, and I was starting to worry, when a drone swooped down from above and fired. I cringed aside, and only then realized it wasn't shooting at me. I turned to look behind and saw the Zhen guard go down. "This way!" I heard, and looked to my side to see a young man with a distant look in his eye, and beside him an elderly woman. "Come on, son!" she called, gesturing into her home. The drone went to the roof, and the young man's eyes snapped back into focus as I passed him.

Once inside, the old woman led me straight to a closet in the back of the house. She opened it, swept the clothes hanging there aside and pushed the back, which swung open to reveal a ladder going down. "Volunteer number 2342, sir," she said. "Emily Hernandez. Take the ladder down. You'll be met there by a guide. Good luck, sir."

I stopped long enough to smile at her. "Thanks," I said. "If they—"

"Pssh. Never mind about me, Captain. I've been dealing with Zhen for years. I know how to stay safe."

I stopped as something occurred to me. "How'd you even know to help me?"

A twinkle lit up her eyes. "Do you really think you go anywhere without the Resistance keeping an eye on you?"

"Guess that makes sense," I said, and went down the ladder as she closed the door behind me. I heard it latch with a metallic *clunk* that told me it was shielded. Reassured, I continued as fast as my no doubt broken rib would let me.

At the bottom, I was met by a young woman. She took one look at me, said, "You seem okay," and led me through a maze of passageways.

"I didn't realize we'd built this much down here," I said.

"We hadn't," she said. "A lot of this is left over from before the Destruction. That's why you need a guide. There's no map for these levels, and they're not all safe." She played her lights around the tunnel. "Some of us started exploring them a while back – even before the Occupation started. Once things started getting grim, we made contact with the Resistance. There's a group of us that are working on charting the tunnels, and we help out with guiding cells when they need to move around without the Zhen finding them."

"Who do you report to? I haven't heard anything about this."

"Usually Injala, but also Ben Denali."

"Ben?" I was shocked. Ben, a trained doctor, had been a member of my crew when we found Earth and retook it a year ago, but when

Earth's population had grown, he'd quit to open a clinic on Earth. "I saw Ben just a few days ago. He didn't say anything about this."

She looked at me like I'd said I wanted to kiss a Zhen. "What kind of Resistance leader are you?" she asked.

"The kind that's barely leading," I said. "Early on I compartmentalized the Resistance so no one person could take it down. I think some of my officers have stuck to that policy perhaps a bit too much."

"Seems like," she said.

Eventually, we came up outside the city. A Resistance member who was known to me picked me up and flew me out to Settlement 19, where I'd been staying since the war began. Liam and Ben met me at the shuttle pad and helped me home, where Ben had me lie down and scanned me, then placed a nanite package on my side and began the work of knitting my ribs back together.

"You've been holding out on me," I said to Ben.

"What?"

"I met one of your scouts in the tunnels. She said she reports to you and Injala. Why didn't you tell me about the tunnels?"

He grunted. "We've been trying to map them. Didn't want to get your hopes up until we knew we could move around in 'em well enough to use 'em."

"And how close are we to that?"

"Well, we can use them to move small teams around, but there's not enough room down there for large-scale movement."

"But we can move teams into position using them?"

"And, of course," he said, "individual escape routes." We laughed, and then continued to talk for hours, catching up and planning new operations.

The next day, I woke to a message that contained an address with no other information. I woke Liam and shared it with him.

"You think it's Zekan?" he asked.

"Probably," I said. "We were supposed to meet again when the probe was finished."

"He didn't give you a time?"

"No. Guess we should check it out."

"I'll get dressed."

Once we were ready, we headed for the address, a run-down apartment block in the outskirts of Landing. It had been damaged in the Rising, and nobody had bothered to repair it yet. Odds were nobody would, if the condition of the place was any indication.

"We just supposed to wait here?" Liam asked.

I frowned. "Seems unlikely, doesn't it? I—" A thought occurred to me, and I switched my visual implants on. The pattern-analysis computer nestled in my brain looked at everything I saw, looking for anything out of— There. A section of wall was highlighted; zooming in on it, I realized the dust had been disturbed by a wall hanging. I pulled the hanging aside and saw nothing out of the ordinary, but my implants called my attention to a section of the hanging. I located a tiny chip, removed from the usual casing such small objects were carried in. I scanned it with my NeuroNet and uploaded the information.

"Got it," I said. "He left the names here."

"How many are there?"

I scanned the list. "Thirty DK, with twenty humans scattered throughout the Resistance. Nobody close to us."

"So, what do we do?"

I beckoned him to follow me and headed back to our flyer. "We send them my message," I said.

*   *   *

Joel Bennet was a middle-aged Resistance member. He'd taken part in several operations, and was a well-liked member of his cell. He was also working for the Zhen, and was, unknown to anyone but me, the source of reports that had gotten several of his colleagues killed in the last few weeks.

Which is why, one calm morning, I walked up and shot him in the head.

The crowd around us reacted about as you'd expect, and I quickly escaped in the confusion. As I ran, I hoped the other teams were doing as well. We'd chosen a small group for today; more of a proof-of-concept for the larger attacks that would be coming in the future.

When I approached my second target, she took one look at my face, turned, and ran. "She's on the move," I said on my comms. "Going south on European Way. Make sure she sees you before she gets to Fourth

Street. Do not engage directly – I want her trapped in the target zone." I chased her for several blocks before finally cornering her in the dead-end alley we'd planned for.

"What the hell is wrong with you?" she cried. "I'm on your side!"

"Enough crap," I said. "We know you're working for the Zhen."

Her face changed, growing harder. "Well, then," she said. Her eyes unfocused slightly, for just a moment, and I realized she'd sent a message, probably to request backup.

"They won't get here in time," I said.

"Then they can avenge me."

"Why fight for them?" I kept my gun leveled at her. "They destroyed our planet!"

"A thousand years ago," she said. "Not the Zhen today."

"Didn't you watch the video I put out last year?" I asked. "When the One told me what she wants of us? They've been grooming us for centuries, trying to engineer us. Do you really think they're ever going to admit us as equals in the Empire?"

"Video can be faked," she said. "And even if it wasn't, I can think of worse things than being honored by the Zhen."

"Honored by them?"

She drew herself up. "They are an old and powerful race," she said. "I'm proud to have been raised by them, trained by them. They make us better than we were. You may have walked away from them, but I never will. *Zhen:ka ne'kal sharak!*"

The words meant 'Zhen never stop fighting'. I shook my head. "You're the perfect product of eight hundred years of Zhen programming. It's almost sad. I want you to take a message to the Zhen – and the rest of their spies among us."

"What message?"

"Leave our world," I said, "or die." Having given the message, I fired. "I'm sorry, but you chose our enemy." I knew the Zhen would access her implants to see what she experienced in her last minutes. They'd know who did this, and why.

In other words, I'd just increased the size of the target on my back.

*　　*　　*

A week later, I was standing in an alley across the street from the local Zhen authority office. Based on our intelligence dossier, my targets were in that office – one of them reporting in to the others.

"Once we do this, there's no going back," Liam said. "This is our last chance to call it off."

"It's too late for that," I said.

"Yeah. But it's going to get worse from here."

I took in a deep breath, held it a moment, and let it out slowly. "I know," I said. After this, the Zhen would probably throw away whatever restraint they'd used to this point.

So far, I'd been protected, as it were, by my popularity back home. The Zhen command figured that if they moved against me, they'd only martyr me and spur even more human resistance. But those days were over once this operation began. After today, there was no way the Zhen could allow me to continue to operate. If they got their claws on me, I was dead.

"It has to be done," I said. "We can't let them continue like this. If it was just Earth, that would be one thing. But it isn't, not anymore."

"Ready when you are."

I looked at Bailey. "You ready?"

"Got your back, sir."

I activated my comms. "All teams," I said. "Go."

My own team, Liam, myself, and Bailey, calmly walked out of the alleyway we'd been standing in and crossed the street. We entered the office and walked up to the desk belonging to our first target. Sitting across from him was a human, wearing cuffs and looking quite nervous.

"You Sebastian Michaels?" I asked the human.

"Y-yes," he said.

"I have a message for you," I said. "We warned you to leave." I drew and fired, shooting him in the chest. As he fell back, a smoking crater where his heart used to be, Liam and Bailey both drew their weapons. Liam fired his at the Zhen who'd been interviewing Michaels.

The room erupted in noise and motion as other Zhen officers drew their weapons and fired at us. Liam, Bailey, and I ducked behind the desk and returned fire as we could.

"That's two!" I said. "Either of you get eyes on the other three?"

"One of 'em," Liam said. "He's the ugly fucker trying to kill us over there by the window." He grabbed a grenade off his belt, hit the activation stud, and threw it, ducking back seconds before it exploded. The room grew bright, and I felt the heat of the plasma wash over me. Liam popped his head around the desk and said, "Good news, got 'em. Bad news, I think I broke our exit."

I rose just high enough to see what he was talking about. The grenade had taken out the entire front of the building. "Great work," I said dryly. "Bailey, you see any other exits?"

"There's a doorway in back," she said, firing at a Zhen. "But I've never been in here. No idea what's back there."

"Well, we'll have to risk it," I said. I flicked a tiny probe up over the desk. A window opened in my visuals, showing me the scene. We had one more Zhen in the office; the others had been hit by Liam's grenade blast. "Give me some suppression fire." The others fired at his location. When the Zhen ducked down behind his barricade, I got up and aimed for where he'd be when he rose again. I signaled Bailey and Liam to hold fire, and the moment the Zhen popped up to return fire, I hit my blaster's firing stud. The shot took him in the head, and his body slumped over. "Let's go." I made for the back door.

It led into a hallway lined with doors on either side. Liam and I glanced at each other, then began working our way down, clearing each door as we went. Bailey came behind, keeping watch on the rear.

The end of the corridor turned to the right. I sent a probe around it. "Clear," I said softly. I continued on, following the corridor around several corners. "Watchtower, this is Hunt. I need an exit."

"Locking to your location," Kiri's voice answered. "Hold on." A few seconds later, she said, "Okay, there's an exit twenty meters ahead of you. Sending you a schematic. But there's a nasty surprise waiting in the street outside."

"Oh, are they planning a surprise party?" I asked.

"A good one, looks like."

As we reached the doorway, I said, "Kiri, can you get me a position plot?"

"Sending now." The feed from Kiri showed me an overlay on my vision, each Zhen in the street outside appearing as a red ghost image, as if I could see through the walls. I shared the feed with Liam and Bailey. "I have the two in the center," I said.

"Got the two on the right," Bailey said.

"Fine, leave me the heavy lifting," Liam said.

"On three," I said. I counted, and on three, I kicked the door open and ducked down as I moved, firing at the two Zhen in the middle of the group. One of them went down with a shot to the face, but the other flinched, his armor taking the brunt of the shot. I felt the heat of his shots pass over my shoulder. My second volley hit his arm, causing him to drop his gun. As he reached for it, I kicked it out of his reach. His claws grazed my boot, but didn't penetrate the armor under the leather.

The Zhen rose to his feet, swinging his off hand in a backhand that knocked me off my feet. I registered Bailey in combat with her remaining target, but my attention was drawn back to my own as he stepped over me, drawing his dagger in one smooth motion. I heard Liam yell, but he was pinned down by fire and couldn't help me. Bailey was busy fighting for her life. I was on my own. As the Zhen raised the dagger for a killing blow, I drew back my legs to kick at his. I didn't think it would do much, to be honest. The Zhen had two feet and two hundred pounds on me, easily. I was about to die.

My impending martyrdom was curtailed by several blaster bolts that hit the Zhen in the back. I rolled out of the way as he toppled into the space where I'd been lying. Another series of blasts took out Bailey's opponent.

One of Liam's remaining foes was down, and the other turned to see who had fired on his friends. "Traitor!" he bellowed at Zekan.

"No," Zekan said. "I am no traitor, Karn. Can you not see that the Twenty and the One are acting without honor?"

"They are our leaders!" Karn shouted. "They command! We obey!"

"What you describe is slavery," Zekan said. "I want more."

"All you will get," Karn said, raising his weapon, "is death."

A blaster bolt hit Karn in the back of his head at point-blank range before he could fire. As the body toppled, Liam was revealed behind him. "Asshole shouldn't have forgotten about me," he said. He looked at Zekan. "We cool?"

Zekan's crest showed his confusion. But he holstered his blaster. "We should leave," he said.

"We?" I asked. "Getting involved now?"

He gestured at the bodies. "Everything that just happened will have been seen. I am no longer safe among my own kind. I would join you."

"You may not be much safer among my people," I said. "They won't trust a Zhen easily. I'll speak for you, but I'm not sure how much I can do."

"It is good enough," he said.

"Then welcome to the Resistance." I snorted. "Hope you survive."

★   ★   ★

As we entered our Landing headquarters – a basement under a machine shop – there was a cheer, which ended the moment Zekan was revealed. Throughout the room, guns were drawn and aimed at the Zhen.

"Whoah whoah whoah," I cried, spreading my arms out and standing in front of him. "He's with us!"

"Bullshit," Henry Boles said, pushing his way to the front. "He's Zhen."

"And?" I said.

"As you're so fond of saying," he said, looking Zekan up and down, "they're the enemy."

I took a breath, looking around the room, before speaking. I could see at least some of the faces were hostile, and others were nodding along, but seemed undecided on Zekan's status. "Yes, I've said that," I agreed. "And in the general sense, the Zhen are our enemy. But that doesn't mean every Zhen is." My eyes swept the room. "I know of several Zhen back on Zhen:da who are on our side. One of them helped me get the information that exposed the Zhen. There are a growing number of them, there and here, who believe the Empire is mistreating us and want to stop it. If we kill every Zhen we see, we are no better than the worst of them." I stepped up to Zekan and put my hand on his forearm. "This is Zekan. He gave me the information that kept Talvikki Suzuki, and a few others, free when the Zhen came for them."

"What about the rest of the council?" one of the fighters called.

"Tynes and the others? They didn't listen to me," I said. "There was nothing I could do. That's not Zekan's fault." I paused, and when no one spoke, continued. "Zekan also killed two other Zhen today, saving me and my team. That's earned him my trust. And he alerted us to the presence of spies among us."

"The Zhen would have no trouble killing their own to set us up," one woman said. "How do we even know all those people on the list were spies?"

One of the others raised a hand. "Mine was," he said. "Shot at us as soon as she saw us."

Other teams indicated that their targets, too, had turned out to be Zhen spies.

"Did any teams not come back?" I asked Kiri.

"Every team made it back, but not all of them got back intact," she said. "Teams eight and ten each lost a fighter."

"And did any teams report their target was clean?"

"No," she said.

I turned back to the crowd. "That would seem to prove he was accurate," I said.

"Still," the woman – Jorene, I remembered – persisted, "the Zhen would sacrifice human assets even more gladly, if it meant having a shot at you. He could be a— what do they call them? A double agent?"

Zekan looked at me, and I said, "A *fijakkan*."

"Ah. She is not wrong that it's a possibility," he said. "I regret I have no way of proving it is not the case."

"I do," Injala's voice rang out. I looked up to see her entering the basement. She stepped down in silence, regarding Zekan the entire way. "Though how you will regard it depends on how you feel about me," she said.

"We trust you, Injala!" Jorene said. Many nodded; Injala had long since proven herself to most of the Resistance.

"Then accept my word," she said. "Zekan is known to me. He has been a source of my own information for some time now." She turned to regard him. "And one I will be hard pressed to replace, though I understand it was necessary."

I watched the room; Injala's words seemed to have placated everyone. "Kiri," I said, "can you get a room set up for Zekan?"

"The one next to me is empty," Injala said.

"I'll take care of it," she said, "but I'm not sure we'll find a bed big enough."

"I do not need one," he said. "Zhen prefer to sleep on warm stone and sand. Give me those things and a source of heat, and I will be fine."

"I said I'll take care of it," Kiri said. "Trust me."

I left Zekan in Kiri's care and checked in with the team leaders, Liam at my side. While we'd lost a couple of fighters, we'd also taken out all of the human spies and half a dozen of the DK targets. "We'll get the rest eventually," I said.

"There'll be reprisals," Liam said.

"Yes."

"What happens then?"

"We raise the brutality level."

"Is that what this is?" he asked. "A race to see who can become the most brutal?"

I sighed. "Unfortunately, that's exactly what it is. We have to show them that they will never control us, and that anything they do to us will only cause us to come back stronger. Eventually, there has to be a point where they just can't afford it anymore."

"What if there isn't?"

"Then we all die," I said. "Eventually, they'll just wipe us all out."

"That's…grim," he said.

"It's not likely," I said. "If they were inclined to that, they'd have done it already, at least here."

"Let's hope it's not on tomorrow's list."

"As my grandfather said, no shit."

★   ★   ★

After the operation, I ordered all Resistance members to lay low. We'd done some damage, now we had to stay off the radar. Some of my fighters had decided to go to the football game at the arena. I had a lot to do, but Liam and Bailey reminded me that I needed to live too, and dragged me to the game. I figured, what the hell – I was certainly already on the wanted list, but a crowd is a great place to be anonymous, especially when the Resistance's hackers were working constantly to keep the facial recognition systems offline.

While many things about Old Earth had been lost, a few remained. We had a collection of video entertainments from Earth up to about 2146. Some were of very bad quality, but others were pristine. It was from these that many of the settlements and streets in our new colony were named.

And we'd retained a game played by millions on Earth before the

Destruction. Football was played by two teams of eleven, each trying to kick a ball through a goal at the opposite end of a field. The Zhen considered it an unworthy game, and had tried to adapt it by adding combat to it in service of the concept of Zhen:saak:arl, but we'd resisted it, holding the game as close to the original as we could.

The game was a good one. After nearly an hour of expert maneuvers from both sides, the game was still a nail-biter, which meant the score at halftime was 2-1. The Landers were one up on the Explorers, but the Explorers had Jaime Ramsay, and on the close-ups projected to our NeuroNets, he looked like he was ready to turn up the heat.

About five minutes into the second half, the gates opened and a Zhen transport came sailing onto the field, where it hovered over the pitch. The hatches opened and a platoon of Zhen soldiers exited, taking up positions surrounding the transport and facing the crowds. Hundreds of people in the stands shot to their feet, standing in worry, waiting for the Zhen to say or do anything else. The Zhen stood in formation, silent.

After a minute of just standing there, one of the players, James Hogan, kicked the ball, which he'd had control of, to a teammate. The teammate passed it to another, and in ones and twos, the teams began to play again, being careful to stay away from the Zhen.

Suddenly the circle of Zhen began firing. Hogan and another player were hit almost immediately, but most of the shots were aimed into the crowd. The people screamed in terror, and the crowd surged toward the exits. Liam, Bailey, and I moved quickly. "Down!" I yelled, grabbing a nearby child and her dad and shoving them toward the floor in front of their seats. "You stay down and don't move, you hear me?" They nodded, eyes wide with fear, and I turned to another person.

I'd left my blaster back at the base, like an idiot. I had a hold-out in each sleeve, but those would do little against the armor the DK were wearing. The DK's fire was relentless; if I stood or moved from my spot there was a good chance I'd take a hit. And if that happened, I was dead. All I could do was try to keep my head down and live.

After about a minute of sustained fire, the Zhen stopped. Without a word, they got in their transport again, which lifted from the pitch and moved toward the exit, the crowds parting – or flattening themselves to the ground – as the antigrav vehicle approached. Many of the latter screamed as the transport's grav-coils pushed them farther into the dirt as the transport passed over them.

When they were gone, the arena was silent but for the sounds of wailing. Liam and I got to our feet and looked around. The scene was chaos. I looked for Bailey and didn't see her. "Where is she?" I said. "Bailey!"

When I turned to investigate a crying child, I found her, riddled with plasma fire, face down over the child. I pulled her off the kid and handed him to his father. The man looked at me. "I was too far away," he said. "I'd gone over to buy a treat for him. I saw her grab him and shield him." He stared for a moment, and I checked Bailey over. She was gone, her wounds so extensive, she'd probably been gone before she hit the deck.

I moved down the stands, to a man holding a teen boy in his arms. He screamed, not in rage, or fear, but anguish. It was the sound of a man who has had the very last thing he cared about taken from him. "They killed my son," he said, sagging over the boy.

Nearby a woman held what I assumed was her husband, trying to stop the bleeding. I ran to her, grabbing my emergency kit from my pocket. I slapped a nano-pack over the wound, instructing it to go to work. It spread, anchoring itself and beginning the process of sealing the wound and knitting the tissues back together.

"Where'd you get that?" the woman gasped, then looked closer at my face. "You're him...."

"Not important now," I said. I ran my hands over the man's body, looking for more wounds. There were a couple of smaller injuries caused by trampling, but no other plasma wounds. I injected him with an analgesic, and said, "He'll be all right."

"Thank you," she said.

Liam and I did what we could, but the supplies we carried on us weren't enough to help more than a few people. I activated my comms. "Kiri, we need emergency services here."

"I'm monitoring, Uncle. They're already on the way. You need to get out of there before they arrive – you're all on the shoot-on-sight list."

"Yeah, I know. Shit," I said. I relayed that we needed to leave to Liam, and we began moving for the seats.

A burly man stepped into my path. "Tajen Hunt," he said. "This is your fault! Your war started this!"

The woman I'd helped earlier stormed over and straight-armed the man, pushing him back. "Knock that shit off, Leroy!" she said. "He didn't start this. He didn't fire into a crowd of people. The Zhen did that." She looked over her shoulder at me. "Get out of here, Hunt. Keep doing what you're doing, for all of us." She turned back to Leroy. "Don't you ever blame a human for what the Zhen do!" I missed the rest, as Liam pulled me along.

We made our way out of the arena just before the police arrived on scene. We went straight to the nearest tunnel's entrance and followed the guide waiting there for us to the Resistance garrison we'd been assigned, now that we couldn't go home again.

"You know," Liam said later, sitting on the uncomfortably hard bunk, "I'm really looking forward to having a permanent address again."

"Tell me about it."

"I want a comfy bed, for one thing," Liam said with a grin. "But a place where I can have windows and sunlight is also high on the list."

"Yeah," I said. "But look at the bright side. We're still doing better than Katherine and Takeshi."

Liam stared at me for several long moments. "You know, sometimes your sense of humor isn't funny."

"Not joking," I said. "They're beyond all this shit."

"You believe in an afterlife?"

I shook my head. "No, not really. But I believe in an end to suffering."

"I'll drink to that," he said. "Preferably without dying, but at this point I'll take what I can get."

He passed me a beer from the unit's small refrigerator and opened one for himself. We clinked the bottles together.

"To Bailey," he said.

"To Bailey."

The moment I said her name, my face began to twist. I fought it, but I couldn't stop the emotions from coming to the surface again. I collapsed into tears.

Liam put his arms around me, rubbing my back, trying to soothe me even as his own tears began. We sat there, crying over our friend, until both of us were too exhausted to do anything but sleep.

CHAPTER FIFTEEN

When the Zhen attacked the match, I'm sure they expected something so horrific would cow us. They expected the human race to recoil in fear, and let them have what they wanted.

They clearly didn't understand us at all.

We'd had more volunteers make contact with the Resistance in the last few weeks than in the months since the Occupation began. We had so many volunteers we didn't actually know what to do with most of them – our whole setup was designed to train a few at a time, and now we had a backlog. Back home, it was even worse.

My command team had withdrawn from Landing, setting up a training and command post in one of the outer settlements again, trusting Injala and Aleph to keep the satellites from 'finding' us out here. Kiri and I were glad to be near each other more, and it kept me out of the crucible of Landing, which my family appreciated. I didn't think it made a whole lot of difference, but I had to concede we'd have more warning of Zhen attacks than if we stayed in the city. We'd brought Zekan with us, but the poor guy wasn't exactly welcomed. Even though everyone knew he was on our side, most didn't trust him.

The Zhen media had attempted to explain and justify the arena attack. They had at first claimed that human Resistance members had fired first – which was easily disproved with the recordings of the event, garnered from the NeuroNets of the people who had been there, many of whom had sent their recordings into the slipnet as soon as they could. When the Occupation shut down the slipnet relays, we just handed the files to Injala and had her Kelvaki agents, lurking in the system, disseminate them throughout known space.

Then the Occupation tried to claim the actions were unsanctioned, and sacrificed the DK who had been involved. This backfired even worse; the Zhen back home clearly didn't believe the story, and mass demonstrations were occurring again – only this time, the majority of the protesters weren't human. One demonstration in the capital city had more Zhen than humans showing up, and the riot that broke out had nothing to do with the government. The fact was, the Zhen no longer agreed about Earth, and fights were breaking out amongst themselves.

The debates in the Talnera were growing more common, and while no movement there could get any traction, there were more and more theatrics. My old friend Jaata and his faction walked out of the Talnera, vowing not to return until the Earth question was settled 'appropriately, with no loss of life'. Some of them returned to their offices and seats when commanded to, but Jaata and some of his closest allies were now sitting in jail, publicly declaring their support for Earth and the human resistance forces.

A few weeks into this new world, Injala handed me a message. In the old days, I'd have copied it to my NeuroNet before playing, but under her tutelage I'd grown more cautious, so even though it came from her network, I played it via a hologram projector.

Seeker, or I guess Jette, now, appeared on the screen, with Quince beside her. "Tajen," she said. "I thought maybe you should see this." The image cut to an exterior view of Shoa'kor Station. In addition to the normal system traffic, there were dozens of ships, some of them huge. "We've been calling disaffected humans to Shoa'kor. They've been coming here for a while now, but even more since the Football Massacre. We're trying to arrange ways to get them to Earth, but the Zhen are blockading the system. They're also destroying any human ships they find fleeing Imperial worlds. If you can find a way to get people smuggled to Earth, get us word. We can't keep these people here indefinitely."

I looked at Injala. "Can we do anything?"

She waggled her fingers. "Somewhat," she said. "Smuggling a few humans in here and there can be done, but it's somewhat pointless. We can't move anywhere near enough numbers to make much of a dent, and the Zhen will notice eventually, which begs the question, why bother?"

"We can't just leave those people hanging in space, either," I said.

"No. Dierka is working the Assembly council, trying to get them to agree to give the humans at Shoa'kor a place to stay. However, it is slow going. As you may recall," she said drily, "they are reluctant to get involved in the war between your people."

"Still playing that song, are they?"

She waggled her fingers again. "Well, to be fair, it *is* an internal struggle of the Empire, if looked at a certain way." She held up a hand as I took breath. "I'm not agreeing with them. Besides, you heard the woman: Zhen are destroying human ships that flee. Dierka has capitalized on this by sending Kelvaki ships to Shoa'kor, with orders to defend the human vessels."

"Which means that if the Zhen attack them, the Assembly will be at war."

"It isn't quite so simple as that," she said, "but you are more or less correct."

"Isn't that an illegal order?"

"It is," she corrected me, "an *unofficial* order. But one the captains and crews of the ships he sent have volunteered to follow. There are benefits to being the heir to the Assembly leadership, and benefits to allying yourself with that heir, as well."

I chuckled. "Did Dierka think of using their ambition to his benefit on his own, or did you have something to do with that?"

"I may have whispered a word or two at the right time," she said.

I looked at her. "You have your own angle to play, don't you?"

Her ears quivered. "We *all* do, Tajen. Myself maybe more than most." She put a hand on my shoulder. "But do not fear. My own goals are perfectly aligned with yours. Your fight is mine."

"For now, you mean."

She met my eyes. "You understand me quite well, but in this case, for as long as Dierka calls you *draka*, which I expect will be a long time yet."

She got a faraway look in her eyes and motioned to the door. "I am receiving a message I must take in private. If you will excuse me?"

★　　★　　★

I was walking with Liam when I heard my name called.

"Tajen!" Zekan yelled, as he ran to me across the Settlement's central plaza. The big Zhen looked stricken. "Tajen, I have received information you must know."

"From?"

"I have friends still among the Zhen forces. One of them reached out to me. The Zhen have found the humans at Shoa'kor."

"How do *you* know about them?" I asked, alarmed.

"I did not, until just now. My friend informed me. They are sending a task group to destroy them."

"To destroy the humans at Shoa'kor?"

"Yes."

"How old is this information?"

"The order was made yesterday," he said.

For once, I noticed Injala approaching. "I have confirmation," she said. "I just received an emergency transmission from my own sources."

"That's pretty quick for information to filter through your spynet," I said.

She tossed her head. "I have agents positioned in the Zhen home system."

"Really?"

"I would be a very poor spy handler if I did not," she said.

I looked at Liam. "I'm going to need the ship," I said.

"You mean *we're* going to need the ship."

I must have changed; I didn't even consider arguing with him. I nearly argued with Kiri when she stepped up and declared she was going too, but I took one look at her face and decided not to. I looked to Injala. "You coming?"

"I would not miss it for the world," she said.

Zekan stepped forward. "I would like to go, as well," he said.

I eyed him. "Zekan, no offense, but I'm still not sure I one hundred percent trust you."

He gestured *obvious fact.* "What better way to reassure yourself, then, than to keep me close and in line?" He rumbled in his chest. "You can always space me if I betray you."

I snorted. "All right, then." I looked to Injala, as if to say *watch him.* She nodded. "Kiri, call in a ride." She made the call as I ran to get my gear.

Liam followed me, and as we burst into our quarters and began to gather our personal equipment, he said, "You as excited as I am?"

"Liam, our people are in danger. If we don't get there in time, thousands of people will die."

"Yeah, that's my point," he said. "Thousands of lives on the line? A race against time? That's when we have the most fun."

I blew my breath out in a laugh. "Yeah, I guess you're right," I said. "Ready?"

He gave me an intense, smoldering look. "I was born ready," he said.

"Gods above and below," I muttered in a deadpan voice, and led him back to the square, where the rest of the crew was gathering.

A flyer came in hot, hovered inches over the square while we scrambled aboard, then took off at full speed immediately.

It was a short flight to the cavern where we'd stashed the ship. On landing, we all jumped clear and, without waiting to watch the flyer leave, we headed for the cavern. I tossed a salute to the crewmen who'd been on maintenance duty there and went straight to the ship. When I opened the hatch, I dropped my gear, trusting Liam to stow it, and headed for the bridge, Kiri on my tail.

We strapped into our seats. I initiated the reactor warm-up and glanced over the readouts. "All crew," I said over the comms, "launch in two minutes."

"Incoming!" Kiri called. "Three Zhen fighters, two minutes out!"

"Shit," I said. "They must have seen us coming out here. Crew, launch in ninety seconds; we're going to cut it as close as we can. Ground crew, if you've got transport, you might want to leave now. Or get on board if you really want to take your chances."

Seconds later, I saw the ground crew heading out, piled into an aircar. I sent them the best escape route based on our sensor sweep and wished them luck. For the next two minutes, my eyes were glued to the plot, watching the three blips get closer. "This is going to be—"

"Fun?" Kiri said.

"Well, maybe," I said. "But until then, there's a very real danger I might pee my pants."

"You should've gone before we left," she said.

At one minute, the reactor had warmed enough I could start the engines cycling. At thirty seconds, I brought the flight systems fully online. "All crew," I said, "brace for launch!" I lifted off the ground, moving the ship out of the cave, and the moment we were clear, I slammed the throttle to full and angled for space.

I could feel the impact of plasma fire on our shields a few seconds later. Kiri shook her head. "At that range it barely affects our shields. Why not wait?" she said.

"No Zhen pilot wants to be the last one to start combat," I replied. "Liam, feel free to fire back."

"I'm on it," he said, and I felt the vibration of our rear turret firing.

As we entered orbit, Kiri highlighted more ships angling toward us from the station. "Find me the closest jump point!" I said. A marker appeared in my vision showing the jump point, and I steered us that way, pouring on the speed. "Ready for jump?"

"Ready," she said. "Jump is plotted."

"Good work." I started an evasive pattern to avoid incoming fire, but tried to keep us on course for the jump. The ship was slammed off course by a particularly good hit. "Dammit," I said, as we swung wide of the jump point. I turned the ship so the belly was facing the direction we were going, shedding velocity while not stopping us. Slowly, I brought us back on course. We hit the jump point with no time to lose, and the system initiated the jump the moment we were in position.

As the colors of slipspace started to flow over the ship's viewport, I sat back, finally beginning to relax.

"This jump will take us to Rinpak. From there we can jump to the outer edge of Shoa'kor's system," Kiri said.

"We going to get there before the Zhen?" I asked her.

"I hope so," she said.

Rinpak was the only system on a path between Earth and Shoa'kor, making it the perfect spot for a Zhen ambush.

If only I'd thought of that before we got there.

★　　★　　★

We burst out of slipspace on the outer edge of the system. Before I could do anything, the plasma blasts of five Zhen ships were slamming into my shields. "Son of a bitch!" I yelled, immediately taking the ship into an evasive pattern. "It was a karking trap!"

I heard Zekan on the comms. "Zhen fighters, cease your attack!" he rumbled. "This ship is on a mission for Commander Grevink of the Earth garrison. Clearance Jek-var-kon-na."

The only answer was more plasma blasts on our shield, and a missile targeting lock. "I don't think they're going for it, Zekan," I said.

"It was worth the attempt," he said.

"Targeting lead ship," Kiri called, flicking the targeting data to me.

"Rear guns powering up," Liam called over the comms net. "Line 'em up and I'll take 'em out."

"Don't get cocky back there," I said.

"Have you met your husband?" Injala asked from behind me.

"Hush. You on sensors or engineering?"

"Engineering," she said. "Maximizing power to engines and weapons."

"Thank you," I said, and rolled the ship on its side, slipping between two Zhen ships. I hauled the ship around, settling in behind one of them, and began chipping away at his shields.

Zekan said, "I suggest you target the—"

"We have a saying on Earth, Zekan," I interrupted. "Don't tell Tajen Hunt how to fight!"

The Zhen was good, but I was better. I stayed on his tail, pouring fire into his shields until they collapsed with a flash of energy. "Gotcha," I said, and fired all my weapons into his unprotected engines. As his ship broke up, I pulled away from the debris and found my next target. "This is fun, but we don't need to finish the dance. Got a jump solution for me yet?"

"I'm trying," Kiri replied, "but I'm doing three things, here. Stand by. And maybe get that Zhen off our tail?"

"Liam?"

"I'm trying. He won't stay still!"

"I'll handle it," I said. I cut thrust completely and flipped the ship around. The Zhen saw my move coming, and increased his own thrust, slipping by me. "Slippery bastard," I muttered, turning back and going back to full thrust. While I'd been faffing about looking fancy, the Zhen had increased the distance between us. He was now at the extreme of plasma bolt range. I locked missiles on and fired two. The missiles, equipped with small chain drives, flashed across the distance to the Zhen. The first one hit the shields, knocking them out in one hit, and the second hit the ship itself, shredding it in an explosion of plasma energy.

"Two down, two to go," I said. "Unless you've got the jump ready?"

"Not yet," Kiri said.

Affecting a bored tone, I said, "Fine, I'll shoot some more Zhen."

"Don't forget about me," Liam said.

"I don't know," I quipped, "you haven't done much yet."

"Well, fly better, and I will," he said.

"Oh, like that, is it?" I saw a Zhen lining up for a shot and went into a crazy series of maneuvers, then came out of it to drop onto the rear of one of the Zhen fighters. While I was lining up my own shot, the second remaining ship dropped onto my six. "Take 'em out!" I shouted, focusing my fire on the ship in front of me.

Liam whooped moments before the ship ahead of me went dead in space, continuing on the same heading without power. I looked at Kiri. "We hit the power distributor?"

She shook her head. "No idea," she said. "But I've got the jump plot."

"The pursuing fighter is gone," Injala said. "I assume that was why Liam shouted."

"You're damn right he's gone!" Liam said. "I got a one-in-a-million shot there. It'll never happen again, but it was a beauty."

"Stand by for jump," I said. "Kiri, how long will this jump be?"

"Twelve hours," she said.

"All right. All hands, make sure we're in good shape. If the Zhen had an ambush here, they could already be at Shoa'kor."

I steered the ship to the jump point and made the jump.

It was the last jump this ship would ever make.

★　　★　　★

We came out of the jump at Shoa'kor and were relieved to find no Zhen ships in-system.

"Shoa'kor Station, this is Tajen Hunt," I sent. "Requesting docking and an immediate conference with Stationmaster Quince."

Quince's voice came over the comms a few minutes later. "Hunt, we have a problem?"

"Affirmative," I said. "I'd rather discuss it in person."

"Understood. Use docking berth seven. I'll meet you there."

I took the ship in and docked where I was told. When I opened the airlock, Quince was waiting. I walked out to meet him. "I got a tip the Zhen sent a task force to take out the human ships here," I said. "Seen anything to indicate they've been here?"

"No," he said. "But that doesn't mean they haven't been. We've got crap sensor coverage on most of the system. But our allies out there haven't said anything, and I'm sure they've got more."

"We'll need a meeting with them, as well as the captains of every human ship."

"In person?"

"If we have to. But a virtual conference should be enough."

"I'll set it up immediately," he said. "What else can we do?"

"How able is this station to defend itself?"

"About as well as any commercial station."

"So, not well."

"That's about right. We've got standard anti-missile defenses and some point-defense plasma cannons, but that's about it other than our patrol craft – and those are piloted by mercenaries we contract with."

I thought a moment. "What about your regulars? The syndicate?"

"There are some ships owned by Seeker," he said, referencing Jette's pseudonym, "and a few by others, but none of them are straight-up combat vessels."

"Get the conference set up," I said. "And in the meantime, I could use a resupply. We got ambushed on the way here."

"Zhen?"

"Who else?"

He gestured to a subordinate nearby. "Get this ship topped up and rearmed," he said. "No limits."

I was touched. "Thanks," I said.

He looked me in the eye. "We're allies. I'll get the conference set. You figure out how you're going to save us all."

I left him to his work, going back to the ship and prepping what I could. A short while later, Quince sent me an invite to a virtuality, and I sat back in my bunk and linked in.

I was standing on a dais in front of a huge room, full of both humans and Kelvaki, as well as a few – a very few – Tchakk. My crew stood around me, along with Quince. "Hello," I said. "For those who maybe don't know my face –" a chuckle went around the room at that, "– I'm Tajen Hunt. I know you've come here from worlds across the Empire, fleeing the human enclaves to join us at Earth. And I'd love to welcome you to Earth itself – but we've got a bigger problem today than getting you there.

"I'm here at Shoa'kor now because a few days ago I got word that a Zhen task force was being dispatched here to take out the human fleet gathering in this system. Based on the usual travel times between Zhen:da and Shoa'kor, we estimate it will arrive here within the next twenty-four hours."

The room dissolved into incoherent babble. I tried to get their attention, but finally looked to the Kelvaki commander. He opened his mouth, took a huge breath, and bellowed a short phrase in Kelvaki. It didn't mean anything important – it was sort of the Kelvaki equivalent of 'Hey, morons!' – but it did the job. Everyone turned back to me.

"I know many of you are frightened. I am too. But I'm here to tell you that we will not give in to that fear. We will stand strong – and we will stand together.

"Because that's the strength of the human race. Eight hundred years of trying to turn us into Zhen didn't work, because we are human first, and everything else second." I looked down for a moment. "I once forgot that basic truth. My friends here," I said, gesturing to Liam and the others, "reminded me, when humans stand together, nothing can stand in our way."

I looked around the room. "I know it doesn't feel like it. We're so few, in an Empire of so many. But even fewer of us kicked the Zhen off Earth. And even fewer of us held it. And even fewer of us have been giving them bloody noses for months now."

Someone in the back of the room shouted, "You had Kelvaki on your side then!"

The Kelvaki commander stepped up to join me on the dais. "And you have us now," he said. "I am ordered to defend human ships – and that is what I will do."

I gave him a Kelvaki salute, and turned back to the rest of the room. "Our Kelvaki allies are few, but they are strong. And not all of us are going to fight.

"Those ships without offensive capabilities are going to take as many noncombatants as possible aboard and jump to a rendezvous point I have prepared. Those ships that can fight are asked to stay and defend the rest. Once they've jumped, you're free to go too." I'd already talked to Quince, and while he hated to admit it, he knew saving Shoa'kor was a lost cause. The Zhen would never allow the station to survive after it had defied them.

"The Kelvaki and I will keep the Zhen off the civilian ships. Once you're all away, we'll join you at the next rendezvous and go on from there."

"Go where?" someone called.

"I can't tell you right now," I said. "Operational security means the destination has to be kept secret until it's time to move. Anyone who doesn't trust me, is free to go elsewhere." I waited a moment, and then continued. "All right, then. I'll let you get on with your repairs. We'll start moving the non-offensive ships as soon as passenger transfers are complete. Stationmaster Quince has volunteered to coordinate that effort. Defense ship captains, we'll have a briefing immediately after this meeting to arrange our defense strategies."

I ended the virtuality, then immediately transferred to the defense-planning meeting, which took surprisingly little time. Thanks to the marauders who often preyed on shipping in the deep dark, most captains had at least a little familiarity with combat tactics, though this time they'd have to fight their instincts to run. The Kelvaki, of course, were utterly professional. I noticed they tended to defer to Injala. Once the meeting was over, I checked in with Quince, who informed me that the passenger redistribution was nearly complete. Luckily, some of the personnel from non-battle-ready ships had volunteered to join the defense ships and bolster their capabilities. Once I finished that call, I went looking for Injala.

I found her on the ship, calibrating the main guns.

"Yes?" she asked.

"Who are you, really?"

"What do you mean?"

"Those captains knew exactly who you were and why they should obey your instructions," I said. "Don't tell me you're just a spymaster."

"What am I then?"

"That's what I'm asking you."

She sighed as if disappointed. "Well, I'm waiting for you to figure it out. When you do, let me know."

What could I do? Whatever it was, it wasn't dangerous to me. I could well believe that. "All right," I said. "We almost ready for combat?"

"We should be ready in— *Skark!*" The sounds of alert klaxons interrupted her. Her ears perked as she looked at me. "Well... now," she said.

CHAPTER SIXTEEN

Standard Zhen battle doctrine was to approach a system from several points, allowing them to corral the system and prevent jumps out. Fortunately for Shoa'kor, it was on the edge of the Empire, and there was no way for the Zhen to have the system surrounded without provoking war with the Kelvaki.

Still, that left them hemming in the system on three sides. The lack of satellites near the station itself precluded jumping from this deep in the gravity well of the star. So every retreating ship had to make a run for the jump limit at the edges of the system before they could jump. In some systems, they could use a convenient jump point, where the gravity of two stellar bodies canceled each other out and allowed for jumps. But the Shoa'kor system was unique in its lack of bodies near the station, which meant there were no jump points in the inner system.

In short, it was a recipe for disaster.

"All ships, protect the jumpers. Jumpers, you are go for the jump limit. Remember your assigned escorts and follow their directions! Handing operational control over to battle command now." I signaled Injala, who took over the job of monitoring and directing our forces, freeing me to lead just my fighter group. I looked to Kiri in the second seat and asked, "You ready?"

"As I'll ever be," she said. "So, not really."

"Undocking now." I hit the release and the ship drifted. As soon as we were clear of the dock I used the dorsal thrusters to move us farther away and hit the main thrust. "Give me a target."

She flicked targeting data to me, and I raised my brows as I got back on the comms. "Alpha flight, on me. We're going to take out that Zhen ship going after the *Night's Bliss*." I pushed my thrusters to max, as the *Night's Bliss* was a bit far out, but Alpha flight was made of the fastest fighters in our arsenal.

As we approached, the Zhen fighter screen turned to engage us.

"Weapons free!" I shouted, juking the ship to avoid incoming fire. "Take out those TAVs!" I locked on to the closest torpedo-assault vessel. They were slow-moving but well armored ships designed to take out larger ships. As soon as we entered missile range, I sent a missile after the ship. The missile's chain drive kicked in as soon as it was launched, and the missile shot across the space between us in seconds, impacting with the TAV. The yield in the missile was enough to shatter the TAV's shields, leaving it open to a shot from my wingman that burst through the ship's armor, turning it into a momentary fireball.

"They got a torpedo off," Kiri said. "Targeting now."

I pushed my throttle past the redline of maximum thrust, pouring more power into the engines. It was dangerous for extended periods, but we needed the speed to catch the torpedo. I fired plasma bolts at it, hoping to take it out before I had to stop firing or hit the *Night's Bliss* itself. I got lucky, and two of my plasma bolts converged on and destroyed it. I throttled back and whipped my ship around, headed back toward the still-approaching bombers.

"Fighter on our six!" Liam shouted from the tailgun. I could feel the ship's guns firing, and a few moments later he signaled his target destroyed.

"Good work, honey," I said.

"Damned right," he replied. "You're lucky you married the best tailgunner in the galaxy."

"Watch it, we don't want your head getting too big," I said.

"Hey, you know what they say, big head, big—"

"Hat," I interrupted. "Remember my niece is on this ship."

Kiri, for her part, ignored us. "New target lock," she said.

Injala muttered, "At least *someone* on this ship is a professional."

"Yes, Mom," I said, and even Kiri smiled. As I closed on the new target, I was distracted by a bright flare of light in the distance.

"We lost the *Mackenzie's Folly*," Injala said. "Escorts have been heavily damaged. Reassigning viable units to Beta flight."

"Dammit," I said. "How many was she carrying?"

"Four crew, fifty-seven passengers."

I shook my head and got it back in the present. There'd be time to mourn those losses later. "*Night's Bliss*, how long until you can jump?" I asked.

"Engines are spun up, Captain," the reply came. "We just need to clear the jump limit. I figure, about a minute."

"Push it if you can, *Night's Bliss*," I said, and signed off. "Oh, no you don't," I said to a Zhen fighter angling for a firing solution on the freighter. I sprayed him with plasma fire, and while it wasn't enough to get through his shields, it did get him to spin away from the big ship. I followed, my weapons continuing to fire whenever the computer got a firing solution.

A bit less than the prophesied minute later, the *Night's Bliss* hit the jump limit and disappeared in a flash of slipspace's weird colors. "That's two away," Injala said. "Alpha flight is reassigned to *Euclidean Nightmare*."

"Acknowledged," I said, and turned to the new ship.

"Zhen group C is moving on the station itself," Injala said. "Tasking Gamma flight to defend. Station evacuation is commencing." I heard her suck in her breath. "Zhen ships are firing on evacuation vessels. Gamma flight, get in there!"

We got the *Euclidean Nightmare* to jump and watched her disappear before Injala reassigned Alpha flight to defend the station. I got in close, Alpha flight following me in, to engage the Zhen right up against the station.

Over the next few minutes, we lost a lot of small ships, and a few big ones. My world contracted to what I could see from my seat and hear from Injala and Kiri. My usual running commentary stopped; these weren't military personnel dying, but civilians we'd promised to protect.

My heart sank when Injala called out, "New ships arriving in-system!"

"Zhen?"

"I— No," she said. "I don't recognize them at all." She passed me a visual, and they looked like nothing I'd ever seen before.

"What are they doing?"

"Nothing yet," she said. "Just flying."

A transmission cut across all channels, speaking in Zhen, though the voice was human – sort of. There was an odd, synthetic-sounding quality to it, as if it were too perfect to be real. "Attention Zhen vessels. The human ships are under our protection. Break off and retreat in the next thirty seconds, or be destroyed."

We kept fighting, because the Zhen weren't stopping. When the specified thirty seconds were up, the unknown ships signaled again – by opening fire on the Zhen.

The resulting change in force distribution rallied our side, and the despair I'd been flying under dissipated pretty quickly. And then came back when a Zhen ship exploded too close to my ship. We were rocked hard by the explosion, and as we fought to recover, the ship lost power, leaving us drifting in darkness.

★   ★   ★

"Can we get power back?"

"I'm working on it," Kiri said. She unstrapped from her seat and headed back to engineering.

"We've got another problem," Liam said from the tailgunner's position. "I'm locked in here."

"I will go get him out," Zekan rumbled, and left the bridge.

"Battle command will pass to the Kelvaki command," Injala said. "If we get power back, we will decide whether to transfer it back or not." She got up from her seat. "In the meantime, I will assist Kiri."

"Thank you," I said. There was nothing I could do from the cockpit, so I got up from my seat, thinking I'd check on Liam. But my comms implant alerted me to a message.

"Tajen! Are you there?"

"Tajen here," I said. "Jette, is that you?"

"Yes!" she said. "Quince and I were about to get on his ship when he got shot! He's alive, but I can't move him, and he won't wake up. And I can't fly."

I thought for a moment. "Can you send me your location?" I asked.

"Yes," she said, and a moment later I got a location ping. "I've locked us into a storage room for now, but they're still out there, I think."

"Who?"

"Zhen soldiers!"

"Wait," I said. "You've got Zhen on the station?"

"Yes!"

"What are they looking for?"

"How in the hell should I know?"

I shook my head. "Is Quince's ship still working?"

"I think so."

"I'm on my way," I said. I switched to Kiri's comms signal. "Kiri, got an estimate on the reactor?"

"Still trying to figure it out," she said. "I'd say it's going to take some time."

"I'm heading to the station. Jette and Quince need help. When you get the power up, let me know and head for the Kelvaki command ship – we'll be coming out in a different ship."

"Be careful."

"I will."

"Tajen, wait for me," Liam called.

"How long?"

Zekan, his voice strained with effort, said, "Maybe ten minutes?"

"Can't, Liam. They need me now."

"Then take Zekan."

I sighed. "Zekan."

"Yes?"

"I expect you to keep them all safe if anyone tries to board."

"Yes, sir."

"Dammit, Tajen!" Liam said.

I cut the feed and made my way to the airlock. I told my flight suit, a nanite-based model from Zhen, to form up for spacewalk. The suit's material flowed over my face, turning me into a tall black specter with blue lights at my shoulders. I turned the lights off with a thought – no sense in standing out against the black of space when there were enemies still in the area.

I cycled the lock. When the outer door opened, I leaped out, activating the grav-nodes in my suit. The station was on the other side of the ship, so I looped around and headed stationward.

I had a lock on Jette's location, and access to the Shoa'kor database. I located the nearest airlock to her and directed the suit to take me there. I had to dodge a lot of debris, mostly parts of the station shredded in the initial assault, and a few broken ship parts.

I got to the airlock and triggered the cycle. When it finished, my suit reconfigured itself for land operations, shifting so my plasma pistol was reachable.

It was eerie, running through empty corridors, signal lights flashing at every intersection while the twin sirens of an attack klaxon and an evacuation order blared. I expected chaos, but not the body I nearly tripped over when I turned a corner.

I crouched down and knew instantly he was dead. The human was dressed in the uniform of station security. He'd taken a plasma blast to the chest, but the armor had taken the brunt of that. Death had come from the claws that ripped out his throat.

I pulled my pistol and crept forward more carefully, which is the only reason the Zhen who spun from the doorway beside me and raked his claws at my own throat missed.

I jumped back and fired at the Zhen. The plasma was dissipated by his armor, and he kept coming, swinging his claws again. I dodged, ducking the claws. I tripped over the body behind me and let gravity take me, swinging my legs over to somersault backward out of his range.

I scrambled to my feet and swept my left arm at the Zhen, releasing with a thought several thousand nanites that formed tiny incendiary bombs. As they neared the Zhen, they exploded in series, causing him to roar in pain and surprise. He stumbled back, and I took advantage of his momentary lack of balance and stepped inside his guard. I stuck my pistol into his screaming jaws and fired several times, then stepped back as his body fell to the deck in a heap.

There was no one else in the room the Zhen had come from, but there were probably more of them scattered around the station, looking for – well, for whatever it was they were seeking.

I directed my suit to send drones out. Several small globs separated themselves from my suit, then fragmented further, tiny invisible machines spreading out in a network through the corridors. I closed my eyes, letting my implants show me the layout in my mind's eye.

There were several corridors to go until I got to the room Jette and Quince were holed up in. And between me and that room was a whole squad of Zhen soldiers. Well, a squad minus the guy I'd already taken out.

The fastest way to my goal was through a museum. Apparently Quince had a soft spot for the history of human space travel, because he'd dedicated a whole section to it. I entered through the main doors and stopped. My nanite scouts had identified several sensors in the room, and I needed to find a way to get past them without triggering them.

I crept as quietly as I could, crouched below the counter level, until I got to a sensor placed to detect anyone walking through a narrow space between kiosks. I told my suit what to do, and it quickly sent microscopic assassins to take out the trap's triggering mechanisms.

The next room, according to my tactical overlay, had a Zhen. Fortunately he was facing away from me, but he was a bit too far to reach without being seen. If I fired, it would alert everyone nearby. I thought about it a moment, and sent an instruction to my suit. A slim launcher formed along the back of my forearm, ending in a small aperture mounted just above my wrist. I leveled my arm and pointed it at the Zhen. When my suit automatically adjusted my aim and reported a lock, I triggered the weapon the suit had built. A tiny lance of solid metal leaped from the tube, gravitic induction nodes propelling it to near-hypersonic velocity instantaneously.

The spike hit the Zhen in the head, which…well, let's not dwell on what happened to it. It was ugly, let's leave it at that.

The Zhen was wearing a nanite-based suit of armor. I reached out to touch it and triggered one of the military subroutines, hoping the Zhen hadn't changed the codes. It seemed they hadn't; the armor lost its shape, flowing like thick liquid into my suit, replenishing the nanites I'd used up so far and stocking up on more.

There were only two more Zhen between me and the next section. I skirted my way around a model of the *Far Star*, the colony ship that had brought humans to the Empire. Both of them were standing over a computer terminal.

"It isn't here," one of them said.

"Somebody is giving them the jump coordinates," the second one said. "The station makes the most logical command post."

I shot the first one, the plasma burning through the side of his head. The other spun to face me as I stood. "He was right," I said. "It isn't here." I stepped to the side, holding my weapon trained on him. "You were right too – but that's why your side will never win."

"What are you talking about?"

"You never seem to get that we're as smart as you – and as tricky. Of course the station was the most logical command post. That's why we didn't choose it. We knew you'd never let Shoa'kor stand after they defied you. So we decentralized command authority. It was on my ship. Now it's somewhere else."

"Bah!" he said. "The Kelvaki model. You humans are so full of your desire to be yourselves, but you will only become slaves to the Kelvaki."

"There's two problems with that theory," I said. "First, you don't seem to get how different the Kelvaki are from you. And second, you still don't get what makes the human race so bloody successful.

"Our history is *full* of governments like yours. But humans take what works, and we toss out what doesn't. So we'll borrow from you, and from the Kelvaki, the Tchakk, hell, even the Tradd have things to teach us – but we'll jettison everything about you that we don't like."

"Tlal spit. In time, humans will be just another client, licking our boots alongside the Tradd."

"Maybe," I said. "But maybe—" I was taken aback when his head simply burst. Behind him, another Zhen stood. "Greetings, Captain Hunt. Forgive me, but that conversation was giving me a headache, and you have things to do. Now, if you would not mind wounding me – but not mortally?"

"You're one of the Zhen objectors," I said.

"Yes. We call ourselves the Dissent. We are a small movement, but… we help where we can."

"Thank you," I said. "Now, have you a preference for the wound?"

He held out his hand. "Here," he said. "It has already been injured. A little more will be convincing enough."

"Not for me," a new voice said. A Zhen commander stood in the doorway. He snarled a phrase in Zhen that was pure nonsense words strung together, and the Dissenter stiffened, cried out in pain, and fell down, smoke curling from his skull, courtesy of several new holes.

"What the hell did you do?"

"A fail-safe that unfortunately did not work on you," he said. "But perhaps…." He raised his hand, and before I could fire, he triggered a device in his hand. A pulse of blue-white fire reached out and enveloped me. It hurt, and I struggled to remain on my feet, grabbing a counter for support.

My armor, on the other hand – the nanite-based suit that was both armor and spacesuit – crumbled into dust, sloughing off me as if it was so much sand.

"What the hell?"

"Now, Tajen Hunt. Let us end this." He lunged for me, and I turned and vaulted over the display behind me, knocking a model of a Zhen ship over. A tiny part of my mind appreciated the appropriateness of that, but honestly? I was mostly wondering how the hell I was going to get through this. My bag of tricks was toast, and all I had was a plasma pulse-pistol.

I popped up and fired at the spot where I expected him to be, but he was fast, and he'd already moved – as I discovered when he backhanded me, sending me flying. I hit the wall and slid down it in a heap, trying to fight my way through the pain and move. I watched the Zhen stalk toward me, slowly, clearly playing with me. I'd lost my gun, and I cast about wildly, looking for it – only to find it behind the Zhen. "Damn it," I said, struggling to my feet.

I faced off against the commander, trying to judge which direction he'd favor. I feinted to the right, but he didn't fall for it. I sidestepped and circled right, trying to get some space. My hand brushed against a piece of the model, and I instinctively grabbed it. Metal – a spar, or something. I could use this.

I leaped in and slashed with the broken metal, scoring a cut on the Zhen's wrist before dancing back. He snarled in pain and reached down to pick up a large crate that was part of a display. He threw it at me, clipping my left shoulder as I tried to dodge. The impact spun me around, but I managed to hold on to my improvised knife, and when he closed with me, I stabbed at his eye with it even as his claws grabbed for my throat.

Hot blood poured over my hand as the shard of metal slid into his eye. He released me as he instinctually reached for the offending object. I let go and backed off, grabbing my gun and turning it on the Zhen, firing repeatedly into his unprotected neck and face. As the body fell, I sagged against the display beside me for a moment, then limped over to the remains of my nano-suit. I reached out to it, trying to connect to it and reform it over me.

Nothing. It wasn't just refusing commands; there was, to my implant system, nothing to connect to at all. It was well and truly dead.

"Fuck," I said.

I made my way farther into the station, out of the museum's back entrance and to another corridor. I ran right into a closed airlock. There was supposed to be a transit tube linking this airlock to another on the next section – but I could see through the transparent doors that the transit tube had been destroyed.

If I'd still been wearing my nano-suit, I'd have been fine, but without it, there was no way I was getting across that. I checked the map for a way around this. There was a way, but I quickly found it was impassable, bulkhead safety doors slammed shut across the intersection. They must have lost atmosphere in that whole section. "Quince? Jette?"

"Jette here."

"Glad you're okay," I said. "I've got vacuum between us. I'm looking for a way around it."

"We're okay. Quince is still messed up. I'm doing what I can, but I need a medkit."

I closed my eyes, thinking. I'd taken care of the squad my scouts had found, but there were still Zhen on-station. I needed to cross the vacuum, but my suit had been totaled. So how was I supposed to survive the jump? I chuckled as I remembered something in the last room. I rushed back to check it. "I must be insane," I said out loud, running my hands over the ancient spacesuit.

It appeared to be functional, and not a replica. The suit was plugged into a power tap; it seemed the museum docents liked to demonstrate the primitive interface of the suit's computer.

It took me longer than I'd like to admit to put the bulky suit on. My respect for ancient humans, who had suits even more primitive than this bulbous, bulky old thing, grew. To trust their lives to fabric and plastic, and leap into the unknown stars, seeking knowledge without conquest? That took more guts than it did for me to fight.

Eventually, I got the damned thing on and sealed. I checked the systems, and found I didn't have any air in the tank. That was fine, I wouldn't be in this thing long enough to need more than I had. The onboard air scrubbers were working well enough to keep me standing for as long as I needed.

I moved to the airlock, being careful not to trip over the displays I'd shattered in that last fight. When I got there, I cycled the lock and stepped out into the vacuum. It looked like I had about four meters of floor before the tube was shattered. After that, it was another twenty or thirty meters of empty space to get to the other side. There was just enough transit tube on the other side to complicate things; if I didn't hit the tube just right, I was likely to get hung up on the sides or tear the suit.

I backed myself up to the airlock door, pressing myself against it as much as I could while I took several deep breaths. It occurred to me I was wasting what little air I had in the suit and I ran, moving as quickly as I could to the end of the tube, where I leaped toward the opposite side.

I was experienced enough in zero-G maneuvers that I didn't flail like a raw recruit, but I definitely held my breath as I crossed the empty void. A Zhen ship flashed by 'beneath' me, followed by a Kelvaki ship firing after it.

Several agonizing seconds later, I drew near the other side. I held my hand out, catching hold of the tube's edge, and swung myself down into the tube. The glasteel edge of the tube cut through the cloth of the spacesuit and into my hand. I swore as my feet landed in the tube, and I instinctively let go of the edge.

I tumbled down the tube toward the door, which was shut. I hit the command to open it, desperately holding my right hand closed around the rip. I could feel the air escaping through my fingers. "Come on," I said to the door. "Come on come on come on."

Finally, the door opened, and I slipped through, hitting the CYCLE command. Of course, the stupid door continued to move until it was entirely open, and I spent a few seconds cursing all designers and engineers everywhere, and also cursing the station builders for using doors sized for Zhen and not humans alone. Once it finished opening, I hit the button again, and the door slid slowly closed. Air started to fill the chamber, and just as I began to get dizzy, the inner door opened. I reached for the helmet, twisted it and removed it as fast as my oxygen-deprived fingers allowed. I gulped in air, breathing deeply for several moments.

Once I could breathe again, I took the rest of the suit off and accessed the station map, getting my bearings. "Jette, you still there?" I said on comms. "Is Quince still alive?"

"Yes to both questions," she replied.

"Good. Hang tight. I'm coming to get you."

★　　★　　★

When I got to the room Jette and Quince were holed up in, I found no Zhen nearby. Apparently they'd moved on in their search – or, more likely, they'd been monitoring my conversation with that commander earlier, and knew the information they'd been trying to get wasn't here. And his ego notwithstanding, even Jeremy Quince wasn't important enough for the Zhen to keep after him, especially when they'd already wounded the poor bastard.

"Jette," I said. "It's me outside. Open up." The door slid open and my eyes widened as Jette turned and leveled a blaster at me. "Whoah!" I said.

She quickly lowered the gun. "Sorry," she said. "I had to be sure. The Zhen have too many tricks."

"Don't I know it." I quickly stepped inside and knelt beside Quince.

He'd been shot in the side, and from what I could tell, he was in bad shape. He was losing blood, and while Jette had managed to slow the hemorrhaging, she couldn't stop it completely. "Gods below, Quince, what did you do to yourself?" I looked up at Jette. "You know this place better than I do. Is there an emergency medkit anywhere close?"

She consulted her NeuroNet. "There should be one nearby." She glanced at the door. "Are we safe here? The Zhen—"

"Are not in this area," I said. "You'll be fine. I'll stay with Quince. Go."

She scurried off, clearly spooked, but she had faith in me.

"Tajen," came Quince's shaky voice.

"You're awake, huh?" I asked.

"For now," he said. "I need a favor."

"Yeah? What's that?"

"Leave me," he said. "I'm gonna die anyway. There's no point in you guys going with me."

"Stow that," I said. "We're getting out of here, and you're coming too. Stay with me, Quince. We need you."

"Tajen. I'm just a bureaucrat. The Resistance needs you, it doesn't need me."

"Horseshit," I snapped.

"What's a horse?"

I smiled. "It's an animal from Earth. They're described in the old records, but I never thought I'd see one. But you know what? There's whole herds of them running wild on Earth."

He looked at me. "They've survived?"

"Yeah." A thought occurred to me. "You told me last year you're a Dreamer," I said, referring to the group of humans who'd long dreamed of returning to Earth, back before we'd found it. "Why haven't you come to Earth?"

"S'got Zhen all over it," he said with an alarming rattle.

"Before that," I said.

"I was…needed here."

"You still are. Needed, I mean. Not here – this place is gone, and we both know it. I'm sure you'd love to play Noble Hero and die here, but the truth is, as much as I hate to admit it, Earth and the Resistance need people like you. It is utterly karking selfish for you to even think about dying here when you've got skills humanity needs. So you shut the fuck up about leaving you behind. When Jette gets back, we'll slap some bandages on you and get you off this heap of metal. We'll set you up somewhere where you'll use all that bureaucratic know-how in that weird little brain of yours and put it to use against the sons of bitches that destroyed this place. You hear me?"

He didn't speak, but he nodded, and I smiled at him. "Good. See how easy life can be?"

He laughed, which caused a coughing fit. Jette got back and handed me a block of gray. "Hey, a nano-medkit. Nice." I placed the kit over the wound, causing Quince to wince in pain, and triggered it. The block began to 'melt' into the wound, sending the nanites that composed it deep into Quince's wounds, cutting off the pain and beginning to stitch him back together.

"We need to wait a bit before we can move him," I said, sitting back. "Where's the ship?"

Jette blinked, then made a motion as if grabbing something out of the air and flicking it toward me. It unfolded in my vision into a map, which showed we had a ways to go to get to Quince's ship. "Nothing's ever easy," I said, and Jette laughed. I still saw madness lurking in her eyes, but she was coming down from it.

The nanite package signaled me, and I stood, stretching a bit before bending to help Quince stand. "Okay, Quince. Time to suck it up for humanity."

He groaned as he struggled to his feet. Jette slipped under his other side, supporting him as I guided him out. We turned outward to the station edge, where the docking bays were, and hurried as quickly as possible.

Passing one bay, I saw an intact ship. "Why don't we use that one?" I asked.

"I've got information on my ship the Resistance can use," Quince said. "Can't be copied; it's on a physical medium hidden in the ship."

He recoiled at my look. "Hey, I never knew how long this place was going to be operational. It was insurance. But it can help you."

"Us," I corrected him. "It can help us."

He gave me a small smile. "Us," he agreed.

★ ★ ★

As we made our way toward Quince's ship, I used his codes to access the station cameras to scout our way. "Well, our good luck had to end eventually," I said.

"What's wrong?" Quince asked, wheezing.

"There's a Zhen:ko ahead," I said. "Any way around this?"

"No," he said. "He's standing just past the only junction on that corridor. And that's the only corridor that has access to my docking bay." He met my eyes with a pained expression. "It's supposed to be a security feature."

I thought a moment. "Can you fly?" I asked him.

"Not like you," he said. "But I can manage, as long as I don't have to fight."

I eased him to a sitting position on some rubble. "I'll draw him off. You two get aboard and launch. Make straight for the Kelvaki ship *Drokkha Nakar*. Use this code." I flicked the code to him. "They'll get you aboard safely."

"What about you?" Jette asked.

"I saw at least one functional ship. I'll lead this guy on a chase until you're clear. Then I'll make my way to one of those and meet you at the rendezvous point."

"Can't we just shoot this guy and go together?"

"You ever fight a red Zhen?"

"Of course not."

"Well, they're stronger and faster than the Zhen:la. And that one," I said ruefully, "is wearing a full nano-suit, which means he's got a hell of an advantage over me. So it's not going to be a fair fight."

"Can you beat him?"

I thought about lying, but what was the point? "Not a chance," I said. "But what I can do is lead him away from here, and then lose him long enough to board a ship and launch."

"Are you sure you can do it?"

I weighed my chances. "Pretty sure," I said.

"But not certain?"

My tone was serious as I said, "Nothing's ever certain, Jette. We do the best we can, and we make the best choices we can, and leave the rest to the universe. Have faith."

"In you?"

"Hell, no. Have faith that the universe doesn't mean any of it personally."

She laughed despite her fear. She looked at Quince and raised her eyebrows. He held out a hand, and she helped him back to his feet, then looked to me. "We're ready," she said.

"Good luck." I moved down the curving corridor, hiding behind debris, until I could see the Zhen:ko, standing proudly in the middle of the hall. He seemed to be waiting for something. Well, he could keep waiting until I was ready. I looked around me, but there was nothing nearby I could use. I had my pistol, but nothing else. "Fuck it," I said, and stood, stepping into his line of sight. "Hey, asshole!" I called out.

He looked confused.

"What's the matter," I asked, "don't you recognize the Empire's Most Wanted?"

"Tajen Hunt," the Zhen:ko snarled. "You have been a thorn in our side for too long. Time to die, meatsack."

"You want to martyr me?"

He hissed. "Martyrdom is no longer a concern. Once the fleet is done wiping out your little rebellion here, we will crush those remaining on Earth."

"You think that's enough?" I asked. "You really think the humans here at Shoa'kor are the only ones sick of the Empire's crap?" I shook my head. "Man, you red Zhen have been inbreeding for so long, your minds have gone soft. You do that, and the entire human race will turn against you."

The Zhen nodded and bared his teeth. "It will be a glorious battle," he said. "A paean to *Zhen'saak'arl*."

"What's your name, dumbass?"

"I am Shonkanaa."

"All right," I said. "I'll send your regards to your kin." I pulled my gun, pointed it in his general direction, and fired. I missed, but I hadn't really thought I'd hit him anyway – at that distance, my gun couldn't get through his armor even if I did make the shot, and I needed to lead him away so Jette and Quince could get behind him. I aimed more carefully at his unarmored head and kept firing.

At first he just stood there in a display of Zhen bravado, letting his armor absorb the plasma charges, but when I got lucky and grazed his head-crest, he ducked, feeling his crest gingerly with one hand. He growled menacingly, then began stalking toward me. He was moving slowly, deliberately, trying to intimidate me with a predatory display of my inevitable doom. I moved down the adjoining corridor, away from Quince and Jette.

Once I knew he was following me down the corridor, I kept going. I wasn't worried about him giving up on following me – I'd drawn blood when I hit his crest, and even after millions of years of evolution and millennia as a spacefaring race, the Zhen were still slaves to their baser instincts. I'd drawn his blood and dented his pride, and he wasn't going to give up until he felt my own blood sluicing down his throat and coating his hands.

"Come on, you big, dumb slowpoke!" I yelled, mostly to let the others know I was moving away from them. I reached a new junction, and was pleased to find a cargo mover abandoned in the intersection. I hooked into it with my NeuroNet and readied it for movement, then took shelter farther down the corridor behind a stack of crates.

When the Zhen:ko reached the intersection, I saw he'd extended his armor to cover his head as well. I accelerated the cargo mover immediately, sending it at full power toward the Zhen:ko. He twisted away at the last second, and the cargo device glanced off his armor, spinning him to the deck but not injuring him.

I ran toward him and launched into a leap. He rolled out from beneath me, lashing out with his arm, and knocked my feet out from under me. I slammed into the ground and immediately rolled away from him, his claws scraping my side, burning like fire.

We both climbed to our feet. I took out my gun again as Shonkanaa flexed his hands, extending his claws fully, the nanites of his armor moving aside to allow the claws through. "Ready to die, Tajen Hunt?"

"Not really," I said, and fired at his head. His armor took the blast, which I'd expected. I ran as the armor repaired itself and cleared his vision. I stumbled in the corridor, suddenly dizzy, and reached for a nearby doorway for support. My side burned where Shonkanaa's claws had raked me. "Oh, shit," I whispered. I'd been poisoned.

I activated my anti-toxin implants, but they didn't detect anything, which meant it was something classified beyond the clearances I'd had. I steeled myself and kept moving, nearly dropping my gun. I grimaced and put it back in the holster for now; it wouldn't do to lose my only weapon.

"Tajen, this is Jette," my comms unit said. "We're away. Are you out yet?"

"Working on it," I mumbled, but I wasn't sure if I'd sent the message or not. I was confused, my mind increasingly unable to grasp what I was doing or looking at. I could feel the rumble and vibration of explosions, both near and far, as the assault on the station continued. As if it wasn't already hard to walk, my legs were beginning to go numb. I needed help.

I tried to access the station to see if there was a med-center nearby, but I couldn't make sense of the readings. I already had a lock on the ship I was supposed to take out of here, so I started making my way toward it. Behind me I heard the Zhen:ko roar, an atavistic act that in today's society was bad form. It meant that Shonkanaa was lost in a primal hunting fugue, and I retained just enough lucidity to know that I was in deep shit.

I made it to the docking bay I'd chosen more or less on automatic pilot. When I got there, my shoulders sagged in disappointment. The bay was a mess; it looked like a ship had crashed through the forcefield. The vessel I'd planned to escape in was toast, slammed up against the rear wall of the bay and missing several important parts, which lay strewn across the bay, burning.

I was about to turn and try to find something else when I heard my pursuer running up the corridor behind me. I turned just in time to be straight-armed, sending me to the deck and sliding for many meters before slamming up against a pile of rubble. Something in the pile was poking me in the back, the pain of which was the only reason I didn't lose consciousness.

Shonkanaa stalked toward me, reached down, and grabbed me by the throat. He pulled me to my feet and then lifted me so my toes were scrabbling for the deck, inches beneath them. I grabbed at his wrist, trying to dislodge his grip, but it was hopeless. The armor of his helmet flowed like liquid down into the collar of his suit, joining with the armor over his chest. "Now, Tajen, you learn the fate of all who oppose us," he snarled, tightening his grip. "Look into my eyes as you die. Know who killed you."

"Th-thanks," I choked out.

"For what? Killing you before the poison takes you?"

"No," I said, my right arm rising once more. "For removing your helmet." I shoved my pistol right up against his left eye and pulled the trigger repeatedly. At that range, I got some blowback from the plasma, singing the flesh of my hand, but it was worth it to watch his eye and everything behind it liquefy and burn. His grip on my throat slackened, and we both fell to the ground in a heap. I shoved myself away from him and activated my comms.

"Liam?"

"I'm here, Tajen. We got the ship back up. Where are you?"

"Docking bay," I wheezed. "Time to say goodbye, my love."

"What are you talking about?"

"The ship I was going to use is destroyed," I said. "I took the Zhen out, but the Zhen:ko bastard poisoned me. It's making it hard for me to move. I think I'm done here."

"Tajen, don't you dare give up," Liam said. "What docking bay? We'll find you."

"Can't tell," I said. "I love you, Liam."

"Don't you do this, Tajen. Get on your feet, soldier!"

"Can't," I said. "Legs're numb. Kinda gettin' hard to talk."

A few moments of silence, and then, "Tajen, don't give up," he pleaded. "There's help coming. Get on that ship, my love!"

I was thinking I must have misheard him, but a ship entered the bay soon after and quickly spun to face back out into space. It was one of the unknown ships that had jumped in at the beginning of the fight. It looked like nothing I'd ever seen before. It was white, and whereas Zhen ships looked bulky and aggressive, this thing looked like a hunting bird. It had atmospheric wings that bristled with weapons, as well as two missile pods mounted on a pylon that connected the fuselage to the wingtips, each of which was tipped with oversized cannons. It was a sleek, dangerous-looking design, and I'd never seen its like.

A ramp dropped, and a voice spoke in English, amplified by speakers:

"Come aboard, Captain Hunt!" I managed to climb to my feet, and staggered up the ramp. The interior ran the length of the ship, it seemed, from the ramp behind me to a door that presumably led to the cockpit. Back here there was a large bed for a ship so small, and not much else, though here and there on the walls it seemed there was equipment hidden behind doors and folded-shut cabinets.

"Sit here," said the voice, and a complicated-looking chair slid out from a recess in the wall. I sat, and the chair extruded several restraints and sensors over my body. The voice said, "You have been poisoned. Stand by for antidote." Several needles penetrated my skin and I felt the pressure of injections.

"Ow!" I said.

"Don't be a baby," the voice said. "While the antidote will take some time to reach full effectiveness, you'll be able to fly in a moment. When you feel better, please come to the cockpit. Stand by for launch."

There was a surge of acceleration. I sat still for a few minutes, then, as feeling came back to my legs, and the chair released me, I got to my feet and went to the door in the front of the ship.

It slid open as I approached. "Welcome, Captain," the same voice said. The ship was flying, but I was astounded to see the cockpit was empty. "Where's the pilot?" I asked.

"Welcome, Tajen Hunt. This ship is yours."

"I don't understand," I said. "Who sent it?"

"Later," the voice said. "The ship is yours." The pilot's chair slid back from the controls and turned to face me. "Have a seat."

I blinked and said, "Okay...." I sat, and the moment I did, the chair turned and slid back up to the controls. The layout was exactly what I'd have done if I'd designed my perfect cockpit. "Whoever built this did a good job," I said. "Now, let's go end this fight."

★ ★ ★

This ship was made for me. I mean, probably not, as there was a whole flight of them out there fighting alongside us. I tried to make contact with them, but nobody answered.

I quickly looked over the battle plot. Most of the human ships had made it safely into slipspace, but a few stragglers were still trying to get to the jump limit. I activated comms. "Tactical command, this is Tajen Hunt aboard unknown vessel. Where do you need me?"

"Captain Hunt," came Injala's voice. "Designating your ship as Alpha leader. Unless you have an objection, Lieutenant Kanish?"

"Not at all," a Kelvaki replied. "Alpha flight is yours, Captain Hunt."

"Alpha flight, escort the *Dreaming Angel* to the jump limit."

"On it, TacComm." I pulled the ship around and headed for intercept on the *Dreaming Angel*. My scopes showed Zhen fighters on a similar course ahead of me. I locked my weapons on them and fired, the energized plasma leaping out of the wingtip cannons and impacting on their shields. The four guns cycled so that two fired at any given moment. As my target's shields depleted, I locked a missile on to them and fired. It flashed across space and impacted on the shield, a fusion explosion shattering the shield and eating a pretty big chunk out of the ship, which tumbled off course.

I immediately locked on to the next ship, but before I could fire, one of my wing-mates took the ship out with a few well-placed plasma bolts. "*Dreaming Angel*, you're clear for jump," I said.

"Thank you!" There was a flash, and the *Dreaming Angel* was gone.

My scopes showed the other ships had jumped clear too. "All ships," Injala said, "noncombatants have all cleared the conflict zone. Civilian combat ships, break for the jump as soon as you can. The Kelvaki ships will cover you."

"All right," I said to myself. "Let's distract us some Zhen."

"Now you're talking," said the voice from earlier. I'd thought it must be a recording, or someone steering the ship via remote – not something I was used to beyond small drones, but possible – but now I wasn't sure anymore. It seemed female, but not entirely human.

"Who are you?"

"My name is Clear Skies at Midnight on a Night with No Moon," she said.

"Okay," I said, pulling the trigger as I skimmed over the surface of a Zhen ship, dodging incoming plasma cannon fire while taking out their turrets. "What are you?"

She waited until I'd completed a high-G turn and begun a second run. "I'm the AI that resides in this vessel."

I was taken aback by that. The Zhen don't use AI systems. In fact, sentient computers were forbidden under Zhen law. But the Kelvaki didn't have that technology, either – only 'weak AI', that is, computers that could recognize and follow commands. I'd already suspected this ship wasn't Kelvaki, but who else could have built it?

My ruminations were ruined when I came under fire from not only the turrets, but several Zhen fighters. I juked left, barely evading a salvo from the lead ship. The salvo hit a turret, and the shockwave of the explosion slammed into the ship, sending us tumbling. I fought to recover the ship, wrestling it back under control.

"That was fun," the AI said. "Can we not do it again?"

"Can't promise that," I said.

"Well, then, I want a new pilot."

"Well, you'll— Shit!" I banked hard, rolling the ship ninety degrees, and hit the ventral thrusters, pushing the ship aside from an incoming pulse of plasma fire. A team of three Zhen fighters flashed through the space where I had been, and as I brought my ship around to pursue, my Kelvaki wingman's ship disintegrated in a fireball.

I settled onto a pursuit course and tried to get a lock for my missile systems. I got one, and fired two missiles at one of the ships. They launched flares, but the missiles ignored them entirely, exploding right up against the Zhen's shields. The ship wasn't destroyed, but it was taken out of the fight, one of its weapon pods sheared right off the ship, the other consumed in the hell unleashed by my missiles.

The lead fighter peeled off, spinning around and shedding velocity, then leaped toward me, firing his own weapons. My forward shields flashed with plasma fire and feedback pulses, making it hard to see anything beyond the shields. But I was used to that, and even at 'close' range, space combat targeting is almost never close enough to actually see your enemy in the first place. I trusted my instruments and hit the ventral thrusters, causing the ship to rise above the incoming fire. My system alerted me to incoming smart missiles, and I grimaced. "I really hate those things," I said.

"Activating ECM," the AI said.

"You can do that?"

The AI's voice turned snarky. "Who do you think was actually flying this ship before you came aboard?"

I took the ship into an evasive pattern. "I thought it was being remotely flown."

"Right, because that works so well? There's a reason nobody uses remote-controlled fighters. Even in the same system, lag is a problem. I was told you were smarter than this."

"Told by whom?"

The AI went silent. I'd have continued trying to get her to talk, but the Zhen leader was getting closer and my attention was totally on him. As he flashed by me, both of us flipped our ships over so we were still facing each other, firing continuously. I kept my ship pointed at his, but applied thrust to keep moving, randomly shifting thrust direction and intensity to throw off his firing solutions.

"Dorsal shield depleted thirty percent," the AI said. "Compensating."

I whittled down the enemy's shields, nervously keeping an eye on my own. He was good, and I was starting to get worried – not so much about his fire as about other ships catching me while my attention was on him.

The AI spoke up. "Damage to the gun actuators. Dispatching repair probes."

"Wait, we have auto-repair?"

"It's limited, but yes," she said. "Shall I take over shield and systems control while you focus on flying and shooting?"

"Sounds like a plan," I said. If I'd had a human sitting in the second seat, that's what would have happened, so it wasn't difficult to hand over control, but the fact it was being done by an artificial intelligence was new. I was a little too focused on not getting shot out of the sky to worry about that, however.

The Zhen pilot decided to try to close with me, which gave me an advantage, as I wasn't worried about the distance. I circled my ship using lateral thrusters, getting out of his firing arc, and poured all the firepower I had into his shields, followed up with a missile. He tried to turn his forward shields back in my direction, but he wasn't fast enough, and my salvo hit him in the weakest part of his shield. The resulting fireball blinded me for a moment.

When my eyes cleared, I realized my wing had taken out the remaining fighter in the group we'd been targeting. "Good work, Alpha," I said.

"Attention all pilots," TacComm said. "The Zhen vessel *Adamant* have signaled they are withdrawing and are no longer to be considered combatants. Ignore that vessel unless it fires upon you."

"TacComm, are you kidding me?" I asked. "What, now that the battle is almost over, they get to leave with no consequences?"

"That is correct, Alpha leader." Almost immediately, Injala switched over to a private frequency. "Letting them go is better for us, Tajen. I'll explain when this is over. I promise you'll be pleased."

"Understood," I said.

With the *Adamant* leaving the field, the other Zhen were outnumbered, but they were Zhen, and they were fighting to the death. I retargeted the nearest turret on my objective and went back in, skimming just feet away from the ship's hull. My old ship could never have gotten this close – we were so low, the turrets couldn't target us accurately, and the Zhen fighters in pursuit had to be careful or they'd hit their own ship. In short, it was the perfect zone.

"Alpha leader, please take out the remaining capital ship *before* it fires that plasma charge at my ship?"

"On it," I said.

Zhen shipbuilders are rather fond of putting huge plasma cannons on their ships. Which is fine, unless someone gets close enough to put some missiles into the assembly. I was fast approaching the plasma cannon now, and I could see the Zhen fighters scrambling. "Alpha flight, keep them off me," I said. "AI, can you send Alpha two my targeting information?"

"Easily," she said. "I have a name, you know."

"Later," I ground out, then got back on comms. "Alpha two, target that plasma cannon exactly where I did," I said. "Fire on my mark." I watched the cannon come closer, and I hoped they hadn't fixed what I was about to attempt to exploit. "Four, three, two, mark!" I squeezed my firing controls.

Alpha two and I both fired everything at the maintenance panel before peeling off and accelerating away. Ordinarily the small door into the cannon was protected, but we'd managed to get in behind the turret's firing arcs. The maintenance door and everything behind it vanished in a hell of white-hot plasma from *outside* the magnetic bottle that usually protected the cannon's internals from the power the gun channeled. The plasma escaped confinement, obliterating the gun from the side of the ship and, before the safety systems could engage, caused a cascade failure all the way back to the engines.

The shockwave of the engines blowing slammed into me, sending my ship into an uncontrolled tumble. I worked to get it under control and checked my scopes. "Wait," I said. "TacComm, am I reading my scopes right? Are we done?"

"We are, Alpha leader. We're evacuating the few people remaining on Shoa'kor and will be jumping soon. See you at the rendezvous."

"Ship," I said.

"I have a name," came the irritated response.

"We were in combat," I said. "Run it by me again."

There was a synthetic sigh. "My name is 'Clear Skies at Midnight on a Night with No Moon'."

"That's...long. How about I call you 'Midnight'?"

"If you must," she said.

"All right then. Okay, Midnight, once we rendezvous with my crew, I can release you so you can go back to wherever you came from."

"You weren't listening, earlier."

"Pardon?"

"The rest of my squadron will return home, but this ship is yours, Tajen Hunt."

"But where does it come from?"

"I'm afraid that information is not mine to divulge."

"Then once we get to the rest of the humans, I'll disembark and you can be on your way," I said.

"Very well."

I threw my hands up. I'd hate to lose the ship, but the truth was I couldn't trust a gift from unknown people.

"Very well," I said. "Plotting jump."

★   ★   ★

When I exited the jump, I looked for the human ships, but didn't see any. Nor did I see any Kelvaki. I quickly scanned the area, but found nothing. There was a star in the distance, glowing bright red, but no planets nearby. I checked the coordinates.

"Midnight, these are not the coordinates I set. Where are we?"

"I do not have access to that information," she said.

"What the hell does that mean?"

"It means I do not have access to that information."

"How can you not know where we are?"

"There is some kind of block in my programming. I can see we are not where we should be, but I cannot access the reason for this. I am sorry." She actually sounded worried.

Moments later, a new ship jumped in. Most ships, whether they're Kelvaki or Zhen, Tchakk or one of the other, rarely seen races that brought themselves into jump-capable society, look like they're piercing something when they come out of slipspace, trailing bits of the weird colors that fade out as the ships manifest in realspace. The bigger the ship, the longer the slipspace effects persist.

This ship was bigger than anything I'd seen in years, but it exited slipspace with nary a ripple of color. It wasn't there, and then reality seemed to ripple, and suddenly the ship was there. And as soon as I saw it, I could feel the blood drain from my face. "No," I whispered. I hadn't seen one of those ships in over fifteen years, I wasn't ready to see it now.

Tabrans.

My ship was already vectoring toward it. I pulled the stick, planning to get to the *Drokkha Nakar* as soon as I could. But the ship didn't respond.

"Midnight, what's going on?"

"We have been directed to report to the *Sudden but Deep Understanding That Comes upon You When Least Expected*."

"The what?"

"The Tabran vessel," she clarified.

"Midnight, are you a Tabran ship?"

"Not as such," she said.

"What the hell does that mean?"

"I am a human ship, but I was constructed by Tabrans."

"Why?"

"I do not have that information."

I tried to override the AI's control over the ship, but nothing I tried made a bit of difference. If I'd had a spacesuit, I'd have tried to get out of the ship, but trying to breathe vacuum wasn't going to help.

We entered the shadow of the Tabran ship, the sun of this system disappearing behind its immensity. Like most Tabran ships, it was unadorned, designed for maximum efficiency and little else.

As Midnight brought the fighter into the cavernous docking bay, I began to breathe deeply in an attempt to calm myself. The Tabrans were a tough enemy, easily more advanced than the Zhen, but I'd never seen one in person. Most battles against them were fought in space, and as I well knew, they never took prisoners.

The ship settled to the deck. As the engines shut down, Midnight said, "Rear hatch open."

I considered resisting, but there seemed little point beside the drama. I wasn't going out there unarmed, though – I rose from my seat, drew my pistol, and exited the cockpit.

Nobody had entered the ship, and I didn't see anyone through the open hatch. I proceeded to the ramp and gingerly stepped down it. The air seemed the same as what I was used to, which was helpful, but not terribly surprising. As I reached the bottom of the ramp, I looked around, and my eyes fell on something – or someone – I hadn't expected to see again.

"Hello, Tajen," she said.

"Katherine? You're supposed to be dead." I'm not sure why, but it never even occurred to me to doubt it was really her.

She shook her head. "As one of my grandfather's stories went, 'the rumors of my death were greatly exaggerated'," she said. She stepped up to me, looking pointedly at my gun. I sheepishly put it back in my holster.

We were alone in the docking bay, so I did what I wanted to do, and pulled her close. "I'm so glad you're not dead," I said, squeezing her tightly.

"Me too," she said with a laugh. We held each other for several moments, and then she gently pushed me back. "How are you?"

I huffed. "Things are bad out there," I said. "Earth's under Zhen control, they've declared martial law across the Empire. And we barely escaped from them at Shoa'kor. They're not even pretending anymore, Katherine. They mean to wipe us out."

She nodded. "I know," she said. "Never a break for us, huh? But I need you to brace yourself, Tajen, because it's about to get much, much weirder." Still holding my arms, she tossed her head toward the exit. "Come on, I'll introduce you to the Tabrans."

ACKNOWLEDGMENTS

Just like the first book, several people helped to make this one a reality.

First and foremost, I owe an absolute debt of gratitude to my wife, Elli, who frequently made it possible for me to hole up in my office, or flee the house, and write this book. Especially in the crunch at the end, she went above and beyond the call in making sure I had the time and space I needed. I love you, El.

My daughter Tegan was incredibly understanding of my taking a lot of our summer vacation together to write. She continues to be one of my most ardent supporters, jumping for joy when good things happen, and even taking me to task when I'm looking at Twitter when I should be writing. I love you so much, Tegan. You're the best daughter that has ever lived.

Thank you to my compatriots in both the 7th Prime and Codex writing communities, who gave input and advice when asked, and cheerleading when needed. You're all amazing people, and I'm proud to know you.

Jim St. Claire, Jerry Kennedy, and Miles Cochran, my ride-or-die buddies: I love you guys. Never forget it. Thanks for keeping me sane when the crazy stuff happens.

And finally, thanks to the Flame Tree Team for all their help and encouragement. There are more people than I know behind the scenes, but the ones I do are: Don D'Auria, Maria Tissot, Josie Karani, and of course Nick Wells. To them, and all the folks at Flame Tree Press whose names I don't yet know, I say thank you.